www.melodramapublishing.com

Library of Congress Control Number: 2011927249
ISBN-13: 978-1-934157-64-0
Mass Market Edition: February 2013
10 9 8 7 6 5 4 3 2

Interior Design: Candace K. Cottrell
Cover Design: Marion Designs
Cover Model: Vanessa

Coca Kola

THE BADDEST CHICK

NISA SANTIAGO

Buy

for Melodrama

Prologue

The understaffed trauma unit at Harlem Hospital was overrun with 9-1-1 calls. It seemed like everybody who had fallen ill, gotten shot or stabbed, or had some unknown sickness had come to that hospital for treatment. The hallway was lined with the sick and injured, some needing to be restrained, others fighting to survive their injuries. The echoes of the men and women in agony seemed never-ending to the doctors and nurses bustling back and forth from one patient to the next.

The EMS bus brought in a patient who was screaming and definitely out of control. She was barely strapped down to the gurney and had suffered serious burns to most of her face.

As the staff hurried her into the center, she screamed out, "I'ma kill that bitch! I'ma kill that fuckin' bitch! Aaaah, shit, it hurts! It hurts! It fuckin' hurts!"

The medical team wanted to treat her as quickly as possible, but she was kicking, screaming, and squirming on the rushing gurney.

"Get the fuck off me! Get off me!" Apple yelled, sounding crazy.

"Ma'am, just calm down. We're trying to help you. Just stay calm," the night RN said, trying to hold Apple down on the gurney with the help of the other team members.

"What happened to you?" another nurse asked.

Apple refused to be cooperative, though. She continued kicking and screaming, feeling her face painfully melting away like the wicked witch from *The Wizard of Oz*.

She screamed out, "My fuckin' face! My fuckin' face! I'ma kill that bitch! Aaaah!"

"She needs to be sedated," the doctor said.

After wheeling Apple into a private room cluttered with staff and security, the nurses started prepping her and the room for an emergency surgery. The sedative was being prepared, and the doctors wanted to tend to the burns right away. From the looks of her injuries, they were confident that Apple would need some major skin grafting procedures.

Apple kicked one of the nurses into a shelf filled with medical supplies, causing them to spill over.

"Hold her down!" the doctor yelled.

It took security and four staff members to hold Apple down while the RN tried to stick the syringe filled with a sedative into her arm, her screams echoing through the trauma center.

"Get off meeee!" she yelled.

She tried to bite the second nurse, but her arms were forced to her side by security. The RN quickly thrust the syringe into Apple's right arm, hoping it worked promptly.

Apple's chest heaved and dropped like a winded athlete's, her wildness slowly fading and her facial expression looking more serene. There was finally some calm in the room.

"Shit!" the RN exclaimed, shocked that the teenage girl was so strong.

Immediately, they began operating on her burns. The doctor tried to operate the best he could on her face, but the acid had done severe damage. It would take a miracle for Apple to look the way she used to.

Apple slowly opened her eyes hours later to find her face heavily bandaged. Still loopy from the sedative, she touched the dressing slowly and gently. She started to cry when she realized how ugly she must be.

When she closed her eyes to try and stop the crying, she heard a nurse say, "You need to rest."

Turning to look at the short, round nurse clad in blue-and-white scrubs, Apple yelled, "I want a fuckin' plastic surgeon now, bitch!"

"Ma'am, you need to rest."

"Fuck that! Look at me!" she cried out.

The nurse had a sad look on her face. She wanted to console the eighteen-year-old but thought against it. Instead, she checked Apple's IV flow, jotted something down on a clipboard, and walked out the room, leaving Apple feeling alone and disgusted.

Apple fell asleep again and woke up hours later in the burn unit. Alone in the room, the only thing on her mind was revenge. Every time she touched the bandages, which covered most of her burned face, she fumed with rage. Then she'd start crying, with the realization that she was no longer pretty.

The doctors gave her another sedative to calm her down.

Chico charged into the hospital, searching for his woman. He argued with security and then a few staff members, shouting, "Where's my fuckin' girl?"

One of Apple's doctors escorted him toward the burn unit, where she was heavily sedated. Her burns were itching and painful, but she couldn't scratch.

Chico stopped at the doorway, a look of shock on his face. He couldn't believe it. She looked like a mummy as she lay in bed.

"What the fuck!"

Apple slowly turned to see her love, Chico, standing in the doorway, but she didn't say a word to him. The medication in her system had her drowsy and dizzy.

Chico rushed into the room, took Apple's hand into his, and looked at her with that firm love in his eyes. "Baby, who the fuck did this shit to you? Just give me a fuckin' name, and they dead. I promise you that."

Apple locked eyes with her boyfriend. "Kola . . . Kola . . . Kola."

Chapter 1

Kola violently awakened out of her sleep with an inexplicable yelp and rose up in a cold sweat, staring into a dark room. She felt something being ripped away from her, tearing into her soul, like a shovel slicing into dirt. Kola didn't want to panic, but the dream seemed so real. She was feeling out of breath with a sharp pain in her chest and agony in her heart. She placed her hand against her chest and looked over to see an empty bed. Cross wasn't home for the third straight night, but she knew he was a busy man, a natural-born hustler who had her living in the lap of luxury.

Suddenly, the dark was making Kola uncomfortable. She got out of bed and turned on the lights. She looked around her magnificent bedroom with the large skylight above the bed, volume ceiling, fireplace, floor-to-ceiling windows, large plasma flat-screen, and high-end bedroom set with a platinum-colored bedspread. It was the only way Kola could live and wanted to live—like a queen and with her man running Harlem like a king.

Kola donned her long peach silk robe and walked over to the large mahogany Serena dresser mirror to peer at her image. She was naked underneath the robe—her curves, ample breasts, and shaved pussy showing in the reflection. She had a body that many women would envy her for, and it belonged to Cross. Her body was his temple. She was in love with him, and he took care of her. She understood why Apple was so in love with him, and she had no regrets snatching away the man her sister had idolized and loved for so long. You snooze, you lose, Kola believed.

Kola and Cross were the Bonnie and Clyde of Harlem, attractive and deadly at the same time. Their illicit empire was growing, and her sex parties were the talk of the town. Kola had made a name for herself generating so much money, and she didn't know what to do with it all. And with Cross by her side, she felt untouchable.

Kola continued to stare at herself in the mirror, trying to shake the eerie feeling. For some reason, she felt her skin itch, and it almost felt like she was being watched. She pulled open her drawer and removed a pack of Newports. She lit the cigarette quickly and took a much-needed drag from the cancer stick.

She then walked over to the bed and took a seat, searching for the remote to the flat-screen. She glanced at the time. It was three in the morning. After taking another pull from the cigarette, she sighed heavily, clicked on the television, and looked at a few infomercials for a moment. Wanting to get her mind out of a bad place, she continued to smoke while looking at the TV, but she couldn't shake that odd feeling.

"Something's wrong," she said to herself.

She got up to dump the contents out of her purse and picked up her cell phone. No messages or missed calls.

She started to worry about Cross, who had told her that he was out on business. She trusted him. She knew Cross could handle himself, and if something was wrong, he would call her. Yet, she couldn't help feeling a little scared.

She walked over to the window and stared down at her new black M-class Benz truck parked in the circular driveway. She loved how she looked in the truck.

Kola loved the suburbs like she loved Harlem. However, being miles away from Harlem gave her peace of mind and kept the bitches and bitch-assness out of her business.

"Where are you, baby?" Kola whispered, staring out the window as she continued to smoke.

She had an itch between her thighs that needed to be scratched, and Cross was the one man able to scratch it for her. Her pussy tingled for his touch, and her nipples felt like pebbles as she thought about his kisses.

Kola sighed, extinguished her cigarette in the ashtray on the nightstand, and walked away from the window. She didn't want to be alone. She felt troubled, which was a new feeling for her. She was a tough girl, but her mind was playing tricks on her. It was the first night she felt uneasy being alone in such a big house. She looked at her cell phone again and was tempted to call someone.

The TV was playing the end of the infomercial, and the vast bedroom looked bigger to her than usual. Kola sat on the bed with the phone in her hand, trying desperately to shake the bad feeling. She felt like a young girl. She finally felt her age—eighteen. She had matured quickly over the years and hadn't felt like that young girl in a long time.

As she sat on the bed thinking, her cell phone rang, startling her. She jumped for a moment and then hurried to answer it. She didn't recognize the number on the caller ID but answered the call anyway.

"Hello?"

"You have a collect call from Cross at the Manhattan Correctional Facility," the automated recording announced.

Kola quickly accepted the call, her heart beating against her chest. She had a million worries in her head, and receiving a collect call from her man in jail had her tripping out.

"Hey, baby," she heard Cross' smooth voice say.

"Baby, what's wrong? What happened?"

"We good, Kola, and don't even worry. I'm wit' Edge. We got knocked wit' a gun in the car."

"What!"

"It's bullshit, baby. We'll be out soon. Don't even worry about it."

"I *am* worried!" Kola exclaimed.

"Baby, just chill out. Don't be trippin', you hear me? We gonna be good, you know what I'm saying?"

"I guess."

"But, listen. Business is always business. Shit don't stop. I hate that I'ma miss that game wit' Eddie, though. It's a really big game. I got money on this game."

Kola quickly picked up that Cross was speaking in code, and being aware that their conversation was probably being recorded, she went along. She listened closely.

"How much was the tickets?"

"Expensive. But you go in my place, baby. Enjoy yourself."

"I don't like football."

"But I don't want them tickets to go to waste while I'm fuckin' stuck up in here. Eddie got me a good deal on them tickets, Kola. Just go wit' the nigga and put 'em to good use."

Kola sucked her teeth. Cross wanted her to meet his connect, Eduardo—Eddie for short—and buy some work. But it wasn't Kola's line of work. She did sex parties and was a borderline pimp. She didn't feel comfortable meeting with Cross' connect. Still, she was a ride-or-die chick and, like her man, a natural-born hustler.

"Baby, he'll teach you the game. Just go and have fun. It's football. And we got seats right on the fifty-yard line. You gonna see everything."

"How close?"

"Really close. The spread on the game is by fifteen."

"I got you, baby," a confident Kola replied.

"That's my baby. I love you."

"I love you too, baby," Kola replied with a smile.

"But I'ma hit you up. And don't worry about this charge. It ain't gonna stick. You know we got lawyers to fuck wit' these pigs."

"I know."

The call ended abruptly, leaving Kola with the phone in her hand and nothing but silence. She sighed and tossed her phone on the bed.

She was being thrust into Cross' world unexpectedly to meet with a Colombian connect. However, with Cross, Edge, and Mike-Mike locked up, she knew somebody had to step up and take charge. Now wasn't the time to be nervous. She was ready to become "that bitch," like she was born and raised to be.

Chapter 2

Earth, Wind and Fire blared throughout the fifth-floor two-bedroom apartment. There was thick cigarette smoke lingering in the living room, bottles of alcohol spread out near the folding card table, and a new deck of playing cards ready to be opened for a wild and crazy game of pitty-pat or spades. It was Denise's night to party, get drunk, and maybe get her freak on, if the right man approached her with the correct game. She wanted to smoke like a chimney, yell and act out behind a game of spades, then get herself some dick by the end of the night. She wanted to be free like a bird tonight. No rules, no restrictions.

Denise strutted around her apartment clad in a miniskirt, exposing her meaty thighs and fresh tattoo, and a tight, tiny, metallic plunging-neckline halter top that showed enough cleavage to make the room feel almost x-rated. She held a glass of vodka in her hand and took casual sips as she walked around the apartment preparing everything for her soon-to-arrive guests.

Denise loved throwing her card-game parties. She loved the loud chatter, the cursing and shit-talking, along with the flirting, heavy drinking, chain smoking, and blaring music. On a good night, her place was as ghetto as they come. The men got tipsy and sometimes would become a little too frisky. And if a certain woman was up to it, with the liquor making her more flirtatious and promiscuous than usual, then she would find herself in one of the back bedrooms with her skirt up or jeans down, with her wet pussy about to make a hard dick come.

Denise didn't mind anyone using her bedroom for sex or sniffing blow, as long as they didn't make too much of a mess and paid to play. She understood that everybody needed to have fun, and being the hustler she was, she was able to pay her rent through her wild weekly card games and renting out the bedrooms for pleasure.

She was still salty with Apple. She couldn't believe her bitch of a daughter had the audacity to throw her own mother out with only the clothes on her back. But Denise had quickly bounced back and was steadily getting herself together again. Yet she still wanted to smack fire out of her daughter's mouth and beat her down on the streets like she was a stranger.

Denise never thought she would find herself back in the projects after living in luxury and being spoiled like one of the Hilton sisters. And though she was laughing and smiling, deep inside, she hated going back to project living again. For her, it was embarrassing.

Denise walked near the window and looked outside,

singing along to Earth, Wind, and Fire's "Shining Star," and swaying to the beat.

While singing, she heard a knock at the door. It would be only one of many knocks to come during the night. She pivoted in her four-inch heels and went to answer the door. She swung it open with a smile and greeted Nina.

"Hey, girl!" Nina joyfully screamed out.

"Nina! Always the first to get your drink on, huh." Denise greeted her with a hug.

Nina was in her late thirties and as whorish as they come. During Denise's last card game, she got pissy drunk, naked, and was fucked by her one-time best friend and his brother. Denise only tolerated Nina because she made Denise look like Claire Huxtable when they were in the same room.

"What you got to drink in here, girl?" Nina asked, rushing into the apartment in search of the Grey Goose. "You know I gotta sip on my Goose."

Denise laughed and pointed over to the bottles. "And take it easy on my shit, Nina. I don't need you actin' a fool before our game even starts."

Nina sucked her teeth. "Girl, I got this. I know how to hold my liquor."

"Mmm-hmm." Denise smirked. "Like last time when the Durant brothers ran a train on you in the bedroom."

"At least they were cute."

"Slut."

Nina ignored the comment and poured herself a half cup of Goose mixed with some cranberry juice. She quickly took it to the head and was ready for another one. As Nina was about to pour herself another shot, she looked at Denise with a look of urgency, ready to spill some important news.

"Girl, I know you heard what happened to Apple the other night."

Denise didn't want to hear that name in her house. She despised everything about Apple and wanted to forget she even gave birth to her.

"Some crackhead walked up to her while she was flaunting in front of her new ride and tossed some acid in her face. She was lookin' a hot mess, Denise. I mean, I know that's ya daughter and everything, but word around town is that she deserved it, the way she was acting."

Denise looked nonchalant after hearing the news. "I could care less."

"I'm just saying, there might be some shit going on behind that. You know Apple."

"I don't wanna hear shit about no muthafuckin' Apple!" Denise barked. "That bitch is dead to me."

"I'm sorry. I didn't mean to intrude."

"Well, bitch, you is."

Nina shrugged and continued to sip on her drink.

Denise removed a cigarette from her pack and lit it. She was more worried about her card game than Apple's predicament. She walked over to the window and looked outside. She sighed heavily as the murder of her youngest daughter, Nichols, loomed in her head. It had been months since her death, and Denise couldn't help feeling guilty.

She was never the heartwarming, reliable mother to any of her daughters. And now, with the youngest gone, one of her twins in the hospital, and the other almost absent from her life completely, she resorted to drinking, partying, and having sex to ease the pain of her troubled life.

"Fuck her!" Denise muttered to herself. She took another drag from her cigarette.

Denise knew she wasn't getting any younger. She didn't have any retirement plan, and tricking off niggas and hustlers was getting old for her. She still had her curvy, attractive figure, but every year there was something changing about her. She was gaining more weight; her breasts didn't sit high like they used to; she had a little pouch; and the younger girls were throwing pussy at every baller they came across, whoring themselves out at a much younger age, and making the competition more fierce for her in the streets.

Nina lingered by the bar, chatting on her cell phone, while Denise stood by the window and smoked. She would be forty soon, and her life wasn't getting any better. She missed Nichols deeply. She remembered how that little girl used to burn in the kitchen some mornings and how she was so smart and sweet. It tore a hole in Denise's heart that her youngest daughter was murdered and dumped in a dumpster like yesterday's leftovers. And she couldn't do anything about it.

Denise knew, if Nichols was alive, she probably would have been in a better situation with her older twins and that Nichols would've done whatever she had to do to bring her sisters and mother closer together. Denise missed Nichols' warm, caring heart.

Denise quickly wiped the tears from her eyes, making sure not to face Nina with her eyes puffy and watery. She didn't want Nina to see her looking vulnerable.

Denise took another pull from her cigarette before turning to Nina. "You ready to wild out tonight, bitch?"

Nina smiled and raised her cup. "Ya know it, girl. Where everybody at anyway?"

Four hours later, Denise's apartment was in full swing with people and loud music. Anita Baker was playing from the stereo, and the thick, lingering cigarette and weed smoke mixing together made some of the strongest lungs in the room cough from contact. The tainted smell carried heavily into the hallway. There was a comfortable mixture of men and women, and they all were cursing, drinking, and carrying on. The bottles of liquor that Denise had set out earlier were almost down to a swallow, so Nina and a friend had to do another run to the liquor store to get a few more bottles.

Denise sat at the card table playing spades, a burning cigarette dangling from her lips and a half cup of Goose sitting in front of her. She smiled at the hand she had and shouted, "It's muthafuckin' on up in here! I'm gettin' my fuckin' rent paid tonight."

The sadness and gloomy mood she'd been feeling earlier quickly disappeared when company arrived, and she was her usual self again—a swearing, teasing, loud-mouthed bitch. Her deceased daughter Nichols was no longer on her mind. The only thing that concerned her was the pot of money resting on the card table and probably fucking one of the cuties chilling in her apartment.

Tipsy, Nina was sitting on a man's lap and her tits were all in his face. He placed his hand between her legs and whispered the things she wanted to hear in her ear. It didn't take long for her to disappear with him into one of the bedrooms.

"Wear a fuckin' condom!" Denise shouted humorously.

Denise focused back on her game and stared into her partner's eyes. It was clear as a sunny, warm June day that they both had a thing for each other. Robert was her spades partner, and they were killing the other team. They were ready to win the five hundred dollars up for grabs.

Robert was tall, lean, and barely breaking his twenties. He sported long braids, smooth, dark skin, and was easy on the eyes from head to toe. He had a winning white smile and full lips that made Denise think of him eating her out. Coming up under Cross, Robert's style of clothing was sharp, and his jewelry was always on point. That night, he wore a lengthy white gold and diamond chain with a diamond-encrusted cross pendant that almost blinded Denise. And he sported a pair of diamond stud earrings, a Cartier watch on one wrist, and a matching yellow gold and diamond bracelet on the other.

Denise wasn't the only woman in the room checking out Robert. He had a few female admirers, but she made it her business to make it known that she was interested in the young hustler.

She smiled at him and bluntly asked, "So, Robert, you like cougars?"

Robert smiled. "I like any kind of cat. Pussy is pussy."

"Oh really? So, maybe I need to take your young ass to the zoo and have you pet one."

Robert chuckled, but Andrea didn't think Denise's comment was funny. She cut her eyes at Denise and said, "Ain't cougars suppose to be extinct anyway?"

"Oh no, she didn't!" someone exclaimed.

Denise cut her eyes over at the young girl dressed in the tight Apple Bottom jeans and tight shirt with the long ponytail and replied, "And cougars are known to kill viciously. Don't get hurt up in my place, little girl. Besides, it's always good for a growing boy to have some meat on his plate."

Andrea rolled her eyes and sucked her teeth. She had a huge crush on Robert and had been trying to fuck him since the summer. Robert was amused by the not-so-subtle catfight between the young and the old. Still, he had his eyes on Denise. He loved his women mature.

Andrea knew her boundaries when it came to messing with Denise. The thirty-six-year-old wildcat was known to cut a few bitches back in her days, so she didn't feel threatened by the girl.

She continued with the card game, and blurted out, looking at Andrea, "Just like my damn daughters—so fuckin' stupid. Don't get fucked up over some dick that don't even belong to you."

Andrea could only roll her eyes and look at Denise sideways.

The house phone rang while Denise was in the middle of her minor dispute and a good hand. She answered the call with an agitated tone, only to hear it was a nurse informing her that her daughter was injured and in critical condition at Jamaica Hospital.

"Well, I'm glad she's alive, but she's now eighteen and fuckin' grown. Besides, I already know about it, so don't fuckin' call here no more about that bitch. Fuck her!" Denise shouted. "I can't do shit for her anyway. You have a nice night."

Everyone at the table looked at Denise in shock. They couldn't believe the apathy she had toward Apple being in the hospital.

After hanging up, Denise exclaimed, "I ain't got no more fuckin' kids!"

"You a cold bitch, Denise," one of the players stated.

"Fuck her! That tramp gonna do me dirty and think I'm gonna have some concern? What goes around comes around."

By this time, it was nearing three in the morning, and the unruly pack was fading. Most of the guests were staggering their way back to their homes.

Denise sat on Robert's lap, sipping on her drink, ready to fuck him. She said to Andrea, "Little girl, ain't it time for you to leave?"

"I'm grown," Andrea shot back.

"Grown?" Denise chuckled. "What makes you grown, huh? What? You fucked a few niggas, sucked some dick, and think wearing them tight jeans make you grown? Bitch, ya coochie ain't even ready."

Andrea remained silent.

"Matter of fact, let me show you how to please a man the right way."

Denise stood up from Robert's lap and pulled him by his arm. She smirked at Andrea while luring Robert into the bedroom, where empty liquor bottles, clothing, and cigarette butts were scattered around. The ashtray was filled, and the sheets looked used and wrinkled. The condition of the room was a clear indication it had been used for sex all night.

Denise sucked her teeth. "I know muthafuckas don't think I'm gonna be the one cleaning this shit up."

Robert laughed.

Denise just wanted some dick and would worry about the bedroom later. It didn't take long before she was on her back with her legs wrapped around his head, allowing the young twenty-five-year-old hustler to eat her pussy out.

"Ooooooh, eat that pussy!" Denise cried out, making sure her cries of delight were loud enough for Andrea to hear, if she was listening.

Chapter 3

Kola punched in the correct numbers to open Cross' wall safe. She went into the stash, almost half a million dollars, and dumped what she needed into a small duffel bag. She counted ninety thousand dollars to buy six ki's of cocaine. Though business had been good in the past months, and money was not a problem for the couple, Kola knew that now wasn't the time for their product to dry up, because then their empire would start to crumble. Somebody needed to hold down the fort, especially with Chico being their main competition in Harlem. Tension was escalating between both crews, and a few bodies had fallen.

Chico and his crew were fierce competition for Cross. Harlem was a gold mine, and Kola wasn't about to give it up, especially to her sister's boyfriend. She despised Apple and anything connected to her and wanted to see her and Chico fall, and fall hard. With Cross and Edge locked up until their arraignment, Kola knew Cross was right. She had to step up and meet with the connect.

Chico was getting his supply from the Haitians and flooding the East Side with coke and dope that had been stepped on too many times. It wasn't as potent as Cross' supply, but Chico was still cutting into Cross' business with his weak product and lower price.

Kola knew Cross was getting a pure product from Eduardo for fifteen grand a ki and reselling it on the streets to different drug runners for eighteen and a half grand, making a profit of thirty-five hundred a ki. She knew it wasn't a huge profit, especially considering the risk they had to take, but they were at war with Chico and his crew, who was low-balling them in the streets. Cross supplied Harlem, and his reputation preceded him. Kola was ready to fight tooth and nail to keep his name respected and his business profitable.

She sat in the apartment with an idea. It was risky, but she knew with the right persuasion and the money on the table, he had to go for it. Kola's heart beat like African drums as she thought about how many things could go wrong. But if her plan worked well, then she and Cross would see much more money and cut out their competition permanently. It was a chance she was willing to take. She reached back into the safe and removed an extra forty thousand dollars to stuff into the duffel bag. Then she secured the duffel bag and was ready to make her move.

It had been twenty-four hours since she had gotten the phone call from Cross about his arrest, and his arraignment was in another twenty-four hours. Kola's time schedule was tight. She had to meet with Eddie at the preferred location, an apartment in New Jersey, and then rush to the courthouse to bail out Cross and Edge.

Kola sighed, looking at the time. It was getting late. She concealed the .380 in her purse, lit a Newport, and stared at herself in the mirror. Clad in a stylish, tight-fitting Chinese jumpsuit with a rhinestone dragon embedded in the back and a pair of Fendi heels, her look was flawless. Ready to conduct business with Eddie, she picked up her keys to the truck and rushed outside with the duffel bag in hand.

She traveled to Jersey City alone with one hundred and thirty thousand dollars in the bag. She crossed the George Washington Bridge and hit the evening traffic, heading into New Jersey.

Kola looked at herself in the visor mirror and said to herself, "You can do this, Kola. You got this. You gonna take care of this deal and then get your man out of jail."

She was worried about Cross but tried to block the worries from her mind and think about the meeting. Straight out of Colombia, Eddie made his way to the top through violence, bloodshed, and intimidation. He'd even killed his own brother because of his betrayal. Kola didn't know too much about him, except that Cross had been doing business with him for over a year and things always went well. She didn't want to fuck it up, so she kept her game face on and tried to be professional.

It took her thirty minutes to arrive in Jersey City. Eddie had a lavish waterfront three-bedroom condo overlooking the Manhattan skyline. The place was used only for business, and it was heavily secured. It was Kola's first time at the condo, because whenever Cross did business with Eddie, he went alone or with Edge. She had gotten the address and information from Cross and put it in the GPS.

She parked in front of the twenty-one-story building and sighed. She planned on changing Cross' business arrangement, which took courage. It would take a miracle to convince his connect, a man she had never met before, to switch it up.

"You gotta make it happen," Kola said to herself.

She checked her makeup and wardrobe, put on her dark diva shades, stepped out of her M-class Benz, and strutted toward the glass lobby entrance carrying the duffel bag. Kola had purposely unzipped the front of her fashionable jumpsuit to expose her ample cleavage, not wanting to look the least bit threatening. Her curves showed in the attire she wore, and her high heels click-clacked against the marble floor, echoing all through the lobby.

"Can I help you, ma'am?" the tall, well-dressed doorman asked. He was wearing a dark blue blazer, white gloves, and a top hat.

"Yes, I'm here to see Eddie or Eduardo."

The aging doorman looked Kola up and down, his eyes lingering on her breasts. As he picked up the phone to announce Kola's presence, she wondered if she would be let up.

"Yes, I have a young lady here wanting to see him," the doorman announced to the person on the other end of the phone.

"Tell them I'm here for Cross," Kola chimed.

"She's here representing Cross," the doorman added. He nodded as he listened.

While the doorman looked over at Kola once again, sizing her up from head to toe, Kola's nerves were on edge. She watched his every move.

"Yes. I understand, sir . . . I will, sir . . . at this very moment." The doorman removed the phone from his ear and said to Kola, "State your business."

Kola eyed the man and replied, "Making money is my business, and I have plenty to do business with." She raised the duffel bag, indicating there was plenty of money inside.

The doorman held a deadpan stare on Kola and spoke back into the phone. "She seems for real, sir." He listened, taking orders, and then looked at Kola. "Top floor, twenty-one, and they will be waiting for you."

Kola smiled and went on her way. She strutted toward the gold elevator doors, pushed the button, and looked back at the serious-looking doorman, who hadn't taken his eyes off her. The way he looked at her sent chills up her back. When the elevator doors opened, she quickly stepped into the blackened cherry wood interior and pushed for the twenty-first floor.

The lift ascended like a rocket taking off, making Kola feel a little bit queasy. She clutched the duffel bag tightly and took a deep breath.

Kola stepped off not knowing what to expect. It had crossed her mind that she could be walking into a setup, and even though she had her .380 stashed in her purse, she knew she wasn't Superwoman.

The second she stepped off the elevator three armed men in dark suits, two carrying Glock 17s and one an M16, confronted her. Trying not to look nervous, she kept up her game face and let the men pat her down.

"I'm packing," she quickly let it be known.

"Where?" one man asked, his voice stern.

"A three eighty in my purse," she said, surrendering her purse.

The man holding the M16 quickly snatched it from her hand and dumped the contents onto the hallway floor. He removed the gun, checked her purse thoroughly, including the lining, and tossed it back to her. Meanwhile, the other two checked the duffel bag and went through the money. Security was tighter than Fort Knox.

"Damn!" Kola uttered.

They continued their pat-down, searching between her legs, her breasts.

One of the men took it an extra step by fondling her near her pussy, making Kola cringe a little. When he was done, he smirked at Kola and said, "Just checking."

"You like that?" Kola asked, not smiling.

The man smiled.

"State your business with Eduardo," one of the men said, his facial expression hard like stone.

"I need to talk to him. It's about business."

"He doesn't meet with strangers."

"I'm Cross' woman, and I think he would want to meet with me. I came bearing gifts and news for him."

The men looked at her and then glanced at each other. One of the guards disappeared into the suite and left Kola waiting in the carpeted hallway. He came back out a moment later and signaled for her to enter.

Kola smiled as she followed the burly six-three man and stepped into a palace.

"Nice," Kola uttered.

After stepping into the living room, she looked around the place and was impressed with the gold pillars and high ceilings. It felt like the remnants of heaven had dropped around her. In her eyes, she saw true wealth and fortune. The place was extravagant, with its sprawling black-and-white marble floors, two giant crystal chandeliers that hung high over the living room, complemented by warm walnut and cherry furnishings, and delightful paintings hanging about. There was a large pool and Jacuzzi in the living room, along with a wet bar, plasma TV, and a few plants and trees, creating a lush atmosphere inside. The full-sized balcony along with the large bay windows provided a direct view to the Manhattan skyline across the Hudson River. The place was made for a king.

She noticed two naked female swimmers in the pool. She laughed to herself, thinking about the movie *Scarface*. She thought, *This is some Tony Montana shit for real.*

The two armed men standing in the living room were

watching Kola carefully, but she knew she wasn't a threat to them. Though unarmed, she hid her uneasiness well. All she wanted was to talk to Eddie face to face, strike up a new deal, and walk out alive.

A few minutes later, a very well-dressed man clothed in a dark-blue three-button Giorgio Armani suit with thin lapels walked out of a back room, a burning cigar clutched between his fingers. He had the look of a Fortune 500 businessman/crime boss.

Kola stared at him in awe. Tall, well-built, with full lips and a pencil-thin goatee, he was gorgeous. He had dark, curly black hair, enticing hazel eyes, and his skin was the color of honey.

Flanked by two men, Eddie walked toward Kola with an imposing stride, never taking his eyes off her. He took a puff from the Cuban cigar he was smoking then said to her, "You asked for me?"

"Yes."

"Why?"

"I'm Kola."

"I know your name, but why are you here? And it better be good. You with Cross?"

"I'm his lady."

"And what's the purpose of him sending his woman to do business with me? I find this very disrespectful."

"I come with respect, Eduardo," Kola replied.

"Where is Cross?"

"Unfortunately, he couldn't make it, so he sent me."

"And why's this? And I warn you now—I don't like

being lied to."

"He's locked up for the moment."

The news didn't sit too well with Eduardo.

He stared at Kola and asked, "For what charge?"

"Gun possession."

"I see."

Kola stood there with her heart feeling like it was on fire. She didn't want to disrespect the man in any fashion, but she needed to be firm and state her business. "I came to do business with you instead," she blurted out.

Eduardo looked at her. He was almost amused. "Business?"

"Yes," Kola said.

Eduardo chuckled then took a pull from the cigar. "I don't do business with women. I fuck them, they fuck me, but business is never good with a bitch."

"I'm not your average bitch."

He smiled and approached Kola closely. He took her chin into his hand and stared into her eyes.

Kola kept still. She hated the way he grabbed her, but she had no choice. He had the upper hand.

Eduardo looked at her closely and said, "Your eyes show the soul of a lion."

"I'm more than just a bark," she returned, showing no weakness.

Eduardo stared at Kola once more. Her eyes veered from him to the two naked young ladies exiting the large pool. They laughed to themselves as they donned their robes that had been hanging over two chairs.

Eduardo glanced at the women then looked at Kola and said, "One of the perks of being me. You like?"

"Cute."

"It is. I have two girlfriends at home . . . sisters . . . two of the most beautiful women a man could ever have. They both live in my sprawling mansion in Colombia, and they both have a son by me."

"Quite the playboy, huh?"

He smiled. "You care for a drink?"

"Would love one." Kola followed Eduardo to the wet bar.

Eduardo continued puffing on the cigar while mixing a gin and tonic. He passed Kola her drink and offered her a seat. He couldn't help but find Kola very interesting. He sat opposite her, and they continued their talk.

Eduardo boasted about his lifestyle, telling Kola about the life he lived. He found her very attractive and young. He talked about Colombia and its beautiful women. He told Kola that, with her beauty, she would easily fit in. He talked about the sisters/girlfriends more and the homes he had. Kola listened attentively, sipping her drink and trying to read him.

Kola thought that the large suite she was in was his home, but it was only his place of business. He also had the apartment next door and the one downstairs, and there were secret doors and passageways leading to both places in case there was a police raid or ambush.

Eduardo didn't care for the place in Jersey City. To him, New Jersey and New York were below his standards, and the weather was too cold. Still, his business was good in the States, and Harlem became a very profitable place for his product.

Eduardo doused his cigar in the ashtray and fixed his eyes on Kola. "Speak your business to me."

Kola locked eyes with the man, her legs crossed, the duffel bag near her feet. "My man has been doing business with you for a long time now, and unfortunately, he's in a situation that prevents him from being here at the moment. So I'm here in his place."

Eduardo took a sip from his glass and listened, his henchmen nearby and ready for anything.

Kola continued. "We've been buying from you at fifteen stacks a ki and moving plenty of supply for you. But I'm here with a business proposition for you."

The look on Eduardo's face already told Kola that her business with him better be good or she might not walk out alive.

"I'm suggesting you give me ten ki's for twelve-five a ki, and as you know, I came prepared."

Eduardo laughed a creepy, menacing laugh, intimidating Kola.

She kept her stern expression and pushed the duffel bag toward him.

"You come with laughs, little girl," he said.

"Just open it."

Eduardo unzipped the bag and looked in. "Lots of money for such a young girl."

"I'm a businesswoman," she countered.

Eduardo laughed again. When he was finished laughing, he took a sip from his glass before saying to her, "Our business arrangement stays the same—fifteen thousand a ki and nothing less. What makes you think you can come in here and change it? You disrespect me. You think flaunting your tits and body will influence me?"

"Of course, I mean you no disrespect, Eduardo. But the situation has changed in the streets. As you may be aware, we're at war with Chico, and with the prices he has from the Haitians, his business is cutting into our business, causing our profits to decline somewhat. I ask for that number for the ki's because I can guarantee you that Cross and myself can move these ten ki's in a much shorter time, producing a quicker turnaround and ridding ourselves of the competition.

"We all know that, when it comes to quality, the Haitians can't fuck with you. And the Haitians are a problem for the both of us. We move six ki's every seven days for you. Well, at the price I'm asking, we can increase that number and get back some of our old customers."

Kola knew she had Eduardo's attention. He was silent, contemplating the idea. Kola just waited for an answer. He took another sip as he dwelled on the thought. Kola's heart beat rapidly, and the palms of her hands were clammy.

Eduardo got out of his seat and walked closer to Kola. He circled her slowly, sipping on his drink and admiring every aspect of her. "I like you. You have courage and smarts. I respect that."

He stopped in front of Kola and looked at her intimately, touching her in a way that made her somewhat uncomfortable. However, she didn't flinch. He was a handsome man and also a powerful man.

He lingered on his reply for a moment and finally said to Kola, "Cross is a very lucky man to have you in his life. Me, personally, I'm a sexist. I believe women belong in the kitchen or on their backs making babies, and I feel slightly insulted that he sent you in his place. But I know a good business sense when I see one. I'll give you the ki's for twelve-five, but only on these conditions."

Kola held her excitement, knowing she wasn't out the flood yet. She sat still and listened to his conditions, hoping they were reasonable.

"From here on out, I deal with you and only you. You make Cross understand that. His sudden incarceration is a problem for me. His stupidity is an issue for me," Eduardo explained slowly.

Kola nodded.

"And then you will have to move twelve ki's within seven days, not ten."

"Twelve?" Kola asked.

"Will that be a problem?"

"No, it won't. I only brought enough for ten, though."

"I'll front you the two. But you move these twelve ki's for me at the price you ask within the reasonable time period that we agree on. Understand?"

"That's kind of pushing it," Kola explained. "I can do fourteen days."

"These are my terms, not yours. No negotiations."

Kola nodded.

"And if there's a problem with this new arrangement on your end, then there will be repercussions, starting with the price going back up to eighteen-five a ki for my aggravation. And any further problems . . . well, let's just say, I don't like problems."

"There won't be any problems."

"I just hope so."

If Kola wanted to come play with the big boys and step into his territory to make deals with him, then he would give her a deal that she would never forget. But there was something about her that was alluring.

Eduardo lit up another Cuban cigar and continued talking to Kola. One of the girls from the pool walked over to Eduardo in a sheer robe and stilettos and began caressing him from behind as he was discussing business.

He told the woman, "Give me a minute, my love. I have to finish up here."

She nodded and strutted off, leaving Eduardo to focus his attention back on Kola.

"We're done here. You will have your shipment, and you will have all my money in seven days."

One of Eduardo's men exited out of a back room carrying a similar duffel bag to Kola's and dropped it at her feet. She quickly unzipped it and saw the twelve kilos of cocaine, and the deal was made. Kola was on edge on so many levels, her legs felt like concrete, and her body felt like jelly.

She walked out of the building wondering how to tell Cross that she cut a different deal with his connect, and that she would be the one meeting with him from now on. Kola knew there was no easy way to tell Cross. He was going to flip, once he found out what she had gotten them into.

Chapter 4

Kola was so nervous, she hadn't eaten anything since before her meeting with Eduardo. Her mind was on business, with her trying to add new clientele to her roster, and then she had to contact the bail bondsman for Cross and Edge. It was a busy morning for her. She stashed the kilos in a secure place and jumped back into her M-class Benz to hurry to the courthouse for Cross' arraignment, her stomach in knots.

It was a chilly November day, and the early-morning traffic on the way to the court was thick, making Kola frustrated. She cursed and pressed down on the gas, zipping in and out of traffic and running through red lights. She missed her man and couldn't wait to feel his strong arms wrapped around her. She wasn't sure when to tell Cross about the new arrangement and was just hoping he didn't get too mad and beat the shit out of her.

It was twenty minutes past nine when Kola finally found parking and hurried toward the criminal courthouse in downtown Manhattan. She ran into the building in her tight-fitting Seven jeans, pumpkin leather jacket, and five-inch heels. Seeing the line of people snaking around the corner, she had a long wait to get through the metal detector. She sighed. *It's going to be a long day.*

It took Kola fifteen minutes to finally get through the metal detector, and the guards gave her a little hassle about the items in her purse. She curbed her attitude and bit her tongue, knowing they were only picking on her. She just wanted to hurry to see Cross.

She strutted down the long corridor searching for the right courtroom. The lobby of the courthouse on Centre Street was flooded with defense attorneys, prosecutors, legal aids, defendants, and police officers.

She had everything set up. The bondsman was in play, and she figured that Cross' lawyer would already be in the courtroom ready to represent his client. He was on retainer for a substantial amount of money, and today he would be put to the test.

Even though she had the money to bail out Cross, they needed the bondsman because, if the judge posted a large bail, she didn't want to be linked with the cash. Since she didn't have a legit income, the courts would be suspicious about an eighteen-year-old having the money to bail out her drug-dealing boyfriend.

As she strutted down the hallway, looking older and more mature than her true age, she noticed the steady fleeting looks that came her way. There was more than a hint of fascination for the young teen. Some of the side looks were even coming from the prosecutors themselves. In fact, she had quite a few admirers from all walks of life.

Kola was sexy, and the way she carried herself was very appealing. Her admirers gazed at the long, defined legs stretched out in the high heels she wore and were fixated on the way her body curved in the jeans. But she wasn't interested in anything but finding her boo and getting him released. She was focused on finding the courtroom her man was being arraigned in and showing him her full support.

She soon found it and walked into the room quietly, looking around at the concerned faces of girlfriends, mothers, grandmothers, and friends waiting for the docket number of their loved ones to be called by the bailiff and their cases to be reviewed by the judge.

Kola took a seat in the middle of the stale, semi-packed courtroom next to a worried mother with two young kids who was there trying to support her oldest son.

Kola let out a heavy sigh. She didn't know what to do with herself. She was the only one dressed with style in the room, and by the looks of things, she probably was the only one that didn't have a court-appointed lawyer. The sea of poor and worried faces was a clear indication that money and a proper attorney for representation would be an issue. It wasn't Kola's business, though.

The mother sitting next to her looked like her son's arraignment was only one of many issues that she had going on. Kola checked her out from the corner of her eye and knew the woman hadn't seen a hot comb in ages. Her clothes looked secondhand, and her younger kids, the way they were acting, seemed to be following their brother's footsteps.

Kola wasn't ready to have kids anytime soon. She was a career woman and, with her sex parties and reluctantly taking control over Cross' connect, having a family wasn't in her plans. She shunned the young, single black women stupid enough to get pregnant without any support. The one good thing Kola learned from her mother was how to hustle and have a nigga trick on her. She wasn't trying to become no one's baby mama or get stuck with a kid whose father was long gone. Kola was high-maintenance, and her man had to be a real man to fuck with her. That's why Cross was her ideal man.

Kola thought of better places to be than stuck in an out-of-date courtroom waiting for the long list of criminal cases to be processed. She sat through petty drug possession cases, misdemeanors, and disorderly conduct cases. It was a waste of her and the taxpayers' time, she thought. The hours passed slowly, and Kola had to fight against nodding off. It was so tedious, she was ready to pull out her own hair for entertainment.

Noon arrived, and the judge called for everyone to take a lunch break. But food was the last thing on Kola's mind. As the courtroom slowly cleared out, Kola remained seated in the pew trying to stay calm. The last one to exit the room, she went outside to smoke, like some of the others.

While taking a few pulls from her Newport, she rolled her eyes at some of the men steady gawking at her. And she constantly looked at the time.

The November wind pinched at her face with its hard gust, and the army of police, prosecutors, and district attorneys made her very nervous. She thought about her own fate and wondered when the day would come when she would find herself standing in front of a judge or jury.

She started chatting with a familiar face from the hood in front of the courts. Her friend Lateen, whom she had known since grade school, was in court for possession. If he couldn't be found on the corners trying to get money, he would be most likely serving time in Rikers Island. Lateen was never a smart man, but Kola enjoyed his company from time to time. And he made her laugh, which was something she needed at the moment. As they both smoked cigarettes, Lateen started joking with her.

"Tight-ass prosecution tryin' to charge me for a gram of crack and shit, knowing I seen that muthafucka on the block tryin' to cop the other night," Lateen stated.

"Uh-uh. Stop lying."

"Shit, I'm serious. Nigga's eyes red as shit right now. Tight-ass white boy gonna cop from me and then charge me. Pale-ass muthafucka high like a kite right now. You know the nigga gotta be high, wearing that tight-ass blue suit."

"You silly, Lateen."

Kola told him about Cross' incident, and the two enjoyed a quick laugh. Then they walked back inside the courts. She readied herself for another long session of procedures, hearings, motions, and other boring bullshit. She moved to the back because the woman with the two kids was starting to get on her nerves.

Two hours later, Cross' docket number was finally called.

"Docket numbers 448525685 and 449858954, Danny Thompson and Maurice Carter," the court officer announced.

Kola perked up, her eyes fixed on the door the prisoners were coming through. Butterflies in her stomach, her eyes lit up with anticipation. It had been a little over forty-eight hours since she had received the phone call, and she didn't get much sleep. Kola smiled upon seeing Cross escorted from the bullpen and into the courtroom, Edge right behind him, both men still in the clothes they had been arrested in.

Cross' eyes looked red and tired, and Edge's face displayed a stone-cold expression as the court officers led them in front of the judge. Right on cue, Cross' lawyer, Meyers Mitchell, entered the courtroom wearing a gray Italian pinstripe suit, wing-tip shoes, and a Rolex around his wrist that screamed wealth. He immediately stood out from the court-appointed lawyers representing the poor and misguided. He had smooth tan skin, slick black hair, and a tongue sharper than a razor.

Meyers moved with confidence, and all eyes were on him as he sat his expensive leather briefcase on the table, buttoned up his suit jacket, and whispered something into

Cross' ear. Cross and Edge didn't even bother to look back to see who was sitting in the courtroom for them.

The lanky, bushy-haired prosecutor spoke first. He already knew he had his hands full with Meyers. He opened up a manila envelope and peered up at the judge. "Your Honor," he said, "the People request that the defendants be held without bail, pending a grand jury investigation."

"On what grounds?" Meyers chimed.

"A loaded nine millimeter was found in the defendants' truck—"

Meyers tore back by saying, "Your Honor, my clients' civil rights were violated when the officers performed an illegal stop and search with no grounds at all. As you can see, this is my clients' first serious offense, and I ask that bail be posted."

There was a little back-and-forth argument from both sides, and Meyers clearly demonstrated he was the better attorney. He was articulate and witty, and the argument took only a few minutes before the judge posted bail at $25,000 for both defendants.

"Your Honor, my clients would like to post their bail right away," Meyers Mitchell announced.

As the prosecutor let out a sigh of defeat, Meyers patted Cross on his back. Kola smiled and wanted to scream out, but she kept her composure. She thought Meyers Mitchell was worth every penny spent on him.

A few hours later, Kola was reunited with Cross and Edge. She hugged her man tight and kissed him passionately. She had the Escalade parked out front and was ready to chauffeur her man anywhere. The men jumped into the truck, and Kola hurried away from downtown Manhattan.

"I need a fuckin' shower and some pussy," Cross said.

Kola smiled, ready to oblige him.

When Kola merged onto the FDR, heading uptown, Cross asked her, "You took care of that thing with Eduardo?"

A quick nervousness overcame her. She didn't want to tell him the truth right away, so she nodded. "Yeah, I got the ki's at the house."

"That's my girl," Cross responded with a proud smile.

Edge, who had been sitting quietly in the backseat, lit up a cigarette and said to Cross, "You wanna tell her about that thing we heard while in Central Booking."

"What thing?" Kola asked.

Cross looked over at Kola. "Your sister is in the hospital with serious burns to her face. Some crackhead threw a cup of acid at her."

"Karma's a bitch, right?"

Edge and Cross looked surprised that she was so cold to her own flesh and blood.

Edge said, "Damn! It's really like that between y'all?"

"I don't give a fuck if Apple lives or dies," Kola responded.

Edge took a pull from his cigarette. He chuckled. "You's a cold-hearted bitch fo' real, Kola. I see why Cross likes you."

"Did you have anything to do with it?" Cross asked.

Kola cut her eyes at him. Her look already said she was insulted that he had to even ask. "How can you ask me that?"

"I was just asking."

Kola didn't answer him, but she didn't deny the accusation either.

After dropping Edge off at his apartment in Harlem, Kola continued to drive without a hint of concern for Apple. She was more worried about telling Cross that she had arranged a new deal with Eduardo than her sister being in critical condition in Harlem Hospital.

Kola pulled into the circular driveway of their New Rochelle home and walked behind Cross into the dark house.

"I need a fuckin' shower," Cross said.

Kola took a deep breath. "Baby, we need to talk about something. It's really important."

"After I get out the shower," Cross responded, stripping from his clothing as he headed for the bathroom.

Kola followed behind him. She didn't know how to tell him the news. She thought about giving him some pussy first. Maybe it would be easier relaying the news about Eddie after he came and was more relaxed.

As Kola listened to the shower running, she stood outside the bathroom door biting her nails. *How do you tell the man you love that his connect doesn't want to deal with him anymore but would rather deal directly with his woman?* Kola thought to herself. After lingering by the bathroom door for a moment, she decided to just come out with it and stop beating around the bush.

Kola went into the bedroom, removed a pack of Newports from her drawer, and lit up a cigarette. She stood by the window peering out at the cool, fall day and waited for Cross to finish with his shower.

Ten minutes later Cross walked into the bedroom glistening like a spring creek, a towel wrapped around his waist. She turned with a smile, admiring the way the water trickled down his chiseled abs and the bulge underneath the towel.

"C'mere, baby."

Kola doused her cigarette and walked up to her man.

He wrapped his arms around her softness. "Mmm," he moaned. "I need some of this right now."

Kola grinned. "I bet you do."

Cross moved his hands down her curves and grabbed her firm, juicy booty. He caressed and fondled her body, causing him to get an erection underneath the towel. He pressed his hard dick against Kola, who was thrilled and ready to fuck him, but she had to tell him the news first.

"You my heart fo' real, Kola. I'm glad everything went smoothly wit' Eddie. Where you put my shit?"

"In the room where you always have it."

"I need to move that shit quick."

Cross didn't like to bring his work home, but under the circumstances, he had no other choice. He wanted to unload the ki's at the stash house and cut it for street distribution as soon as possible. He kissed Kola fervently and was ready to undress her, but she pulled away from his hold.

Looking Cross in his eyes, she bluntly said, "I made a new deal with Eduardo."

Cross couldn't believe what he'd heard. He glared at Kola and shouted, "You did what?"

"Baby, it's a better deal for us. I got the ki's cheaper."

Cross screamed, "Bitch, are you fuckin' crazy? What the fuck is wrong wit' you?"

Kola took a few steps back from him, fearing he would strike her.

Cross charged at her and slammed her into the bedroom wall, clutching her tight by the arms. "Are you fuckin' stupid?"

"Baby, I had to," she screamed back. "I fuckin' had to!"

"I sent you there to do one fuckin' thang, and you fuck me up! What kinda deal?"

Kola hesitated with her answer. She stared at an angry Cross, who was so close, she could feel the blood boiling in his veins. He gave her no room between them.

"I did what you told me to do, but Eduardo was upset with you for not showing up yourself."

Cross barked, "I was locked up. He don't fuckin' understand that?"

"I tried to explain it to him, but he wasn't listening. I got the ki's for twelve-five."

"At what risk?" Cross knew ki's didn't come that cheap.

Kola hated to reply, but she had no other choice. "We gotta move all twelve ki's within seven days, or he'll go up on the price to eighteen."

Kola heard the sudden explosion as Cross put his fist through the wall behind her.

"Are you fuckin' crazy!" he yelled. "What the fuck did you do that for? You just killed us. We're barely moving the shit we get from him now."

"Baby, we can do this. We can! All we gotta do is cut out the competition that's in our way and get our old customers back."

Cross stepped back and looked at her. "You ain't nothin' but a young fuckin' bitch!"

Kola resented the statement. Her feelings were hurt.

"There's more."

"What the fuck else did you fuckin' do?" he shouted.

Kola swallowed hard. "He only wants to deal with me, not you."

Cross went berserk and charged at Kola again, slamming her against the wall with force, knocking the breath out of her. She screamed out. He was strong. Cross then punched a larger hole into the bedroom wall and shattered the plasma flat-screen by throwing it to the floor.

"Get Eddie on the fuckin' phone," he shouted out.

Kola reached for her purse and pulled out her cell phone. She quickly dialed Eduardo's number. It rang twice, and before she could say hello, Cross snatched the phone from her hand and exclaimed, "Yeah, Eduardo?"

"It is me," Eduardo answered coolly.

"It's Cross. We need to fuckin' talk."

"Cross, lower your tongue toward me."

"I'm sorry, but what's this I hear about you striking up a new deal with my girl? I didn't sanction that. You had no right, man."

"Right? I have many rights. She was here for business, and you weren't, plain and simple."

"Man, I got locked up on a humble, some gun charge that ain't gonna stick. You ain't gotta worry, Eddie. I'm still the man."

"I'm not worrying," Eduardo replied nonchalantly, "but the situation has changed."

"You can't do this, man. I deal wit' you, not my girl. You keep her out of this."

"She's smarter than you think. I like her. She's to come to me, not you. That's the new arrangement from now on."

Cross couldn't hold his temper as he marched around the bedroom with the phone glued to his ear. He glared over at Kola, ready to toss her through a window.

"This ain't fuckin' right, Eduardo. I've been dealing wit' you for over a year now, and you wanna cut me the fuck out? This is fuckin' bullshit!" Cross screamed.

"Watch your words, Cross. Now I suggest you hang up before I get upset."

Cross wanted to kill him, but he knew it would be a huge mistake. Cross understood that if he were to lay one hand on Eduardo, there would be a mob of armed Colombians busting down his front door. Cross felt that his hands were tied.

After ending the call, his eyes cut into Kola with a fierce stare. He tossed her the phone and sarcastically said, "I guess you the boss now."

Kola's heart sank into her stomach. She hated to see her man so upset. She watched him take a seat on the edge of the bed and stare at the wall with a look of despair. He was hunched over, resting his elbows on his knees and cracking his knuckles.

She took a chance by walking over to him slowly. She wanted to talk to him and smooth things out. She refused to believe that she fucked up and had hope that things would turn out OK.

She climbed onto the bed with Cross and tried to ease his worries by massaging his shoulders. "Baby, I'm already on it. I started making phone calls, hitting up some of our old customers to negotiate with. We gonna cut out Chico and that bitch and run Harlem like it should be. We're a team, baby, and together we can move this shit."

Cross remained silent. Still fuming inside, Kola's support didn't mean shit to him at the moment.

Kola realized she had to do more showing than telling, which was exactly what she planned on doing.

Cross dryly responded, "I hope you ain't kill us wit' your shit." He removed himself from Kola's touch and walked into the bathroom, slamming the door behind him.

Kola tried to hold back her tears, but she couldn't help crying at seeing Cross so upset. After sitting there for a moment, she snatched up her cell phone and began making more phone calls, determined not to fail.

Chapter 5

The two weeks Apple spent in the burn unit were excruciating and degrading. She couldn't look at herself in any mirrors. She once took pride in her beauty, but that was snatched away from her viciously. The physical pain was subsiding somewhat with the medication she was given, but her spirit was crushed. The only thing on her mind was revenge. She hated everybody and everything. The bitter spirit that resided inside of her was ready to cut loose and wreak havoc on whoever disfigured her. If they thought she was a bitch before, then Harlem was about to get a rude awakening.

Detectives were in and out of her room, wanting her to file a report or press charges against her attacker or attackers, if she knew who they were. But Apple was defiant toward them and wanted to enforce the code of the streets. She was ready to handle her own problems and didn't need the help of the police.

The one good thing that Apple had in her life was Chico. She was surprised he was still by her side trying to comfort her and make the situation easier. Still, Chico had a hard time dealing with her sudden disfigurement. It took a strong stomach to stare at the burned side of Apple's face.

The doctors had planned to do many skin graft operations, but her face wasn't healing right. They had to treat her face with antibiotics for infection that had developed in the wound and operate on her burns countless times. Chico paid for all her medical bills. He was supportive and constantly by her side, which confused his crew. They figured that, with Apple's beauty gone, Chico would have been long gone too.

Chico sat by Apple's bed, holding her hand gently while she was asleep. His phone kept buzzing, but he ignored it for a moment. It had been another long day with medical treatments—the skin graft, the medication, and Apple's hollering and bitterness. But he understood her pain. He was ready to do anything for her, even kill every single last soul that was responsible.

Chico fell asleep in the chair next to the sleeping Apple. His phone had been ringing all night, but he was too tired to answer anyone's call. He planned to deal with business in the morning. Apple was his main concern for the night.

Chico woke up at four in the morning to see Apple out of bed. He wiped his eyes, looked over at her, and asked, "Why you out of bed?"

"I can't sleep."

"You OK?"

Apple turned and looked at him with an expression that said she was far from OK and wouldn't be for a very long time. The bandages on her face were itching and sticking. The painkillers she was taking were doing her fine but taking a small toll on her. She was drained of tears and felt so bitter that her hands were constantly balled in a fist. She couldn't think about anything but revenge.

Apple was saddened, though. It was her second week in the hospital, and there were no visitors, no concerns, no get-well cards, flowers, balloons, or anything sentimental from anyone. It was like everyone had forgotten about her, including her own family. Chico was her only support, but everyone else—all of Harlem—had left her for dead. It made Apple want to cry, but tears trickling down her face would be painful. So she held back her tears and substituted it with anger, and plotting against all of her enemies—even her sister and mother. Her heart was more bruised than her face.

Apple couldn't believe how drastically her life had changed within the year. She had transformed into so many people in such a short time that she was becoming bipolar. It felt like she was about to go crazy. She would just sit there for hours, looking into space, not saying a word. Chico tried to help her, but some days she would just ignore him.

"Baby, you need your rest," Chico said.

"I don't need shit!"

Chico went up to her and tried to console her, but

Apple pulled away from him, not wanting to be touched or comforted. In fact, most of the time she wanted to be alone.

Holding in his frustration, Chico checked the numbers in his phone and then looked at Apple. "I know what will make you feel a whole lot better," he said.

Apple didn't respond. She just continued to sit on the edge of her bed staring at the wall. The television was on mute with the dimmed room lit up from its azure glare.

"Just give me the word, Apple, and I'll hunt them all down and kill 'em," Chico proclaimed through clenched teeth. He was a killer and ready to spark up death all through Harlem.

"What about Kola?" he asked. "I'll start wit' that bitch. You said she had something to do wit' this shit."

Apple looked at him confused.

"The first night you were here that bitch name kept coming out your mouth. You kept blaming her."

Apple didn't remember anything. She was delirious at the time and hurting really bad. But she didn't rule her sister out as one of the culprits.

Chico, known to protect what was his with an iron fist, felt the attack on Apple was a direct attack on him. The streets and his woman were his. He had a brutal reputation on the streets, and there had to be serious retribution for Apple's disfigurement. People had to pay; they had to die. Or he would look weak, and he refused to be weak.

"Give me a name, Apple," he demanded.

Apple couldn't think. The only thing that came to her mind was the crackhead that walked up to her and changed her life forever.

"You need to kill him!" she cried out. "That's who I want fuckin' dead!"

"Lower your voice, baby. We in a public hospital."

Chico wanted to know every detail about the crackhead. The only thing Apple remembered was, he was always around her old building, and he went by the name Joe.

Chico nodded, taking a mental note of the information. He was ready to go to the projects with a few goons and talk to Joe the way he knew best, using hands-on violence.

He moved closer to Apple, took her hands into his, fixed his eyes on her wounds, and clearly stated, "Baby, whoever did this shit to you, I guarantee will get dealt with in the worst way. Fuck that shit! Niggas think they can throw acid in my girl's face and there ain't gonna be any repercussions? I'm about to light up Harlem fo' real over this shit."

Apple turned her head away from his stare and looked at the wall. She just wanted her normal life back. There was a deep-rooted pain and jealousy stirring in her stomach, making her green-eyed about the fact that her twin sister Kola now had all the beauty and wealth, while she was looking like a monster.

She turned to look back at Chico and saw how serious he was with his statement. He was ready to kill for her. She knew he was capable of carrying out the hits. He reigned with violence, some of which she'd witnessed personally.

Apple managed a smile. "Kill 'em all for me, baby. Kill 'em all, starting wit' that fuckin' crackhead."

"I will. I will."

Chico left the hospital room on a mission. The second he exited the lobby, he began making a few phone calls. He hated to see Apple in pain and felt the only way to make her feel a little better was to find out who was behind the assault and take care of it via bloodshed and torture.

He called Dante, his cousin.

"Yo, speak to me, Chico. What's good?"

"I need you in New York," Chico said.

"Problems?"

"Yeah."

"I'm there, cuz."

Chico nodded as he ended the call.

Dante was the main reason why Chico was running some parts of Harlem today. He had so many bodies to his name, he was nicknamed Body Count. Dante was six three and weighed over two hundred pounds and used various methods to kill his victims—guns, knives, and even strangulation.

Eight years ago, Chico was warring with a rival dealer named Manson, and it was getting ugly for him in the streets, until Dante arrived from Miami. Within two weeks of his arrival, Dante took out four of Manson's top men in brutal fashion, and Manson began looking weak in the streets and in the eyes of his men. A few months later, they found Manson's body in the trunk of a burning car. His own men had killed him.

Dante had locked down Harlem with fear. He was known to sometimes use a machete to hack off the limbs of his enemies and leave them to bleed to death. Originally from Cuba, the ex-militant and illegal immigrant was always ready to kill and cause havoc for his cousin. Chico meant the world to him, and it only took one phone call to bring him back to New York.

Chico walked to his car knowing that his foes would regret the day they attacked his girl. He loved Apple and would continue to do so, even with her scars.

Chapter 6

Kola secretly watched from the crevices of the dimmed doorway as Sunset rode the police sergeant's dick like she was a jockey.

Sunset straddled the officer like a tight noose around the neck as his dick plunged upward into her dripping wet pussy. "Ooooh, fuck me, daddy! Fuck me!" she cried out, digging her manicured nails into his chest as the sergeant slapped her ass repeatedly.

"Damn!" he moaned. "You feel so fuckin' good."

A regular at Kola's sex parties, Sergeant Charles was a large white man with a distinctive mane of thinning white hair and a pork-size penis.

After Bunny Rabbit's death, Sunset had become Kola's number one girl. Kola took the girl under her wing and was training her on how to get money and satisfy a trick. They were becoming close like sisters, and Kola felt she could trust the girl with anything.

Sunset stood no more than five feet without her heels, and with her butter-like complexion, almond-shaped eyes, and full lips, she was able to stir any man's heart. She carried herself like a lady at all times and was a class act. And she was the freak that every man dreamed of. The men chased her down at the parties and weren't shy about offering her all-expenses-paid trips to the Caribbean and spending huge amounts of cash on her.

Kola backed away from the doorway, hearing the moans and cries coming from the sergeant. She smiled as she walked down the corridor to tend to her party, which was in full swing.

Kola's parties were still private affairs with invites only, and they were creating a huge buzz throughout the underground. Well-established men—brokers, investment bankers, entrepreneurs, a few big-time street hustlers, cops, and even a senator's aide—were willing to pay up to two grand to frequent one of her parties, knowing that the women attending would be top-notch and disease-free. One time, a senator himself showed up at one of Kola's parties.

Kola was strict with her business, taking charge of everything, from the type of music that she wanted playing, to the refreshments served, to the attire the girls needed to wear. She even had her girls checked on a regular for any STDs, and she made sure security was on point.

R. Kelly's "Bump N' Grind" was blaring throughout the party, while the girls walked around the hall with their body parts exposed, eyes and hands flirting. Kola strutted into the hall in a *V* set, the bra and V-string encrusted with colorful Swarovski crystals, and bright red stilettos. The raunchy attire showed off her wonderful shape, but she was the only woman off-limits to the men. She belonged to Cross, and Cross was a jealous lover most times.

Kola chatted with a few of the men who were seated by the bar sipping on a bottle of Moët. Wearing boxers and T-shirts, and their dicks hard like rocks, they came from Wall Street to unwind and fool around with the best ladies in the room.

She smiled and asked, "How are y'all gentlemen doing?"

One of the men raised his glass to Kola and replied, "I think I'm never going home to my wife."

The men around him broke up laughing.

Kola smiled at his comment and moved on. She was only eighteen and already the boss of things. She looked around to see if everything was going smoothly, and she was proud of what she saw.

Still, Kola had other business to take care of. She had a few ki's to move in a limited period, and she wasted no time getting on the phone calling up people. She even used her sex parties as an avenue to network.

She had an interest in three particular fellows at her party. One of the men was Perry. He was a fierce Dominican from the East Side in Spanish Harlem, and one of the hustlers who got his product from Chico. Kola saw this as an opportunity to get into his ear about business.

She watched Perry closely, observing him flirt with the girls. He was a pretty boy with long, thick braids, hazel eyes, and smooth brown skin. He had some height on him, and every inch of him was physically built. The ladies in the hall were drawn to Perry like he was NBA ball player. They loved his swag and knew he was somebody rich and important. He was swathed in bling, smoking his Black and Mild and laughing with his boys by a table.

Kola pulled Sassy to the side. She pointed to Perry. "You see him over there?" She watched as he grabbed a few of the ladies' booties and tits.

Sassy, one of Kola's Asian assassins in the bedroom, nodded.

"I want you to take him a bottle of Cristal and tell him it's on the house from me."

Sassy nodded again.

Kola wanted Perry's attention. She observed how he and his crew were downing bottles like water and figured it would be polite. She watched Sassy walk to the bar, get a bottle of Cristal, and sashay over to Perry and his boys with a flirtatious smile and scantily clad in a black off-the-shoulder stretch lace micro chemise with nothing underneath.

The men smiled, and Sassy worked her magic, especially on Perry, taking a seat on his lap and whispering something in his ear.

He smiled and said, "I like your style, ma."

"And I like yours," Sassy returned.

What Sassy lacked in ass, she made up for in plump

breasts and her exotic features. She had full lips, round hips, and sultry Asian eyes that could arouse a man's heart without even trying.

Perry rested his hands between her thighs and played with her pussy. "Damn! And shaved too. I like that, ma."

"I bet you do." Sassy felt his fingers digging into her slippery insides, rubbing against her clit. A pleasing moan escaped her lips.

"You like that?" Perry teased.

Sassy squirmed in his lap and exhaled a breath of satisfaction.

Perry's men laughed. They wanted a piece of the Asian beauty too and were ready to run a train on her in one of the back rooms.

Kola watched from a short distance. She respected how Sassy worked the table. She let Sassy have her moment and then walked over.

"I see you got my girl trippin' over here," Kola said with a smile.

"I like her, Kola."

"Yeah, she's one of my best."

"I wanna fuck," Perry blurted out, the yearning showing in his eyes.

Sassy felt the bulge in his jeans and was highly impressed. She wanted to wrap her lips around his hard dick and suck it like a porn star.

Kola steadied her eyes on Perry. "It's good to see you

enjoying yourself, Perry, but I need to talk to you about something . . . in private, if you don't mind."

Perry nodded. He respected Kola and knew she would never waste his time. Sassy stood up from Perry's lap, and as he stood out of his chair, his hard-on was evident.

Sassy smiled and said, "I'll take care of that when you come back, sweetie."

"Oh, I know you will." Perry returned the smile.

Perry followed Kola into a private room. After Kola closed the door, he looked at her with a lustful gaze. He massaged his crotch leisurely, licking his lips. "You look nice, ma."

"Thanks."

"I'm sayin'. . . what's good wit' that? I see your boy ain't around tonight."

"He takes care of business."

"I bet he do, like I want to right now." Perry stepped closer to Kola.

"Put your dick on chill and relax, Perry. I'm here on business. I ain't tryin' to fuck you."

"I'm sayin', ma . . . it's only you and me in the room. Ain't nobody gotta find out. You is so fuckin' sexy, Kola. I'm sayin' . . . what's really good wit' that?"

She smiled. "Business."

"What about pleasure?"

"Business is my pleasure."

"I respect that." Perry knew not to push it, knowing that Cross and his crew were nothing to play with. Kola wasn't the average hood chick he could just have his way with. "What you got me in here for?" he asked.

"I have a proposition for you. A really nice one."

"Like what?"

"We both about making money, right?"

"It's why I get up every morning, baby."

Kola smiled. "How are things goin' wit' Chico?"

"His shit is weak, but it moves."

"Listen, Perry, I'ma be up front wit' you. I want you to come over and fuck wit' our shit at a better price."

Perry chuckled. "At eighteen-five? Nah. Chico's shit might be stepped on a lot, but it still moves, and no disrespect, but y'all shit too rich for my blood."

"I'm ready to cut you a deal."

"What kind of deal?"

"Sixteen."

"Chico lets his go at fifteen."

"But Chico ain't fuckin' with the quality we fuckin' wit—straight connect from Colombia, and uncut. Maybe stepped on one or two times when you get it ready for street distribution."

Perry still looked reluctant. Kola moved closer to him, staring him in the eyes. She was sharp with business and wanted to pull Perry into the deal.

"Look, either way our shit is sweet like pussy. Gonna sell like it too, and it's gonna get out there on that grind shit, making niggas plenty of money. We got far better quality than that weak, stepped-on shit Chico is pumping out. I'm hollering at you first because I got love for you, Perry. But sooner or later Chico's gonna dry out. He ain't about quality, but we are."

Perry couldn't take his eyes away from Kola. She had him thinking. "I've been fuckin' wit' Chico for a minute."

"Yeah, I respect loyalty, but at the end of the day you a businessman, I hope, and business shouldn't be personal. Are you tryin' to get rich, nigga, or make fuckin' friends?"

"I feel you, ma."

"Nah. If you feel me, then get the fuck on board."

Perry rubbed his chin, thinking about the proposal. He knew it was a sweet deal. Besides, he was becoming weary of Chico. In the past week, Chico had been ignoring his phone calls and hadn't been getting directly back to him when needed. Word on the streets was that Chico was too wrapped up with Apple being in the hospital, and business was the last thing on his mind.

"A'ight, I'll fuck wit' you, Kola."

Kola couldn't contain her huge smile. "My nigga!"

"Sixteen a bird, right?"

"My word is my word, Perry."

"And Cross is good with this?"

"Believe me, we're partners. He knows."

"A'ight, put me down for four. I'll have the money for you by tomorrow evening."

They shook hands on the deal, and Perry exited the room and went looking for Sassy.

Kola was elated. It had been two days since her meeting with Eduardo, and already she had gotten rid of four ki's. She soon would have the streets locked with product.

She walked out behind Perry and looked around the room for other potential buyers. She spotted Fumes and Lennox in the room. Fumes was a heavy hitter from Jamaica, Queens who came up as a teenager under Fat Cat's crew and was now a major player himself. In his early forties, he had done time for drugs and assault.

Fumes was a witty businessman who knew how to use the elements of the streets and book smarts to get ahead. He was established in so many business ventures, the streets called him "the black Donald Trump."

Kola was surprised to see that he actually came to one of her parties. Fumes spent most of his time in the South and abroad, since he had homes everywhere, from New York to the Bahamas. He excluded himself from the day-to-day street operations of his illicit business, but everyone knew he was still the head nigga in charge.

Lennox wasn't as well established as Fumes, but he was a heavy hitter too. He was a Dominican from Washington Heights and owned a barbershop and some bodegas. The only reason Kola invited him to her parties was because he was a big spender and a show-off. He would make it rain dollar bills in the strip clubs and spend twenty thousand dollars at the bar on women and friends.

Kola planned to have a one-on-one conversation with both men before the night was over. She figured Fumes would be harder to pitch to than Lennox. Fumes had seen it all, been there and done that, and was the type of man that needed an accurate blueprint about everything. But, with Lennox, if it was about making him more money, then he was down for anything.

Kola stood close by watching both men. She observed Perry disappearing into one of the back rooms with Sassy.

Kola went after Fumes first, cornering him by the bar while he was with one of the girls. "What you want, teenybopper?" Fumes said.

"A minute of your time."

"My time, huh. Well, unfortunately, my time is taken."

"Well, when will it not be taken?" Kola focused her eyes on his, holding a firm posture, letting him know she wasn't intimidated.

"I'll call you."

"You need to do that."

"I don't need to do shit, little girl, but breathe and fuck."

Fumes puffed on his cigar with his eyes and attitude clearly illustrating that he had little respect for Kola. He saw her as a baby in a grown man's business. Fumes felt she didn't belong anywhere around adult dealings. Fumes was from the old school and felt girls like Kola should stay in their place, fucking men like him and taking care of their babies. He tolerated Kola's parties because he felt that pussy was allowed to sell pussy, but drugs and other things were too much for a female to handle. Fumes always stated that women were too emotional to do what he did and couldn't get their hands dirty like him.

Kola didn't like Fumes' attitude toward her. She passed him her card and strutted away.

Fumes stared at her, a wretched expression across his face. "Cross needs to put that little bitch over his lap and spank her ass for getting in his fuckin' business," he said to one of his men.

His friend laughed.

Kola went looking for Lennox next, knowing he would be much easier to talk to. Lennox and Kola chatted in one of the backrooms, and he was ready to jump in bed with her.

Kola felt she was on her way. She couldn't wait to see Cross and tell him the good news. She had it all lined up, and those who doubted her would soon be copping from her. Kola felt that between her sex parties and moving weight for Eduardo, in no time, the world would be at her feet. She wanted to be that bitch and was well on her way.

Chapter 7

Kola strutted confidently toward the towering building in Jersey City to meet with Eduardo, carrying a duffel bag filled with money. Her nerves were much better than in her first meeting with him. She walked into the building like a diva, wearing a pair of tight-fitting Seven jeans, and a white cable cashmere turtleneck underneath a black denim trench coat. Her legs appeared longer in a pair of sexy high-heeled boots. The same doorman recognized her from a week earlier and quickly called the floor she wanted to go to.

Kola waited in the lobby to be allowed up, and it was quickly approved. It was the same routine when she stepped off the elevator. The same three men in dark suits were waiting to search her.

"Hey, boys," she greeted with a smile.

The men didn't smile back. Instead, they did their job searching her thoroughly, and the same man caught a quick, cheap feel at Kola's expense.

Not taking it personal, Kola smirked at the man. She

was a big girl and wasn't going to cry over some quick fondling. She was there on business and wanted to keep it that way. "Keep this up and I'm gonna have to start charging you."

When they were satisfied, the same man went into the suite to inform Eduardo about Kola's arrival. He was in and out, and gestured for Kola to enter. Kola followed him, eager to do more business with Eduardo. The suite wasn't as overwhelming as before. It was like seeing the same act twice. She set the duffel bag down, removed her coat, and took a seat in one of the many chairs.

Eduardo approached Kola a short time later clad in a long terry cotton robe, his expensive gold chain peeking from underneath, and wool slippers on his feet. He had just gotten out of the pool from an evening swim with two of his beautiful female companions.

He smiled at Kola. "On time. I like it."

"I told you that I'm about my business."

Eduardo stared down at the duffel bag.

"I'm here for that re-up. There's an extra twenty-five thousand dollars in the bag from what I owed you from last time."

"Impressive."

Eduardo picked up the bag of money and quickly went through it. He nodded in approval and passed the bag over to one of his men. He then focused his attention back to Kola.

"I never thought you would do it."

"Never doubt a sister. I told you, I'm a businesswoman."

Eduardo chuckled. "I see this now. Relax. You need a drink?"

"I just want to get this shit done with."

"You in a rush?"

"Kind of."

"Don't be. *Mi casa es su casa.*"

Eduardo eyed Kola's beautiful figure. He admired her sassiness. There was something about her that was different. He walked over to the bar and fixed a drink for himself and one for Kola, even though she'd refused. Eduardo was the type who didn't take *no* for an answer.

Kola remained calm. She sighed lightly, crossed her legs, and looked around the room. Eduardo walked over, smiled at Kola, passed one of the glasses to her, and sat opposite to her. He crossed his legs, sat back in the chair coolly, and asked Kola, "So, same as before?"

"Nothing more, nothing less."

He nodded. "I rarely meet women like you . . . ambitious in this game."

"I told you, I'm a different kind of bitch."

"Young too."

"I get money at any age."

"Business is good, I see."

"Business is fuckin' great." Kola smiled.

Eduardo raised his glass toward her and toasted. "To us . . . to business."

Kola raised her glass. "To business."

They both took a sip from their glasses. Kola couldn't believe she had a direct link to a Colombian connect. It was something out of a movie for her. She was ready to run with it until the wheels started to fall off. She wanted Eduardo to trust her, and the only way she saw that happening was to keep making him a lot of money by being a loyal customer over time.

Kola still felt like she betrayed Cross somewhat. She wanted to be on his good side and was determined to make it up to him in some way. Cross looked out for her, and she could never forget about him. She wondered why Eduardo only wanted to deal with her in the future, when it was clear to her that he was a sexist.

After a half hour of drinking and talking with Eduardo, she started feeling comfortable around him. Eduardo was a very intelligent man, knowledgeable in history, politics, and other fields. Kola was highly impressed by the way he talked. He was a gangster, but carried himself like a businessman. She learned that he owned buildings in Colombia and had most of the government officials there in his pocket.

Eduardo stood up from his seat with the empty glass in his hand and called over one of his men. The burly armed guard in the dark suit walked over with a duffel bag clutched in his hand. He dropped it between Kola and Eduardo and walked away.

"Twelve ki's," Eduardo uttered.

Kola nodded.

Eduardo locked eyes with Kola. The look in his eyes showed his attraction for her. Kola immediately picked up on it and knew it was time for her to leave. She had what she came for. She set her empty glass on the table near her chair and stood up to reach for her coat.

Eduardo moved closer to her, his eyes on her stylish attire. He had the urge to reach out and take her into his arms. "You're a very beautiful woman, Kola."

"Thanks."

Kola put on her coat while Eduardo just stood there watching her. He was a man of power and influence, and he always got whatever he wanted. With the money and muscle he had, the world was at his feet.

Kola had concern that Eduardo wanted her, but she was not for sale and was ready to be stern with him, if necessary.

As she picked up the duffel bag, she heard Eduardo say, "Next time."

"Yeah, next time," she replied coolly.

Eduardo tipped his chin her way and allowed Kola to leave. Eduardo kept his eyes on her until she was out the door.

Kola hurried out of the building and to her car, feeling that her looks were both a blessing and a curse. She tossed the duffel bag into the trunk, jumped into the driver's seat of her Benz, and sped back to Harlem. She rushed to the city to see Cross. Business in Harlem had picked up for them significantly, and Cross' name still rang out through the blocks of Harlem like he was an icon. Kola didn't want to take that away from her man, and even though she had the connect, Cross still had the reputation. The only people who knew about their arrangement with Eduardo were themselves and Edge, who'd made it known that he had a problem with Kola running the show.

The two men had gotten into a heated argument over the situation. Edge feared Kola would become a problem and come between his friendship with Cross.

"That bitch double-crossed you, nigga," Edge had shouted to Cross.

"It is what it is right now, Edge. I'm dealing with it, not you," Cross had sternly replied.

"Fuck that, nigga! She's in our shit. She fuckin' back-doored you, Cross. I don't fuckin' trust that. I don't fuckin' trust her! Wake the fuck up!"

"Watch yourself, Edge!"

Kola pulled up in a quiet middle-class neighborhood in Harlem, where the residents minded their business, and the police rarely patrolled. It was a windy fall evening, and the narrow tree-lined block was cluttered with parked cars. She parked in front of the three-story brownstone on 138th Street with four ki's in the trunk and a .380 under her seat. She dialed the core man inside, and he picked up after the second ring.

"I'm outside," Kola said.

"A'ight," the man replied.

Kola waited a minute until DJ exited the brownstone dressed in a brown Nautica jacket and a Yankees fitted. She watched his approach from the rearview mirror, and when he was closer to the car, she popped the trunk. DJ knew the routine. He removed the duffel bag from the trunk and slammed it shut. He was one of their preferred clients because he could afford to pay in advance. He trusted the couple and had the sixty-four thousand in cash to drop on pure, uncut coke.

DJ was from Harlem but had moved out to Cleveland, Ohio a few years earlier and set up shop there with a rough crew. He was a heavyweight in the Midwest, making frequent trips into New York for his re-up with Cross.

Kola watched DJ from the rearview mirror as he nonchalantly walked back into the brownstone with the bag. She started smoking a cigarette, thinking to herself, she would be able to move more than twelve ki's a week.

Kola walked into her magnificent home on the hills and dropped the duffel bag filled with money on the table in front of Cross—$500,000.

Cross sat back in his chair and looked up at Kola. He couldn't contain his smile any longer. His girl was a true hustler, and he respected that.

Kola beamed. "That's all us, baby."

"Damn!"

"I told you, we gettin' this money, baby. We puttin' Chico out of business with the shit we putting out there. They can't get enough of our shit."

Kola took a seat on Cross' lap and began kissing on

him. She loved the way his lips felt against hers, and the way he pushed his tongue into her mouth made her pussy flow. She couldn't get enough of him.

Before long Cross no longer cared that his woman was dealing with their connect. The flow of money became his main concern along with dominating the streets of Harlem. Kola was able to handle herself, and his doubt and anger was gone once the money started pouring in. Chico was slowly fading out of the game.

"Let's go out, baby . . . celebrate," Kola suggested.

"Like where?"

"Anywhere. I just wanna look good for you tonight and have a good time." Kola straddled Cross in the chair and started kissing on him again.

Cross reached around Kola and grabbed her ass firmly. He loved how her succulent ass cheeks felt in his grip. Kola felt the hard-on bulging in Cross' jeans, and that made her yearn for the feel of him even more.

They kissed passionately while Kola grinded her pussy into his lap. She wanted to fuck him, to feel every inch of him thrusting inside of her.

Cross picked up Kola into his arms and carried her into the bedroom as she laughed like a little schoolgirl. He gently placed her on the bed and began undressing himself.

Kola stared at the treasure that was hers, admiring the rippling abs that lined his stomach and his rich, dark skin that was tight like Saran Wrap around his bone structure.

"Damn, baby!" she uttered with a smile.

Kola hurriedly unbuttoned her jeans and tore off her blouse like a lunatic. She didn't have time for the foreplay. She wanted some dick. She was naked in a heartbeat and reached up for Cross to pull him down on top of her.

"Fuck me, baby!" she exclaimed in his ear.

She positioned herself on her back, spreading her long legs for Cross to take her like the beast he was. She loved the way Cross took control of her body. He wasn't scared to fuck her the way she liked it—rough and with the hair-pulling.

Cross situated his thick, naked frame between Kola's legs and thrust his steel dick into her, making her squirm in his hold.

Kola arched her back and threw her legs around Cross tightly. "Ooooh, fuck me, daddy," she cooed.

Her eyes watered and her legs quivered. The dick inside of her felt like the sun in her face after spending too much time in the dark. She panted in his ear and ran her manicured nails down the center of his back, feeling his sweat saturating her skin as he pressed down on top of her with her tits mashed against his chest. Cross then held her legs in a vertical position while continuing to ram his steel pipe deep into her.

"Ooooh, baby! Ooooh, I fuckin' love you," she cried out.

The missionary position felt too good for both of them. Kola had him weakened and clawing the sheets. She nibbled at his ear while pressing her thighs into his side as he fucked her until she babbled. She felt her body about to go into a convulsion from the pounding she was enduring. The dick was always good to her.

"I'm coming!" she purred.

Right then Kola felt his explosion inside of her and held her boo tight against her sweaty frame. She never wanted to let him go. She always felt secure around him.

Kola lay across Cross' chest and massaged a small piece of him, soothing his need. The way Cross fucked and kissed on her was a pure indication of how much he loved her. Their sexual rendezvous was always memorable night after night, with Kola always feeling stimulated and complete.

Though it was getting late, Kola was still in the mood to go out somewhere and have a good time. She felt that now was the time to mention buying more bricks from Eduardo.

She raised herself up from his chest, looked her man in the eyes, and said, "Baby, I was thinking maybe we should step up our purchase next time around."

"What you mean?" he asked.

"I mean, business is good, baby. So let's step it up a few more bricks. I mean, as soon as I get them, they gone, baby."

Cross looked at Kola with a deadpan stare. She didn't know what he was thinking. She was nervous about bringing up the subject, but it would be a lot more money for them both.

"How much more you talking about?"

"I was thinking maybe fifteen or twenty bricks."

"That's a lot of weight, baby."

"I know, but we got the clientele and the muscle. Who gonna fuck wit' us, baby? I mean, our shit's moving like pussy out there. Chico is getting weak, and since we locked down this wholesale thing, we'll be able to tap into muthafuckas in so many fuckin' states."

She hugged up against Cross, kissed him on the lips, and continued with, "Think about it, baby. You and me, we can run all this shit. Who's gonna touch us?"

Cross liked the idea of it, but state-to-state trafficking was risky business. They were about to step on plenty of toes, including Chico's.

"Fuck it! Let's do it, baby. I'm down."

"You serious?"

"You and me together, with our brains and the muscle we got, you're right—who's gonna touch us? We in this to win it, right?"

"Of course, baby. Ooooh, I love you so much."

Cross grinned. "You do, huh?"

"Yes, baby."

"So show me how much you love me."

Kola grinned. She was more than willing to show her man the love she had for him. She disappeared under the sheets and caressed his nut sack gently, massaging and twisting his balls like it was Play-Doh. Her lips caught the head of his thickening pole, and she flicked her tongue away at the mushroom tip as she stroked it with her soft, manicured hands.

Cross gasped and shuddered. "Oh, baby, that feels so good," he moaned.

Cross tried to control it, but using her skills, Kola toyed with him. She could feel the pressure building in him, feeling the semen mounting as she continued to jerk and suck his dick.

"Oh, baby, I love you," Cross cooed. "Oh shit! Ooooh, shit!"

Kola stopped, squeezed his balls hard, bit his nipples, and purred, "Give it to me, big daddy."

No sooner, Cross released himself into Kola's mouth, and she swallowed every bit of him without a second thought. She nestled in Cross' arms, thinking it was going to be a really good year for the both of them.

Chapter 8

Chico sat in the passenger seat of the dark blue Impala on Fifth Avenue, across the street from Lincoln Projects. His cousin Dante was a menacing figure in a pair of dark shades and a dark hoodie as he sat behind the wheel, both men watching everything that moved.

Dante had arrived in New York via LaGuardia Airport twenty-four hours earlier and was ready to get back into business with Chico right away. He saw Chico in despair about Apple's condition and wanted to make it right. He had in his possession a .50 Desert Eagle, his favorite gun. The weapon was intimidating like him, and once a man was shot with it, he wasn't getting back up.

It was late in the evening, the sun being a memory as night loomed over the city. The traffic was dying as the time ticked toward midnight.

Chico wanted to find the crackhead named Joe, even if he had to tear Harlem apart looking for him. But he knew a crackhead wasn't going to be that hard to find. He'd sent a few goons out on the streets, putting the buzz in a few people's ears that he would pay a hundred dollars if they knew where to find Joe.

Within a few hours, it had gotten back to Chico's goons that Joe spent the majority of his time in the stairwell of the Lincoln Projects or at a hole-in-the-wall spot off Lenox Avenue. He wasn't at the spot on Lenox, so Chico figured he was hiding in a stairwell of the building.

Chico was eager to have a word with Joe in private, and then he would be ready to tear the man apart. He was burning inside thinking about the incident.

"What's on your mind, Chico?" Dante asked.

"Nothin' much. Just thinking."

"We gonna find this muthafucka, Chico . . . make the *puta* talk and then fuck his whole shit up."

"Muthafucka disrespected mines, Dante. You should see her. She's a mess right now."

"And I'm here to make it right."

Chico took a pull from his cigarette and reclined in his seat. He felt untouchable with Dante back in town. He gripped the .45 in his hand and stared out the window, his mind wandering.

Chico had learned that Cross had cut his price down to sixteen thousand a ki, and even though Chico was selling his birds cheaper at fifteen, his clients were choosing quality over his lower price.

"How dare these muthafuckas! They come at my bitch, and now this nigga Cross tryin' to move in on my shit. I want 'em dead. Fuckin' dead!"

"I'm gonna make it happen, cuzzo. Just be patient."

The two continued to sit and wait, knowing Joe would be found sooner or later. They had too much muscle and too many informants spread out everywhere in Harlem for him not to be spotted.

Dante looked over at his cousin with a curious stare. "What's up wit' this bitch anyway? Why you so into her, Chico?"

"She do her thang, yo. I mean, she's smart, and when we met, she wasn't looking for a handout like most of these bitches. She had her own thing going wit' this loan-sharking, and she had her own soldiers too. I liked that, man."

Dante nodded. "A'ight."

"And, besides, she reminds me of Nikki."

"She do?"

"Yeah, her style, and the way she carry herself, sometimes I confuse Apple with Nikki."

"She ain't her, though, Chico. That was a long time ago. You gotta let that shit go, cuzzo. I know that shit is still eating away at you."

"I try, man, but I know it's my fault. If I was only there, it wouldn't have gone down like that."

"But you weren't, and it did. You were locked up. What the fuck were you able to do? Nothing!"

"Nah, I promised I would always be there for her and protect her. I loved her, and for niggas to violate her like that . . . Muthafuckas!"

"I got two out of five, and believe me, Chico, the two I caught suffered like they were in the hands of the devil himself. I tried to get them to talk. Even had both their balls squeezed in a pair of vise grips and under a hot flame, but they were tough. They knew, after that, not to fuck wit' you."

Chico thoughts went from Apple to his first love, Nikki, who was killed ten years earlier. He was eighteen then. He was incarcerated on drug charges and beefing with a rival crew for control of a profitable drug corner in Washington Heights. Chico's name had been ringing out since he was fifteen, and Nikki had been his sweetheart since they were fourteen.

One night, while he was doing time on Rikers Island, five rival gang members rushed into his home looking for money and drugs. They found Nikki asleep in the bedroom. They raped and beat her repeatedly for hours and then shot her three times in the head. The horrendous crime sent shockwaves through the hood. It was a clear message to Chico—they were coming for him next.

Dante hit the streets in his cousin's name and found two of the men responsible for Nikki's death in a week's time. He made sure they suffered before hacking them into pieces with a machete. Chico was distraught for months and spent most of his time on Rikers Island in isolation. After a year on Rikers, he came home a more ruthless man, vowing to never let anyone take anything away from him again.

Chico watched Dennis emerge from one of the project buildings and approach the parked Impala with wild-looking eyes. Slim and grungy-looking with unkempt hair, he had a devastating addiction. Crack had controlled his life for years, and he was willing to do anything for a payday, even if it meant selling out a friend. He could taste the hundred dollars Chico was paying him for information. It was going to be put to good use in a crack pipe.

Chico rose in his seat. "What you got for me, nigga?"

Dennis smiled, showing the few teeth he had left. "I got good news, Chico." He fidgeted near the Impala, looking around nervously. He then grabbed the car door with his greasy hands.

"Nigga, get ya fuckin' dirty hands off the car. You fuckin' crazy!"

Dennis jumped back, his eyes widening with fear. "I'm sorry, Chico. I'm sorry."

Chico stepped out of the car and glared at Dennis with a cold stare meant to send chills into him. "Where he at?" Chico sternly asked.

"Joe in the stairway now gettin' high," Dennis said in a nervous tone.

"Which one?"

Dennis pointed to the first building directly across the street. "He on the third floor smoking now."

Chico stared at Dennis for a moment, making the

fiend even more uncomfortable. He just wanted to get his money, run off, and get high.

Chico reached into his pocket and pulled out a wad of money. He peeled off five twenties and slowly handed it over to Dennis.

When Dennis went to reach for his reward, Chico pulled the cash back. "Nigga, if ya lyin' to me, I'll kill you."

"I'm not lyin', Chico. He up there in the stairway now, alone and gettin' high."

Dennis was beaming after Chico handed him the hundred dollars. It had been the most money in his hands in a long time. In fact, he felt like he had won the lottery.

"Get the fuck outta here!" Chico exclaimed, and Dennis took off running.

Dante exited the car with the .50 concealed in its holster. He stared over at Chico. "You want me to take care of this alone?"

"Nah, I wanna be there for this."

Both men walked toward the building and entered the cold, empty lobby. They walked straight into the stairway and slowly headed up the stairs. Dante had his Desert Eagle in his hand and Chico had his .45 cocked and ready. They got to the third floor and found Joe slumped against the wall with a crack pipe in his hand. He looked up at Chico and didn't say a word.

"You Joe?" Chico asked.

Joe remained quiet.

Chico approached him closer and glared at him. He glanced at Dante, while Joe just sat there.

"Joe, Joe . . . who's Joe? I'm good, though. Nah, you good," Joe mumbled incoherently, the crack pipe dangling from his fingers..

Joe's eyes were sunken, red, and spaced-out. He was wearing a thin, tattered jacket and dirty, torn jeans and had a foul odor. He had smoked "red devil's lay," the talk of the town, which so happened to come from Cross, and it had seeped into his system, making him feel like he was on a different planet.

"Yo, take this nigga up on the fuckin' roof!" Chico said to Dante.

Dante holstered his gun and grabbed Joe from the stairway by his jacket. Then the two men forced him up the steps. Joe didn't put up much of a fight.

Dante kicked open the door to the roof, pushed Joe out, and kicked him in the ass.

Joe fell against the hard gravel and didn't bother to get up. Joe was still mumbling, "I ain't do it. He done it. It ain't me."

"You ain't do what, muthafucka?" Chico exclaimed.

Joe turned over onto his side and looked up at Chico and continued to mumble.

"Yo, this nigga is really fucked up," Dante said. "He high, man."

"I don't give a fuck what he is. He knows something."

Chico walked over to Joe, snatched him up by the collar of his jacket, and dragged him to the edge of the roof. Dante walked behind them. Chico lifted him off his feet and dangled him over the edge.

"Who paid you to throw acid in Apple's face?" Chico asked sternly. "Huh, muthafucka?"

"Apple? I don't know Apple. I wanna go home. Home. Home," he replied, looking lost.

"Yeah, you do. Don't play wit' me, nigga!" Chico tightened his hold around Joe and pushed him farther over the ledge.

Joe didn't cringe, and it angered Chico. Joe was a full-blown crackhead. His skin was ashy and scarred, and he, unknown to Chico and Dante, suffered from dementia.

"Who the fuck paid you, nigga?" Chico repeated, with Joe dangling from six stories up.

Joe just stared into his aggressor's eyes, looking unfazed by everything going on around him, and mumbling to himself.

"He ain't gonna talk, Chico. The nigga's really fucked up."

Chico looked over at his cousin, knowing Dante was right. He threw Joe to the ground and stood over him.

"Just end this nigga and let's go," Dante said.

Chico removed a lethal shot of dope mixed with rat poison from his jacket. He was ready to inject Joe with it, but then he looked down at him and decided against it.

"Crazy muthafucka might wanna go out this way," Chico stated.

Dante laughed.

"Nah, I ain't giving him the pleasure." Chico took out his .45, hovered over Joe with the gun, and fired two shots into his skull, spilling his brains out on the gravel. "Stupid muthafucka!"

"C'mon, cuz, we out."

Chico and Dante rushed down the stairway and jumped back into the Impala. Chico still wasn't satisfied. He didn't get a name.

Two hours later, both men were at a local bar on Broadway having drinks. Jack's spot was teeming with people, a mature crowd of men and women in their thirties and up. Jack was a really close friend and customer to Chico and would purchase a few ki's from him every month. In fact, he was one of the few who still showed loyalty to Chico.

Chico downed a rum and coke, all the while worrying about his business. He'd been spending so much time at the hospital with Apple, Cross had crept up on his customers, and territory. A lot of his money was tied up in Apple's medical bills, since he was paying for everything, from the medication to her surgery. He wanted his lady to come out a hundred percent, but he wasn't sure if that was possible.

Jack walked into his establishment clad in a dark, pinstriped suit, bejeweled in diamonds and bling, and flashing a catching smile. An old-school player in his mid-forties, he was a well-groomed man with a casual demeanor. He was a well-liked guy, but he had a dark side. Jack's spot was a front for money-laundering and drug distribution. He was a businessman first and considered himself a gangster second. He was greeted with love and respect the minute he stepped into his bar.

Jack locked eyes with Chico and gestured for him to meet him in his office in a few minutes. Then he went into the bar's back office, followed closely by his right-hand man, Antonio, and shut the door,

Chico nodded and finished off his drink. He waited for a short moment and then walked through the crowd, headed toward Jack's office. He knocked once on the door, and Antonio opened up.

Chico and Dante locked eyes with Jack's right-hand man and bodyguard.

Dante was far from impressed. He smirked at Antonio and followed his cousin into the office.

Jack was seated behind his red oak desk, tilted back in his leather chair and smoking a cigar. He stood from his chair and greeted Chico with a handshake and a smile.

"It's always good to meet with you, Chico," he said.

"Likewise," Chico replied. "You remember my cousin, Dante?"

Jack nodded at Dante with respect, and Dante returned the nod.

"So what brings you around, Chico? If you're here to question my loyalty, you have nothing to worry about. I'm too old to switch over, and I don't care nothing about Cross and his crew."

"That's good to hear."

"Have a seat then. Let's talk."

Jack sat in his expensive leather chair and continued to smoke his cigar. He poured himself a shot of Henny. Chico took a seat opposite Jack and poured himself another drink.

Jack looked at his friend. "You better take it easy on that stuff, Chico."

"Don't worry about me, Jack. I'm good."

Jack shrugged. "How's your woman?" he asked.

Chico downed his drink. "She could be better."

Jack was a little worried about his friend. He hated to see Chico drinking and worrying about Apple so much, but he wasn't his daddy. It was always business between the two, and he wasn't too fond of Cross and his goons. Even though Chico was a thug himself, Jack felt he could trust him somewhat.

The two sat in his office and talked for a moment while drinking Hennessy. They talked mostly about business. Chico wanted to know, if the streets got ugly, would Jack have his back in a time of war. Jack confirmed his loyalty to Chico, and the two men toasted.

Chico exited Jack's office with a smile on his face, and pussy on his mind. A young woman standing by the bar had caught his interest from earlier, and with Apple lying in the hospital, he needed to relieve some tension. He approached the petite, young woman with her long, flowing hair and said a few kind words to her. He offered to buy her a drink, and she accepted.

"What's your name?" Chico asked.

"Melissa," she replied with a smile.

"Melissa, you wanna go somewhere private and talk?"

She smiled, knowing who Chico was already. He was making her blush with his smooth talk and thuggish mannerism.

"Sure."

After telling Dante he would be back in a moment, Chico took the woman by her hand and exited the bar.

Melissa slipped her full, silky lips back up to the top of Chico's dripping wet shaft and wedged her teeth gently underneath the swollen mushroom tip, causing him to groan and whimper.

"Ooooooh shit!" Chico's eyes rolled into the back of his head. Melissa's tongue and soft lips had him weak.

The windows in the car began to fog up from their breaths of passion. Melissa removed her panties, lifted her skirt to her hips, and slowly straddled Chico in the backseat of the Impala, drowning him in her juices as she slid down on his ready-to-burst organ. She clutched him tightly, groaning and howling in his ear as their bodies came together, sweat pouring from her skin.

Chico was fucking Melissa raw, and when he came, he made no effort to pull out, exploding inside the woman.

Melissa rested her head against him like a girlfriend, and they both took in the moment. Until he felt the urge to throw up.

Chico shoved Melissa off his lap, opened the door, and began hurling out chunks on the sidewalk.

"You OK?" Melissa asked.

"Shut the fuck up, bitch!"

She scowled at him.

"I'll kill 'em all! I'll kill 'em all!" Chico kept chanting,

Melissa looked at him strangely and figured it was time for her to leave. She didn't do cuckoo.

Chapter 9

Dr. Changer examined Apple's face closely and felt that her burns would take more time to heal. He thought it was time for her to go home and rest after enduring weeks of intensive care.

With the money Chico was spending on her care, Apple had the medical attention that money could buy, and it was costly—almost totaling two hundred thousand dollars. The doctors had done reconstructive surgery and countless skin grafts, mostly removing skin from her butt cheeks and surgically grafting it onto the site of her injury. Although the process improved her scars a great deal, she was still disfigured, emotionally drained, and distraught.

Dante sat in the Impala while Chico went inside to help with Apple's discharge. He caught looks from the female staff members as he sauntered down the hallway with his long chain swinging and gleaming, dressed in his urban attire straight out of *XXL's* fashion section.

The doctor had a short conversation with Chico, advising him about Apple's condition and the continuing treatment she would need over time.

"She's going to need a lot more rest, and I'm prescribing a cream that she needs to apply to her burns every night, along with wearing a mask," Dr. Changer stated.

"A mask?" Chico questioned with a raised brow.

"Yes. It's a clear plastic mask that she needs to wear twenty-three hours a day for a few months. It's to help ward off any infections and to ensure her skin continues to heal properly without any keloids developing and her having to take a load of antibiotics."

Chico nodded. "I got you, doc."

"She also needs to eat more and to drink plenty of fluids."

Chico nodded again.

"Thanks for everything you've done, doc."

Chico liked Dr. Changer, a Jewish doctor in his early fifties with countless degrees and a highly regarded reputation. Dr. Changer shook hands with Chico and then walked away to tend to his other patients.

Chico walked into Apple's hospital room and saw her sitting in a wheelchair with fresh bandages on her face. She was already dressed in a pair of jeans, white Nikes, and a sweater, and her hair was pulled back into a long ponytail and tied with a gray ribbon.

He tried to smile, but his mood wouldn't let him. He sighed as he walked up to Apple. "C'mon, baby, it's about time you leave this fuckin' place and go home."

Apple didn't respond to him. She had her good

moments and a lot of bad moments, and today was one of her worst.

After gathering her things, Chico pushed her out into the hallway and toward the elevators, having signed her out earlier. He stepped off the elevator and wheeled her through the main lobby. She was quiet the entire time. Chico could hear Jay-Z blaring from inside the Impala as he approached the car.

Dante stepped out of the car when he noticed Chico with Apple. It would be his first time meeting his cousin's girl. He couldn't help staring at Apple's scarred face.

Apple noticed him looking. "What the fuck you lookin' at?" she shouted.

Dante glanced at Chico. Out of respect for his cousin, he kept his cool. "I'm just here to help, that's all."

Apple sighed. "I just wanna get the fuck outta here."

Once Chico helped her into the front seat of the car, they peeled off in the dusk. Apple slumped in her seat and peered out the window. It had been a while since she had seen outside, and it was eating her up inside that she had to walk around with a plastic mask over her face like some awful creature in a horror film.

A few hours later, Apple sat in her quiet bedroom staring at the walls, while Chico and Dante were downstairs drinking and smoking. She had a lot on her mind. The rage inside of her was growing stronger and stronger every time she looked at her scarred image in the mirror.

She got out of bed and walked over to the dresser mirror. She pulled off the clear, plastic mask and gazed at herself for the umpteenth time. Apple hated what she was looking at, but she didn't wish she could miraculously change back into her old self or turn away from her reflection like she usually did.

She moved her face closer to the mirror and slowly touched her scars, examining her burns like they were alien to her. She gently touched the disfigured side of her face and held her eyes on the wounds.

She closed her eyes, experiencing a quick flashback of the incident, and then reopened them. *Make 'em pay,* she heard a voice shout in her head.

Apple thought she was going crazy for a moment, but she heard the voice again even louder. *They did this to you. Make 'em pay. Show 'em how ugly you can really become.* She looked around the room and realized she was alone. She thought hearing voices was one of the side effects of her medication. She turned to stare at herself in the mirror again, hate and anger showing clearly in her eyes. She knew the voice screaming in her head was right. *Make them all pay.*

She went over to the drawer and pulled out a pen and some paper. She sat on the edge of her bed and began to write up a list—a list of all of her enemies. Thinking about revenge excited her. Apple wrote down the names of those she thought responsible. At the top of her list was Kola, then her mother, Denise, along with Mesha and Cross.

She then tore up the paper, tearing each individual name apart.

She walked to the bedroom door and called out for Chico, who rushed up the stairs and into the bedroom.

"What up, baby?" Chico stared at Apple seated on the bed, holding one of his Yankees fitted cap in her hand. He walked over to her and noticed the torn paper on the floor.

"What's this about?" he asked.

Apple gazed at her man with a sinister smirk. "I'm gonna pick a name, baby."

"For what?"

"Who I want dead next."

Chico smiled. "I like the way you think."

Apple shook the cap with the names like it was a raffle. Chico stood close by her side. Whatever name she picked, he was ready to kill. He was a heartless thug who wanted to take joy in murdering his foes.

Apple reached into the cap and pulled out a name. She smiled as she stared at the name written on the small piece of paper. She felt good. She felt she had the power of life and death in her hands. She handed the name to Chico.

He nodded. "Mesha, it is. She's the first to go," he said after reading the name.

"Kill 'em all for me, baby."

"It will be my pleasure."

Chapter 10

Mesha was partying hard in the downtown Manhattan nightclub called Swags, grinding her thick hips and phat ass against the tall, handsome stranger she had come to know as Tabs. He had thick, long, shoulder-length dreads that looked like a lion's mane around his chiseled features and a complexion like brown sugar. Mesha fell in love with him at first sight. She threw back a cup of Grey Goose and pulled down her tight miniskirt to keep from exposing too much of her precious goodies. Mesha loved the way Tabs' body pressed and rubbed against her to Keri Hilson's "Knock You Down." It felt like they were having dry sex in the middle of the dance floor.

The night continued with her flirting and dancing with Tabs, and downing drink after drink. Tabs made it obvious that he was enjoying her company but wanted a little something extra on the side. He rubbed against Mesha, taking advantage of her inebriated condition, one hand massaging her breast, his other hand sliding between her smooth thighs, and Mesha didn't mind at all.

She exited the club at three in the morning with her two girlfriends, Sammy and Jacqueline, and Tabs. Tabs and Mesha chatted near Sammy's Escalade for a moment. They quickly exchanged numbers, and then Tabs went on his way.

"He's cute," Jacqueline said.

"I know. I think I just found my husband."

Mesha stepped out of her friend's Escalade on the corner of 135th Street and Fifth Avenue, the Goose still fresh in her system. "I'll see y'all bitches later," Mesha said joyfully.

"Later, ho!" Sammy returned from the driver's seat.

Mesha shut the door and strutted down 135th Street as her friend peeled down Fifth Avenue. The block was quiet and the traffic sparse. She walked down the lighted street covered in her brown, crinkled leather jacket. It was a windy, but clear night. Her mind was on sleep and Tabs. She couldn't wait to call him.

Mesha didn't notice the black Impala approaching her from behind in a slow creep, with the passenger window rolled down.

"Hey, beautiful," Chico said with a feigned smile.

Mesha glanced at him, quickly turned her head, and kept on walking.

"I just wanna talk to you for a moment."

Mesha continued to ignore him. She knew who he was and wanted no dealings with him. He was bad news.

Chico told her, "If you're worried about Apple, I'm not fuckin' wit' that bitch anymore."

"Why not?"

"'Cause I ain't. But I like what I see right now. I just want to holla at you for a moment. I ain't gonna bite."

Mesha slowed her steps and looked over at Chico. He smiled. She didn't. Nervousness quickly overcame her. Her instincts were telling her to keep walking. She watched him park his Impala and step out.

"Leave me alone, Chico."

"I just wanna talk, Mesha, that's all," he said, a little roughness in his voice.

Mesha turned around to walk in the opposite direction. She wanted to get away from him, but Chico followed behind her. She glanced over her shoulders and saw him coming. She had the urge to run and scream out for help.

Chico marched quickly toward Mesha, and before she could do anything, she noticed the gun aimed at her side and his menacing stare.

"Like I said, I just wanna talk to you."

Suddenly, Mesha was flanked by Chico and Dante.

"What you want from me, Chico?" she asked, her voice shaky, panic in her eyes.

"Just walk wit' us, and we'll pull your coat to it."

Reluctantly, Mesha followed both men into one of the nearby buildings. They pushed her into the lobby and then into an elevator. Chico pressed for the top floor, and the elevator took them thirteen floors up. Chico grabbed and pulled Mesha out of the elevator by her jacket collar, and they continued down the narrow hallway and entered the stairway leading to the rooftop.

Chico pushed Mesha out onto the rooftop, and Dante wedged the door with a rock, so they wouldn't be locked out. She stood uneasily on the gravel rooftop, clutching her small purse, her eyes on Chico. There was nowhere to run. Mesha was so scared, she struggled to not pee herself.

Chico approached her. "I know you heard what happened to your friend."

"I didn't have anything to do with that, Chico."

"You sure?"

"She was my friend."

"*Was* your friend."

"How is she?" Mesha asked.

"You didn't care enough to go visit her in the hospital. I thought she was a friend."

"I've just been busy."

Chico chuckled.

Dante stood off to the side, silent like death itself. He gripped his .50 and had it pointed downward at the ground. Mesha kept glancing at him.

"Don't worry, he won't hurt you—unless I tell him to."

"I still care about her, Chico. I really do."

"Well, that's why we're here . . . to talk and get some questions answered."

Mesha remembered what had happened to Ayesha a few months earlier. She was shot twice in the back of her head as she was leaving her building. She also remembered her own encounter with Apple while she was coming home from work one evening. Apple had assaulted and robbed her in the hallway, right in front of her grandmother's door, over some money she'd owed. It was an ugly memory that she wanted to forget. She thought her ties to Apple were done.

"What you want to know?" Mesha asked.

"Suspects."

"Huh?"

"I just want to talk to the people that you might know had a grudge against Apple. I know you hear things in these projects. You always hear things, Mesha."

"Look, all I know is that maybe her brother might have something to do with it."

"Whose brother?"

"Ayesha. You remember she was shot in the head last summer because she had a beef with Apple. I'm just saying, maybe you need to talk to Memo about that incident."

"Memo. You know where he be at?"

"I don't know. We don't talk."

Chico nodded. "What he look like?"

"He's tall, light-skinned with braids. I just wanna go home, Chico. I didn't do anything." Mesha's heart was racing like it was in the Indy 500.

Chico moved closer to her, and she took a few steps back away from him. He smiled. "I told you, I'm not going to hurt you, Mesha. I just wanted to talk."

Chico thought Mesha was a very beautiful woman. She had a runway model's posture and enticing eyes.

He suddenly became green-eyed over her beauty. She still had hers, while Apple looked like a burn victim. An uncontrollable rage stirred up inside of him. He'd heard enough. He looked over at Dante.

Dante nodded, understanding the look. He holstered his weapon and approached Mesha, who continued to step backwards, nearing the ledge, her eyes registering fear.

"Chico, what's going on?" she cried out.

"It's just business, Mesha. I mean, I gotta send a message, right?"

Mesha took off running in a panic, like she could fly, but Dante snatched a hold of her. She tussled with him, but her strength was no match for his. Mesha screamed out, clawing at his face, but Dante was unfazed by her weak blows against him.

"No! Get off me!" she screamed.

Dante hoisted the petite woman over his shoulder like the wind had lifted her off her feet and walked toward the ledge.

Mesha was squirming and screaming, "No! Please, don't do this! Don't do this!"

Dante stood close to the ledge and peered down at the ground below him, a thirteen-story drop. Mesha gripped his wrist, struggling not to be thrown off the rooftop like she was trash.

"Chico, please!"

Chico said to Dante, "Toss that bitch."

Dante didn't hesitate throwing Mesha off the rooftop. She screamed on the way down and plunged rapidly like a brick from the sky, crashing face first onto the concrete pavement below. Both men stared down at the contorted body splattered against the sidewalk with crimson blood pooling underneath.

"Think that will send a strong message?" Dante asked.

"Strong enough. We just gettin' started, cousin."

Dante smiled.

They hurried from the rooftop and jumped back into the Impala. Chico slowly turned the corner and drove by the body at a snail's pace. Mesha was almost unrecognizable, her face pushed into the concrete and parts of her skull exposed.

As dawn peeked from the sky, Fifth Avenue was shut down with yellow crime tape and flashing police lights from corner to corner. It seemed like the entire precinct was out there investigating Mesha's death. The bystanders stood a short distance behind the tape, peering at the body under a blood-stained sheet. Word had traveled throughout the projects faster than the wind itself. There was speculation that the woman had committed suicide, but Mesha's family and friends highly doubted that. And witnesses claimed they'd heard a woman screaming.

Mesha's two friends were in tears, trying to console each other.

"She was just with us," Sammy told one of the detectives. "She didn't do this to herself. She was happy. She was murdered!"

The gray-haired detective tugged on his bushy mustache as Sammy spoke. Then he wrote something on a small notepad he'd taken from the pocket of his crinkled suit. Meanwhile his partner was canvassing the area, looking for potential witnesses, but the tight-lipped residents were scared, all claiming they were asleep.

The coroner took the body away, but the grieving remained. Detective Rice knew it wasn't a suicide. He figured it was too much of a coincidence that a friend of Mesha's, Ayesha, was murdered in the same projects a few months earlier. The thing that both women had in common was, they were both friends of Apple.

Detective Rice was very familiar with Apple, having investigated her younger sister's death almost a year earlier. The thought of the young girl being murdered and tossed into a city dumpster still haunted him. It was still an open case, but the lead went cold when J-Dogg, the main suspect, was gunned down in the Bronx.

Detective Rice continued to question everyone. He was determined to get to the bottom of everything. In his mind, everything was leading back to Apple. Still, he had no solid proof that she was behind the murders. He was aware that Apple had been a victim herself, with her sister's murder, and by having acid thrown in her face. When it came to mentioning her name about any cases, folks in the neighborhood either went mute or had amnesia.

Detective Rice couldn't understand how such a nice, lovely-looking young woman could become such a monster. Apple's name was ringing out, and the department became keenly aware of her fierce reputation.

Clad in a long, dark blue robe, her hair pulled back into a ponytail, Apple lay in bed staring at the television. She noticed her old neighborhood in the backdrop as the pale, brown-haired field reporter talked on camera, surrounded by a small crowd. She quickly took it off mute to listen to the incident.

She smiled as the reporter talked about Mesha's death. A chuckle escaped from her lips. "Fuck that bitch!" she uttered softly. *One down and three to go.*

Suddenly Apple was hit with a wave of uneasiness. She sighed heavily. She got up and walked over to the window. She peered outside into the dark tree-lined street outside her bedroom window. She had a creepy feeling that someone was watching her, like someone was standing outside her home at that very moment. Dante was the only person who knew of their location.

She closed her curtains and walked away from the window. The past few weeks had her somewhat paranoid. She hadn't been outside since her arrival from the hospital, too ashamed to go anywhere. She looked over at the clear, plastic mask on the dresser next to her medication.

She thought about her failing loan-sharking business. She had made plenty of phone calls around Harlem, ready to get back into business, but business looked like an ugly trip up an icy hilltop. Some of her debtors had heard about the acid incident and thought it was a way out of their debts. They would hang up on her, and some even mocked her, feeling like she didn't have the muscle to collect. The situation was driving her mad.

One of them had said to her, "Fuck you, bitch! You're MIA."

Another one told her, "I thought you were dead."

She heard movement downstairs and decided to check it out. She placed the mask over her face, retrieved a .380 from the dresser, and exited the bedroom with caution. She descended the stairway and came across Chico and Dante, who were just arriving.

"Hey, baby," Chico greeted.

"Hey."

Dante looked over at Apple and gave her a cold stare. He didn't want to stay too long because she made him uncomfortable. He was used to seeing Chico around beautiful women, and even though he knew about the attack, he was still surprised that Chico kept her around. He felt like she was a burden on his cousin. Chico had explained his reasons, but Dante wasn't buying that she reminded him of Nikki. Nikki was a good girl, and she wasn't.

"I'm not gonna stick around, cuzzo," Dante said. "I got business to take care of." And he made his exit.

Apple waited for him to leave and then said to Chico, "I don't like him."

"Why?"

"I hate the way he looks at me."

"I mean, look at you. No disrespect, baby, but he ain't

used to seeing something like you."

Apple could smell the alcohol on Chico's breath. She didn't have a reply. She discarded his comment and focused on business.

"I'm ready to pick another name."

"Well, you might have another to add," Chico said.

"Who?"

"Ayesha's older brother. Before we tossed Mesha off the roof, his name came up."

"Memo?"

"That's the name."

"Kill him too then."

"It's already been arranged. I got people looking for him already."

Apple turned and walked back up the stairs, while Chico stood at the bottom of the staircase watching her. He felt bad about what he had said to her, but he wasn't going to apologize for it. He truly loved her and was showing it by the bodies he was dropping in the streets of Harlem, in her name.

Chapter 11

The East Side of Harlem was becoming a tense place. With the crime rate rising and the corner hustlers on high alert, the police were on constant patrol. Chico and Dante were becoming a known entity in the hood. A few gun battles had broken out with Cross and his men.

Mesha's death was the talk of the town. The people were furious over her murder, and although there weren't any witnesses to her death, word was circulating that Apple was involved.

It was on a clear, cold night that Chico and Dante sat parked across the street from the Blue Note, a hole-in-the-wall lounge on St. Nicholas Avenue with a back-alley doorway that was tucked away in the dark like a dirty little secret.

Chico took a few pulls from his cigarette, while Dante played with the radio. They were hunting for Memo. An informant had told them that the Blue Note was one of Memo's favorite places to hang out and get drunk. Both men weren't about to let the opportunity slip away from them, so they went to the lounge immediately after they got the news.

Dante took a drag from Chico's cigarette, nodding to 50 Cent rapping, admiring the gangster's lyrics and his reputation.

"What's on ya mind, Dante?"

Dante answered immediately, like it was urgent. "Why we doin' this, man?"

"What you mean?"

"We on the wrong hunt, Chico. We should be going after niggas that matter, not some off-brand muthafucka gettin' drunk in a bar. This is news that came from a bitch's mouth just to save her own ass from being thrown off a roof."

"It matters to me."

"What should matter to you is goin' after what's yours—these streets. Cross and his niggas . . . I want them, cuzzo."

"And we will, but this shit here is personal, Dante."

"I don't like that bitch!" Dante spat.

"Why not?"

"'Cause she ain't right for you. I know you say she reminds you of Nikki, but she ain't Nikki, Chico. Far from it. You still riding on this guilt trip about what happened to her. Yeah, it's fucked up, but that was years ago. You tryin' to make up for her death by doin' this shit, carrying out hard revenge for this broad?"

"Niggas need to understand not to fuck with what's mines."

"And they will. But the more time we waste doin' this shit, Cross is getting stronger, making money out there, him and his bitch. I don't like it."

Chico took a long pull from the burning cancer stick. He turned his stare away from Dante and looked over at the bar, observing a few patrons that stood outside. He didn't want to hear what his cousin was saying to him.

"I'm just saying, cuzzo," Dante continued, "business is business. I could spend my time on the hunt for the come-up instead of doing this shit. We find this muthafucka, Memo, and I'm ready to kill him for you. But this shit is eating up too much of our time. You know Cross and Kola moved in on a few of your customers. Yeah, they hitting them with that better quality, and niggas is biting at their bait. Here you are selling ya shit at a stack less, but niggas is still biting for what Cross is throwing out there."

"Nigga, I don't wanna hear about no muthafuckin' Cross or his bitch right now!" Chico shouted.

Chico didn't want to admit that Dante was right. He didn't want to look stupid and played. He had heard the name "Coca Kola" being floated around. Word on the street was, she got that nickname for all the weight she was unloading. Cross and his bitch were moving so much snow, they were calling his team "The Perfect Storm," which was hard for Chico to swallow.

"I'ma go talk to a few not-so-loyal muthafuckas and negotiate," Chico said.

"It's your court, cuzzo."

"And I'm still holding the ball."

Chico sat silently, disturbed by everything going on. He only wanted to have a few words with Memo and then kill him.

An hour later, the two men were still sitting and waiting in the stolen, dark Chevy. It was evident that Dante wanted to be elsewhere. Becoming weary, he fidgeted with the radio continuously.

"We should have brought some CDs wit' us," he said.

"Worry about that shit some other time. Just focus on this muthafucka comin' out," Chico replied, his eyes glued on the tacky lounge across the street.

"You sure he really in there? You trust the chick that's tellin' you this?"

"She's a hundred percent."

"And why's that?"

Chico turned his focus toward Dante. He was silent for a moment before saying, "Because I say so."

"Well, she better be. I'm gettin' tired of this waiting around. It's making me feel like it's a setup."

"You a gangster, right?"

"Fuck kind of question is that?"

"Nigga, then act like it."

Dante glared at his cousin. The bickering was normal between the two. Dante was the only person Chico trusted and the only man with the balls to question him.

It wasn't until after two in the morning when a few patrons began exiting the rusty side door that led into the dark alley. Both men in the Chevy rose up and retrieved their guns. Chico cocked back his .45 and kept a steady eye on the small crowd pouring into the streets, mostly bottom-class residents of Harlem inebriated with liquor, their source of heaven.

"Look hard for this muthafucka," Chico said.

"I always do. You wanna talk first, or just open fire?"

"Talk to this muthafucka for a moment, but if he raise up, shoot to kill this nigga."

Dante nodded.

Memo followed behind the other patrons onto St. Nicholas Avenue. He was easily recognizable by his height alone. He stood six three with long braids and was dressed in a pair of beige Timberland and a classic varsity-style jacket with wool/polyester body and soft, lambskin sleeves. He was high yellow, like afternoon daylight, and slim, and his beady eyes carried an angry stare.

Memo exited the lounge with a friend by his side, shorter in height but carrying the same thuggish demeanor. The two men looked like they were nothing to play with.

Chico observed his mark closely, blowing cigarette smoke out of his mouth. He said to Dante, "Let's fuckin' do this."

Chico jumped out of the Chevy and walked quickly toward Memo and his friend, and Dante was right behind his cousin, both men carrying their guns at their sides, ready to open fire.

Memo headed for the Accord parked at the corner of St. Nicholas and 148th Street. He staggered toward his car with the keys in his hand, unaware of the oncoming threat across the street. His friend Mooky was steps behind him, laughing to himself. The liquor in his system was making everything much funnier to him. He almost lost his footing and caught his balance against a parked car.

"Yo, I'm ready to go smoke," Mooky said.

Memo turned slightly to comment on what Mooky had said, but his eyes caught the sudden trouble heading his way. His eyes squinted, zeroing in on Chico and Dante rushing his way. He saw the guns, noticed their bizarre movements, and read into it immediately—They were coming for him.

He reached under his shirt for his pistol. Before he could warn Mooky about the danger, a shot was fired, striking Mooky in the back of the head, and Mooky fell dead on the pavement in front of Memo.

Memo shouted, "Muthafuckas!" and fired back.

Bam! Bam! Bam!

He took cover behind his car, while Chico and Dante rushed ahead with their guns blazing at him, sending bystanders scattering for cover, lighting up the block like a firecracker.

Shots whizzed by Memo's head shattering car windows, but he wasn't afraid and was determined not to die. "Fuck y'all!" he screamed.

Memo exploded on both men with his 9 mm like a trained soldier and proved to be a good shooter, barely missing Chico's head by mere inches and pushing Dante back.

Dante began pulling his cousin by the collar, shouting,

"C'mon, nigga, let's go!" He knew the police would be on their way soon.

Chico continued to let off a barrage of shots, each one tearing into cars and windows. "I want him dead!" he shouted.

Dante was successful in pulling his cousin away from the gunfire and back to the car with Memo still shooting wildly at them. Both men jumped inside the Chevy and sped off, knowing they would get the chance another day.

Chapter 12

Wrapped in a white towel, Kola was running a hot bath in the large, oval tub that was cemented around marble foundation. She couldn't wait to dip into the soothing water and soak like a boiling egg in her plush bathroom to the sound of Mary J. Blige coming from the small CD player on the granite countertop with dual sinks.

She wanted to relax. It had been a stressful day for her, but life was good. She'd made some strong connections, and the money was pouring in by the boatloads.

Slowly but surely, Chico was getting pushed to the side, his clients now copping weight from her. But she wanted the nigga out of business permanently. Chico was still a threat to her and her organization as long as he was alive and dating her sister, so she put shooters out on the streets to look for him, with the order to kill on sight.

Kola sighed as she slowly slid into the warm tub and felt the water calm her body and soul like a much-needed afternoon nap. She closed her eyes, tread the water calmly with her hands, and thought about the upcoming trial date that Cross and Edge had for their gun charge. They had to meet with Cross' attorney and see which way the prosecutors were going with the case. Kola couldn't imagine Cross being out of her life. That would've been a nightmare for her.

Kola remained relaxed in the tub for a moment, enjoying the sweet sounds of Mary J., a loaded .380 resting on the sink. The CD started playing one of her favorite songs by Mary J. Blige, "My Life," and she started singing along.

Kola had a beautiful, soulful voice like Mary J. Her friends had always said she could become a singer if she wasn't in a life of crime. She had the vocals, and she definitely had the looks. But singing full-time wasn't for her. She had no desire to sit in a dark studio and suck a producer's dick for a hot instrumental track. She was making money moving weight and had respect wherever she went.

She briefly thought about Apple and wondered what her twin sister's face looked like, knowing they were no longer identical. *Who had the balls?* she thought. She wanted to meet that stranger.

Kola continued to soak in the tub for an hour, listening to the entire album. She wanted to forget about her troubles, but Cross' gun charge kept creeping into her mind and stuck around like a cancerous cell.

As the water began to chill, Kola lifted herself out of the tub, her body glistening like a gem. She stepped out the tub and reached for her towel resting on the marble.

Kola sighed and walked toward the window. She peered outside just in time to see Cross' H6 Hummer come to a stop in the driveway. He and Edge stepped out of the mountain-sized vehicle looking like two rap stars, their long chains swinging and gleaming. It was always good to see her man home.

She hurried into the bedroom to change into something decent. She would have remained in the towel and given Cross something nice and warm to come home to, but seeing that he was with Edge, she knew now wasn't the time.

She swung open the dual doors that led into her walk-in closet and picked out a dark blue cashmere robe, wrapped herself in it, tying it closed at the waist, put on some cozy socks, and headed toward the great room, where she heard Cross and Edge talking.

Cross was fixing himself a drink at the small bar, while Edge was splitting open a cigar, about to roll a blunt. Edge sat slouched in the plush, stylish chair next to the glass coffee table that had an ounce of weed sitting on it in a large Ziploc bag .

Kola greeted him with a smile. "Hey, baby."

"Hey."

The two quickly kissed.

Cross didn't look too worried about the meeting with his attorney in a few hours. He took a sip of his scotch on the rocks, walked farther into the great room, and told Edge, "Yo, roll up two of those."

Edge nodded.

Kola positioned herself behind Cross and wrapped her arms around him, nestling the side of her face into his back and hugging him like he was a giant teddy bear.

Cross took a few sips from his drink, but Kola stayed attached to him like she was clothing. When his cell phone rang, he quickly took the call. It was Meyers Mitchell, his attorney. He removed himself from Kola's loving arms and walked toward the large cathedral windows to speak privately with his lawyer, while Kola stood opposite Edge, the glass coffee table separating the two.

While Edge rolled the second blunt, there was an uncomfortable silence between the two of them. Edge had made it clearly known that he was against the new arrangement. He thought a female needed to stay in her place. Kola made it known that she was nothing to bet against and wasn't going to be intimidated by the twenty-six-year-old. In her eyes, age didn't matter; it was how smart and vicious you could be. And she was as vicious in a dogfight in the bloody pits, just like any of the male dogs.

Edge finished rolling the second blunt. He removed a lighter from his pants pocket, placed the long blunt between his lips, and lit it quickly. He then leaned back into the chair, his eyes lingering on Kola with a deadpan gaze. Kola noticed his dark eyes staying on her a little too long for her comfort.

Edge exhaled and handed the burning joint to Kola. "You smoking?" he asked in his raspy tone.

As Kola reached for the blunt, Edge smiled at her. She stepped back from him and took three long tokes.

She coughed after the first pull and took a deeper pull the second time. The third had her feeling nice. One thing Kola respected about Edge, he knew how to cop quality weed, and what she was smoking was straight potent shit, probably directly off the banana boat.

Kola stared over at her man for a moment as he stood by the window talking on the phone. His body language told her that whatever Meyers was saying to her boo wasn't good. She wished she could take his troubles away.

Edge took the blunt back from Kola and continued to take deep pulls from the intoxicating purple haze like it was a cigarette. As he lounged in the chair with the blunt between his lips, his eyes hooked on the shape of Kola's ass under the bathrobe. He rubbed his crotch slowly while studying her shapely figure from head to toe and wished that someday he could slip his dick into her pussy. He longed to fuck the shit out of her. For Edge, young pussy was always the best pussy.

Unknown to Kola and Cross, Edge had had a profound crush on Apple ever since she was fourteen. In his eyes, age didn't matter. In fact, he was attracted to girls, sometimes as young as twelve or thirteen. He used to watch Apple from a distance. He would sit in his car and stare at her hanging around with friends in the projects, and would even follow her around in his car for blocks. But since Apple was no longer around to fuel his fantasies, his lust shifted to the twin sister. He would watch Kola from the side of his eyes, lick his lips, and even touch himself slowly when she or Cross wasn't looking.

"You wanna take another hit of this?" he asked Kola.

She turned on her heels and reached for the blunt. This time, she took two short pulls and immediately passed it back to him. He took it from her and savored the taste around the tip of the blunt, subtly licking it like it was candy. Kola, more focused on the conversation Cross was having with his attorney, wasn't aware of the foul looks directed her way.

Cross didn't look too pleased when he got off his cell phone. He walked toward the two and was silent for a moment.

"What he say?" Edge asked.

"We'll talk in his office today."

Edge shrugged it off and continued smoking.

Cross turned to Kola. "Baby, why don't you go put some damn clothes on? Why you standing out here naked underneath a bathrobe in front of my man?"

"'Cause I can," she teased.

Cross cut his eyes at Kola.

She understood what his look meant. "Fine!" She spun around in her socks and headed toward the stairway.

Kola entered the bedroom with a troubled gaze and sat on the edge of her bed, worried about Cross and his open case. She wanted to know what his lawyer had said over the phone. She heard the men talking downstairs, but it wasn't about the case.

Kola had to re-up with Eduardo soon, but since he was going to be out of town for several weeks, she was forced to do business with Tony, one of his trusted lieutenants. He had a harder-looking face and a much tougher demeanor. Short and robust with a grizzly beard, huge arms, and beady eyes, he was a stern, ugly man. The first time Kola met him, he reminded her of a Colombian Mike Tyson. She had to compose herself to avoid laughing out loud when Eduardo introduced him.

Tony was an easy man to work with because he was about his business. He didn't flirt with her like Eduardo did, even though he didn't have a chance in hell to get with her.

One time, Eduardo came out of a room shirtless with his six-pack exposed. Every inch of him was ripped. His chiseled structure made the young Kola blush and caused her to become moist between her thighs. She had to turn her head away, just so she could focus on business. The attraction between them was definitely there, but she loved Cross. Eduardo made it harder for Kola every time they did business together. She was glad he was back in Colombia with his girlfriends and sprawling mansion.

As Kola sat on the bed daydreaming, she heard an engine start up outside her window. She went to the window and saw Edge jumping into the driver's seat of the monstrous-looking Hummer sitting on 26-inch chrome rims. She was happy he was leaving. Edge brought about an uneasiness in her that she couldn't explain to Cross, especially since they were like brothers. Now she and Cross could talk. She wanted to know what Meyers Mitchell had said to him that had him looking kind of worried.

After watching the Hummer back out of their long driveway, she walked to the foot of the stairs and saw Cross walking up. "What's up, baby?"

Cross looked up at her, his eyes showing the hardness in his life. There was no smile or response from him. He walked by Kola and went straight into the bathroom, slamming the door behind him.

"Baby, you OK?" Kola asked, knocking on the bathroom door. She heard the water running. She knocked harder and raised her voice. "Cross! What did the lawyer say?"

The door suddenly opened. Cross stood there shirtless with a mini-towel over his shoulder. He peered at Kola. It looked like he had something heavy on his mind, but he was reluctant to say what was troubling him. Kola knew it definitely had something to do with the gun charge and his attorney's words.

Cross walked into the bedroom. He went straight to the windows and looked outside. He seemed to be more focused on the breeze blowing the leaves on the trees than what Kola was asking him.

"Cross, what the fuck! Talk to me, nigga!" Kola barked, becoming impatient with him.

He turned around and locked eyes with her. "I just need some time to myself."

"What the fuck you saying?"

"It ain't good."

"What?"

"Meyers said the prosecutor's trying to go hard, saying, either someone cop to the gun charge and eat it, in which case, it's a mandatory three to five years minimum with a plea. We got until Monday morning for our reply. If we take it to trial, it could be more, but it ain't gonna go away. Seems like the DA got a hard-on for us."

Kola couldn't afford to lose Cross to a lengthy jail sentence. There had to be a way around it. She tried to brainstorm but had nothing at the moment. She sighed heavily and went up to Cross to comfort him as he stood by the window, the afternoon sunlight filtering through the open blinds.

Kola reached up to wrap her slim arms around her man, but he pulled away from her. He didn't want any comfort and made it evident by his actions. She twisted her face up at him. She didn't understand why he was acting the way he was toward her.

"We fucked up."

"Who was driving again?" she asked.

"Edge."

"So there's no other way around it. Edge is gonna have to take the charge for you."

"It was my gun."

"And? He's your subordinate. You tell that nigga what to do. Without you, there is no him."

Cross looked at Kola in disbelief. "We brothers!"

"And it's only business. Edge will understand. He knows how to jail, right?"

"He did juvie back when we were young, but nothing else."

Kola nestled against Cross, touching him in a way that would soften his mood. She kissed him tenderly, massaged his chest. She had to come up with a good reason as to why he should have Edge take the charge. Cross didn't believe in snitching or letting his right-hand man take the fall. It was one of the things that Kola loved about him. He was real—a true, thorough muthafucka.

She looked him square in the eyes and said, "I might be pregnant."

"What?"

"We might be having a baby."

She had been feeling weird lately, and they had been fucking like rabbits. She'd thrown up a few times last week, but she doubted it was due to pregnancy.

"You serious?" Cross asked.

Kola nodded.

Cross didn't show any reaction. Expressionless, he stepped back and gawked at Kola.

"You gonna say something?" she asked.

"I don't know what to say right now."

"You might be a father. And I can't have the father of my child locked up. So you gotta work something out with Edge. He'll understand. Let him know that we'll take care of him and his family while he's away. But you can't do this time, baby. Edge is expendable, you're not."

Cross' mind was heavy with thoughts. He said to her, "I gotta run to the city to meet with my lawyer and discuss this."

Kola nodded.

Cross stepped away from her.

"I love you, baby," she said.

He turned around. "I love you too."

Cross departed the bedroom, leaving Kola to ponder what his decision would be.

A few minutes later, she watched him exit their home and get into his cocaine-colored BMW. He sped out of the driveway, tires screeching.

Kola turned away from the window and walked toward the mirror, where she dropped her robe at her feet and gazed at herself. Naked, she placed her hand against her stomach and tried to picture what she would look like pregnant. Even though she was a pit bull in a skirt and a hard woman to fuck over, she couldn't imagine getting that same respect with a growing belly. She felt that pregnancy would make her look weak.

Unbeknownst to Cross, Kola was once pregnant with their child a few months ago. The moment she found out about it, she set up an appointment at the local clinic and terminated the pregnancy. Now she was lying about being pregnant, to try and keep her man out of jail.

Chapter 13

Cross and Edge left Meyers Mitchell's plush downtown Manhattan office with a blank stare, his words lingering in their heads. "My advice is, someone needs to take a plea," Meyers had said, like it was a parking ticket.

Meyers was doing everything he could with the case, meeting with the prosecutor to negotiate on his clients' behalf. He had clout and influence with a few people, and had the case postponed as long as he could, but the charge wasn't going away. He had informed his clients about the chances of going to trial, and they had the weekend to think about a plea bargain, their best option.

Cross and Edge walked toward the parking garage, both men absorbed in their own thoughts. Edge smoked his cigarette, while Cross was on his cell phone. Edge pressed the button to the alarm on his Hummer, deactivating the device. He jumped in the driver's side, and Cross sat in the passenger seat, his cell phone still pressed to his ear. Edge knew from the conversation that

Cross was talking to a woman, but it wasn't Kola.

Cross' infidelity was nothing new to Edge. As long as the two men knew each other, neither of them had ever been faithful to one woman, their reputations and illicit riches attracting the ladies in droves.

Edge started the ignition to his Hummer. The thunderous engine roared to life, and Jay-Z instantly began blaring in their ears. He immediately turned it down, giving Cross the respect. He took a few more pulls from his cigarette and tossed it out the window. He then reclined in his seat and went through his CD collection, which was mostly rap, from old-school Big Daddy Kane to 50 Cent and Kanye West.

Tired of listening to Jay-Z, Edge ejected The Blueprint 3 from the high-end car stereo and replaced it with Lil Wayne. He pushed in the CD and pressed for his favorite track. He liked Lil Wayne's style and the entire Cash Money roster when they were the Hot Boys representing New Orleans.

He began making his exit from the parking lot. He maneuvered his truck into the downtown rush-hour squeeze of Manhattan on a Friday afternoon. The Lower East Side was jammed with traffic and pedestrians bustling from one block to the next. Edge sighed, knowing it would take them forever to get to the FDR and head uptown into Harlem. He lit up another cigarette, nodding to the catchy, upbeat lyrics of Lil Wayne's "A Milli," which was playing low enough for him to hear it and for Cross to conduct his call.

When Cross finished his call, Edge turned up the music until the speakers rattled the truck. Men and women from Wall Street and prestigious law firms in nearby cars glanced at the truck like it was an eyesore, their white faces scowling at the loud rap violating their space, interfering with their easy-listening music. But they only gave Edge and Cross foul looks because no one dared to say anything.

Edge navigated the Hummer north up Broadway and then made a right turn onto Houston Street, headed toward FDR Drive. When Edge finally merged onto the jam-packed FDR Drive, Cross reached for the volume to the radio and turned it down a notch.

Edge glanced at his friend.

Cross said, "You know, Kola might be pregnant."

"She is?"

"She hit me today wit' the news."

"Congrats, yo," Edge replied matter-of-factly.

The traffic on the long stretch of highway from the Battery Tunnel was bumper to bumper. The only thing Edge saw from his windshield was the brake lights of cars.

"Shit, it's gonna take forever to get back uptown," Edge said.

Cross took a cigarette from the pack Edge had stashed in the console between them. He lit it, took a deep drag, and glanced out the window for a moment. "I was thinking about this case."

"What about it?"

Cross exhaled. "I might be a father soon, so I need you

to take this charge for me."

Edge couldn't believe what he was hearing. "What you sayin'?"

"I'm sayin', take this hit for me, Edge. You heard what Meyers said—three years easy and then you're out."

"Nigga, it was *your* gun. And I got kids too, Cross. What the fuck you sayin' to me?"

"I know, but we're gonna take care of you, Edge."

"Who the fuck is *we*? Kola? Yo, you got that bitch speaking for you now?"

"Edge, watch your tone."

"Nigga, she got ya connect. Now she got your heart and balls too?"

"Fuck you, nigga!"

"Fuck you, Cross! Why you lettin' this bitch come in between us, my nigga? Huh? Are you sure she's even pregnant?"

Cross wanted to hit Edge, but he kept his cool. He smoked the Newport and glared at him. "Fuckin' respect her, Edge, or I swear . . ."

"Nigga, look what the fuck she's doin' to you. To us. I don't trust her, Cross. You giving her too much power, fo' real, my nigga."

"You jealous?"

Edge chuckled. "Nigga, I don't need ya chick."

"Nigga, I still run this shit, these streets. Don't get it twisted, my nigga. I'm still the muthafuckin' boss out here. You hear me, Edge? Fuck what ya heard or think. Ain't nothin' soft about me. And if you hatin' on a nigga and his bitch, then let it be known, muthafucka!"

"I ain't hatin' or jealous of you." Edge had been yearning for Kola for a long time now. He wanted to fuck Cross' bitch and move up on the food chain. When he heard about the pregnancy, his mood just snapped. But he was still willing to fuck Kola, pregnant or not.

The heated argument between the two men continued until they got to the 59th Street Bridge. Edge just wanted to drop Cross off and be by himself. It wasn't their first argument, but it was the only one they'd ever had over a woman.

Edge was suspicious of Kola. She had her hooks too deep into Cross. He also questioned why a man like Eduardo would suddenly only want to deal with Kola. In his eyes, it didn't make any sense. Eduardo and Cross had been good associates for a long moment, and business was always good. It dawned on him that Eduardo wanted to keep Kola around because he was attracted to her. It was easy to cut out Cross and get closer to Kola if she was the one coming around for work.

Edge smiled. He thought, *Sneaky muthafucka.* Eduardo wanted what everyone else was chasing, a piece of pussy. Edge believed Kola was fucking Eduardo.

Cross and Edge were quiet until they reached Harlem, turning onto 125th Street. Because of the dense traffic, a twenty-minute drive from downtown to uptown took forty-five minutes.

"Drop me off at Tiko's spot," Cross said. "I'll catch a ride back to the crib wit' him."

Edge pulled up to the Lenox Lounge on Lenox Avenue and stopped outside the long-standing Harlem bar with its retro entrance pushed between the crevices of a growing and faster-moving Harlem. The fading neon sign looked like it was on its last bulb.

Cross stepped out of Edge's truck without saying good-bye. Edge shrugged as he slammed the door and walked toward the bar like he had just gotten out of a cab. Cross didn't even turn back. He walked into the bar without as much of a head nod in Edge's direction.

Edge felt disrespected. "Fuck him," he muttered to himself.

Edge shifted the truck in drive and sped away. He wondered if Kola was actually pregnant. It had to be a lie. He figured Kola to be the type to get an abortion if she was truly pregnant. He knew her kind. They were about business, making money—no time for family or kids. Still, he wanted a piece of her. Cross was a friend, but the game had no boundaries. Besides, Edge didn't respect him as much, with Kola calling the shots now. He saw his friend becoming weak, despite the speech he gave, which he thought was just a charade.

Cross stepped into the dimly lit Lenox Lounge, walking past the time-scarred front bar, and met Tiko at one of the circular, padded booths near "the zebra room," where pictures of music icons hung above the patrons' heads.

Tiko sat alone, sipping on a dry martini. The aging hustler with graying beard and wise-man mentality had seen it all—been there and done that—and it showed in his eyes and the creases on his face. He remembered Harlem back in the days when gangsters like Nicky Barnes and Frank Lucas had a stranglehold over its streets. He grew up with Cross' family and had done time with his ' father in Attica when crack was at its peak. Cross was like a son to him.

About to turn fifty in a few days, Tiko was wearing a stylish black suit with white pinstripes, his matching round derby with the hard narrow brim resting on the table near his drink, and a gold Rolex on his left wrist and a diamond pinky ring on his right hand.

Cross slid into the booth and sat opposite him.

Tiko gave him a head nod, showing respect. He picked up his drink and took a few sips. He looked over at the young lady working behind the bar, admiring her shape and the way she moved. She looked over at the handsome man and smiled, and Tiko smiled back. He took his time with everything, from dressing to business.

He slowly turned his attention back to Cross. "How you been, youngblood?" he asked, his raspy voice trailing like a bumpy road.

"I could be better," Cross responded.

When Tiko was in his prime, he would move hundred of ki's, heroin and cocaine, on a weekly basis, but the game had changed. The young boys coming up in the game didn't go by rules anymore. They were reckless and didn't respect the art of being a hustler, didn't know what being a gangster was supposed to be about. Besides, he'd done his stint in jail and wasn't looking to go back. He was too old. He wanted to die in Harlem, not in some ugly prison in a rural area around a bunch of men and white guards.

He hustled quietly, like a puppy walking on cotton, moving only a ki a month, and only to his loyal clientele that he trusted. He didn't need the headaches and left the corners for the young boys to fight over.

Tiko took another sip from his martini. He then raised his hand slightly and gestured to the passing waitress for another drink.

He looked at Cross for a moment. The young man reminded him of himself when he was that age. He admired Cross' character and thought he was articulate and business-minded, but Cross still had flaws that Tiko wanted to bring to his attention.

"You know Chico came to me?" Tiko mentioned.

Cross raised his eyebrows when he heard the name come from Tiko's mouth. "What he want from you?"

"My business."

"And what did you tell him?"

"I don't deal with his kind, Cross. You should know that about me. He's reckless . . . dangerous."

"He'll soon be dead."

"Well, this war you have with him, you need to end it. It will bring too much attention on you."

"I know, but Chico ain't gonna go out quietly, Tiko."

Tiko nodded. He spoke in a hushed tone. "But the

violence needs to stop. You bring attention to yourself, then it trickles down to my business and me. I've been off the feds' radar for years. Things have been quiet for me. I don't need to become another blip on their screen because of you." "I understand, Tiko."

"I don't think you do, Cross. Violence will bring police, the police will attract the feds, and then business will come to a crawl. The feds up our asses will be like diarrhea. The feds don't get off the pot until they all take a shit. And they *will* shit on us. I've been there, Cross. The last thing you or I need is a RICO case. Once it starts, it won't go away."

Cross nodded. "So how should I handle this muthafucka?"

When the waitress came over with Tiko's drink, the conversation abruptly stopped. She placed the dry martini on a napkin in front of Tiko, who flashed her a nice smile.

She returned the smile. "Anything for your friend?"

Cross shook his head. "I'm good."

"OK."

As she walked away from the table, Tiko's eyes lingered on her for a moment. He stared at her thick backside. She was the type of woman that always caught his eye—dark skin, thick in the waist and hips—a nice girl with a country accent. He had plenty like her, six kids by three beautiful women.

Tiko placed his eyes back on Cross. "You can't continue to go back and forth with him. Four bodies in the past month, the numbers go red on the homicide board in the precincts, and so do our numbers for business. Red is red anywhere . . . brings shit down."

"Yeah, I understand, but you ain't telling me much, Tiko. You talkin' in riddles right now."

Tiko stared at Cross. "What do I suggest? Do what the Mafia used to do back in the days when there was a problem between two factions."

"And what's that?"

"A sit-down."

"A what?"

"You and Chico need to sit down and work this shit out. There's enough money in Harlem to go around without us killing each other over it."

"I'm not sitting down wit' that muthafucka, Tiko. You must be crazy."

"You watch yourself, Cross. You're being ignorant right now. You keep going in the direction you're going, and you'll be nothing soon . . . only a name in the streets blowing with the wind."

"I'm not sitting down with him, Tiko. It ain't an option."

Tiko sighed. He massaged his gray beard, while Cross continued with his hard image, a scowl on his face.

"Youngblood, think about it."

Cross shook his head and stood up from the booth. He was tired of talking. He had respect for Tiko, but he wasn't about to listen to him talk about a compromise with Chico. He looked up at Tiko with a deadpan stare. "No disrespect to you, Tiko, but fuck that nigga!"

Cross caught the attention of other patrons in the lounge with his sudden outburst. The two ladies behind the bar turned to look at him.

Tiko knew there was no talking sense into the young hustler at the moment. Cross' attitude and ego were his flaws. He gestured toward the seat. "Youngblood, sit and talk."

"Nah, I'm done talking, Tiko. I'ma handle mine, you feel me?"

As Cross turned and headed for the exit, not once did he look back at Tiko. He walked outside, reached into his pocket, and pulled out his cell phone. He called Kola.

"What's up?" she answered.

"Come get me. I'm at Lenox Lounge."

Chapter 14

It was after midnight when Memo stepped out of his Accord, his pistol tucked snugly in his waistband. The rapidly graying skies above started to produce rain, and the wind was getting heavy. He zipped up his jacket and looked around briefly, making sure there wasn't any threat looming, as he made his way across the street into the Lincoln Projects.

Memo had his hand close to his pistol just in case. He wasn't taking any chances, because of the shootout with Chico and Dante a week earlier. He didn't understand why Chico was after him. He remembered what had happened to his sister, and decided he wasn't going out like that—shot dead on the streets.

He entered the quiet lobby and looked around again. The rain started to come down heavier. He pressed for the elevator and waited nervously. He was taking a chance by being in Harlem, but he needed to see his girlfriend Cherry, who was four months pregnant with his baby and crying about her bills and the rent. A small-time hustler selling weed and stolen goods, he made enough to live nice and drive around in a 2002 Honda Accord that he'd bought cash.

The elevator door slid open, and Memo stepped in. He pushed for the fifth floor, stepped back, and waited. He stepped onto the fifth floor and walked down the narrow, graffiti-covered hallway toward the apartment, which was the last one down the long stretch of hallway. To the right of it was the stairway exit.

Memo knocked on her door. He could hear 2Pac blaring in the apartment.

He knocked harder, shouting, "Cherry, open the damn door!"

He heard the music being lowered. He glanced around before turning back to the doorway. He knocked even harder. "Cherry, hurry the fuck up!" he shouted.

As Memo focused on the apartment door, the stairway door to the fifth floor swung open like a gust of wind had pushed it. He turned in time to see Dante emerging toward him with a 12-gauge, sawed-off double-barrel shotgun aimed at his head.

Memo's eyes widened with fear as he stepped back and fumbled with the pistol tucked in his jeans. He gripped it, but it was already too late.

Dante didn't say a word. The 12-gauge exploded in his grip, causing a loud echo in the narrow hallway. Memo's head shattered like a water balloon hitting concrete, and his brain and blood splattered against the walls and apartment door.

Dante walked over to the body and smiled at his handiwork. Then he stepped back into the stairway and disappeared into the night like a shadow, leaving Memo's contorted body on display for the neighbors to see.

Denise, eyes closed and legs open, squirmed underneath the sheets as the young stud was eating her out in the comfort of her bedroom. She dug her nails into the top of his skull when his long tongue wormed inside of her.

Her twin daughters and their problems were the farthest things from her mind. It was all about her and Robert. She loved the way the young hustler sexed her. Robert was a beast with his eight-inch erection, and she loved everything about him.

"Ooooh!" she cooed.

Robert inclined her legs at an angle where her knees were vertically pointed at her, and dug his face deeper into her throbbing pussy, his tongue sliding easily between her lips and making her legs quiver. Each stroke of his tongue and the movement of his fingers sliding in and out of her lit up her body with pleasure.

"I want that dick in me."

Robert smiled. He lifted his face from her wet, throbbing pussy, ready to oblige his cougar.

Denise gazed at his chiseled physique. Her eyes traveled down to his penis, which was hard and ready, and her pussy jumped. Their last encounter had her spent and mouthing, *What the fuck!* The dick was good. Really good.

She couldn't complain. The young boy knew how to work her body.

He snatched the Magnum condom off the nightstand near the bed and tore it open with his teeth. Denise waited patiently with her legs spread for him to enter her. He slowly rolled back the Magnum onto his thick penis, and just as he was about to thrust himself inside her, the two suddenly heard a loud cannon-like explosion outside her doorway.

Startled, Denise jumped up and hollered, "What the fuck was that?" Then she heard a woman screaming.

She jumped out of the bed, grabbed her robe from off the chair, and rushed to her front door, and Robert followed her, stumbling over the carpet in the hallway as he tried to put on his jeans.

Denise was barely covered in her robe when she opened her door and saw the body sprawled out right next to her apartment door, half his face gone, and blood and brain matter everywhere. She placed her hands over her mouth in shock, wanting to scream, but the pregnant young girl in the hallway with her was doing enough screaming for the both of them.

More neighbors started to come out of their apartments, every one of them carrying the same horrified gaze, and the hallway quickly began to fill with people.

One elderly woman wearing a long bathrobe and curlers in her hair screamed loudly, "Oh my God!"

A mother grabbed her six-year-old and pulled him back into her apartment, not wanting him to view the scene, which made her skin crawl. A middle-aged couple had to restrain the pregnant girlfriend, who was crying hysterically.

Robert's face became ghostly white. "Yo, I know that ain't my nigga Memo!" he shouted.

Though the body was barely recognizable, Robert noticed the bloody chain around the neck and the pendant attached to it. Memo was the only one known to wear the distinctive gold piece—a pair of 14k gold boxing gloves with a small skull embossed into the gloves—a reminder of his time spent in the gym preparing for the Golden Gloves competition a few years earlier.

Before long, the building and fifth floor were flooded with cops and detectives, another reminder to the residents of their dangerous, violent environment.

Chapter 15

Chico turned his high-priced BMW into the brick, hilltop driveway. He pulled up to his stylish home and remained seated in the car, not in a rush to get out. It had been a long day for him. He had so much going on, at times he would forget what day of the week it was. He had a few liens against him for debts he owed through construction and other companies filing against him. Then the bank had given him ninety days on paying his mortgage because he was behind by two months. His world was slowly falling apart. His investments had evaporated over the months, and it was beginning to look bleak for his legal investments.

He and his cousin were making a strong statement throughout Harlem, completing Apple's death list, which was a pleasure for him. And Memo's murder in the projects had the hustlers and his enemies thinking twice about messing with him and his business.

Chico had made his move on the chessboard and was ready to topple kings. But with the death toll rising in Harlem, people were becoming scared of him, and his clientele started backing out of deals with him, fearing the ramifications of such involvement. Also, his regular customers were complaining about his inferior product.

Chico sighed heavily, staring out the windshield of his BMW. His birthday was approaching, but he wasn't in the mood to celebrate or do anything, since his money was dwindling. He had ki's of cocaine to get rid of, but they weren't moving fast enough for him.

He removed the pistol from under his seat and stuffed it into his jeans. Then he stepped out of the car into the brisk wintry air, the cold wind nipping at his skin. The chilled air was blowing just hard enough to cut through his heavy clothing, even though the sun was shining brightly. He zipped up his coat and walked to the front entrance of his mini-mansion with the sprawling green lawn, wraparound deck, large glass-enclosed patio, walkouts from both the wine cellar and the basement, and expensive furnishings and top-of-the-line appliances, all for Apple's well-being and happiness.

Chico walked into his quiet home, turned on the lights in the living room, and placed his pistol on the coffee table. He didn't call out for Apple, assuming she was asleep. He looked around his home and then headed to the stairway. When he got to the top of the stairs, he saw the light on in the bathroom and heard the shower running. He gently walked toward the bathroom door and peered inside. Apple was in the shower, her clear mask resting on the bathroom sink.

He lingered near the doorway for a moment. The steam from the hot shower was fogging up the room. He saw Apple's shapely silhouette behind the glass shower door. He continued to watch.

The shower stopped running, and the glass door opened up. Apple stepped out of the stone standup shower dripping wet. Though half her face was badly damaged, she still had the body of a goddess. She reached for a towel hanging over the rack and started to dry herself off, peering in the mirror. Her look still troubled her.

The fog in the bathroom began to clear. *She's a strong woman*, he thought to himself. He smiled at her side view. The bodies piling up in Harlem was because he loved her so much and would do anything for her, despite what anybody said.

Apple thought she was alone, until she turned and noticed Chico staring at her from the doorway. She quickly wrapped herself in the towel and reached for her mask. "I didn't hear you come in," she said.

Chico entered the bathroom. "Didn't know you were still up."

Apple turned the damaged side of her face away from him and attempted to put on the mask, but Chico stopped her. He grabbed her wrist and said, "Nah, you don't need that."

She stared at him, unable to hide the sadness in her eyes. Chico pulled her into his arms. Apple tried to resist, but Chico was relentless. They hadn't been intimate with each other since the incident. Chico was always out with his whores—fucking and drinking, trying to escape his reality with Apple.

At first, it was hard for him to look at her, when her wounds were fresh. Tonight, though, he saw her in a totally different light. He saw the woman he fell in love with. She looked enticing, like fresh fruit to a hungry animal.

Chico pressed her into his arms, but she tried to move away from him. He pulled her back, reached down, and slid his hand beneath her towel.

"Chico, no," she protested.

"Why not?"

"Look at me."

"I don't give a fuck. It's been a while."

Apple squirmed in his grip. She hadn't been feeling sexual lately. In fact, sex had been the farthest thing from her mind, but his touch and his kisses were making her blush.

Chico had her pushed against the sink, his right arm wrapped around her upper torso, while the other arm was feeling in between her legs. He quickly unwrapped the towel and allowed it to drop around her feet. He cupped her breasts and kissed the back of her neck, and she moaned.

Chico unbuckled his jeans and dropped his pants. He bent her over the bathroom sink, spread her ass cheeks, gripped his hard-on, and thrust himself into her. She groaned from the sudden entry. He leaned forward, placing a hold around her slim neck and gripping her ripe hips, and kept his rhythm going as he stared at himself in the mirror. Her pussy was still good.

"Ooooh! Ah shit! Ooooh!" she groaned.

Chico's deep thrusts became more rapid. His heated breath alone tickled her every nerve ending. He reached around her to pinch her nipples and do some soft breast-cupping.

Apple pressed one palm flat against the mirror, while her other hand clutched the sink for stability. Chico was fucking her so hard, she had to grab onto something to keep herself from smashing into the mirror. The dick was good. She lowered her face over the sink and bit down on her bottom lip.

"I love you, baby." Chico focused on his image as he said it. He was intense in the pussy, almost possessed. Apple's pussy was tight and feeling too good. "I'll do anything for you. You know that, right?"

She moaned. "Ugggh!"

Chico was hunched over Apple's back and breathing hard. "I'm comin', baby," he hollered.

"Fuck me! Get yours, baby." Apple body was quivering as she came, her back arched and her face down into the sink.

Sweaty from the workout, Chico massaged her tits soothingly. He then rose up and turned her over to face him. He hoisted her up onto the sink and kissed her. He held her face in his hand. He wanted to show her the affection she deserved. He didn't care about her scars.

The couple ended up in the bedroom, where Apple donned her long silk robe and placed the clear, plastic mask over her face.

Chico walked over to the window and looked outside, his back turned to her and his arms behind him. He was staring at his parked BMW. "Pick another name from the hat, Apple," he said.

There was one name that Apple didn't place in the hat—Guy Tony. She didn't forget about him; she'd left his name out deliberately.

Guy Tony was Apple's main suspect, but the last thing she wanted was Chico to catch up with him and have him spill everything about Supreme and how she'd manipulated Guy into killing his former boss and mentor. She wanted to erase that from her mind and would deal with Guy in her own time and in her own way.

All the same, she felt it in her bones that she hadn't seen the last of Guy, that he was probably lurking out there, plotting against her.

Apple reached for the baseball cap. Chico turned to look at her and observed her picking out a name. She unfolded the small piece of paper to see who she had picked. It was her mother, Denise.

"Who you got for me, baby?" Chico asked with some pleasure in his tone.

Apple swallowed hard. She wasn't sure if she could make that decision about her mother yet. As Chico turned and looked out the window again, she slipped the name back into the hat and pulled out the only one left.

"Kola," she announced.

Chico removed himself from the window and walked over to her, seated on the bed, the wrinkled white strip of paper and cap in her hands. She looked up at him.

"That bitch, huh?"

Apple noticed the strange look on his face. "What's wrong?"

"We at war with Cross right now, and getting at Kola is going to be hard. Business is tight, baby, and niggas ain't tryin' to cop this work from me because they think I'm a threat to them. Before we truly get at that bitch, we gonna need to settle up first. That shit is gonna really heat things up, and I'm gonna need the cash to finance certain things right now."

"So what you saying?"

"I'ma murder that bitch and her man, but right now, we need to settle up wit' these bills we owe on this house and other things, baby. I'ma take care of us, I promise.

"Then I'ma hit the streets wit' these ki's and get my money right. Niggas ain't gonna have a choice but to cop from me," he said gruffly. "'Cause we gonna be the ones left standing after this smoke clears."

Apple crushed the paper with Kola's name. She held Chico's stare. She stood up from the bed and walked out the bedroom, uttering, "My sister doesn't get to win."

Chico remained standing in the center of the bedroom, his eyes following her as she left the room. He understood her frustration.

It was a chilly evening when Dante pulled Chico's BMW in front of the two jacked up cars in front of

Moe's Tire Repair Shop on Amsterdam Avenue, Chico in the passenger seat. Moe's, a front company for a drug distribution operation, had been operating on the Upper West Side for years, and Chico was one of his main suppliers. Until Kola negotiated a deal with him that he couldn't refuse. Chico wanted to have a word with him, change his mind about that.

Dante and Chico stepped out of the BMW. As usual, both men were armed, but they came to talk business with Moe first. Employees in greasy overalls, working on customers' cars in front of the tire shop, glanced over at the two men entering the place and continued on with their work.

"We just talk first," Chico said to Dante.

Dante nodded.

The tire shop was noisy with the loosening and tightening of nuts and bolts from tire rims, and it smelled of labor. In the back of the shop was Moe's makeshift office, which was really four walls of sheetrock and a rickety door barely on its hinges, and no covering overhead, just the roof to the tire shop. And mountains of tires and rims clogged the doorway, making entry and exit difficult.

Dante and Chico walked in to find Moe seated in a chair behind his desk, on his cell phone. Inside the office there was paper scattered everywhere. The walls were stained with grime and plastered with dusty posters of naked women of every race. And his stained desk was overrun with old fast-food wrappings, old and discolored newspapers, and miscellaneous junk. And the office reeked, as did Moe.

Moe acknowledged Chico with a head nod then gestured for them to have a seat. Both men chose to stand. Moe's chairs were as dusty as him and his office.

Moe was a stout black man with nappy hair and a shaggy beard, and he looked like he was born in stained, greasy overalls. He had inherited the tire shop from his father ten years earlier, after his father passed.

One time Moe had fallen behind in payments with creditors. He then got down with Chico in the drug business, and business picked up for him. Soon he was hooked on the money coming in from both sides—his shop and the four ki's a week he was moving.

Chico didn't have time for Moe to finish up with his conversation. He walked closer to Moe. "Get the fuck off the phone," he said, glaring at him, "you fat fuck!"

Moe became silent over the phone. He looked up at Chico in confusion.

"We ain't got time to wait for you," Chico told him.

Dante closed the door to the office, giving them some privacy.

"Let me call you back," Moe said to the caller on the other end. He hung up and leaned back in his chair. "Chico, what's up?" he asked calmly, raising his hands. "Why you gotta be disrespectful?"

"Nigga, what's this I hear about you gettin' into bed with that bitch Kola and her man?"

Moe knew getting into bed with Cross and Kola would have come back to bite him, but he didn't think it would've happened that soon.

"Chico, look, it's just business, man. Kola came to me the other day and said she had an offer for me that I would like. The bitch knows how to talk, Chico. She's about her business. I mean, her shit is pure, man. My peoples couldn't get enough of her shit. It sells."

Moe's eyes darted back and forth between Chico and Dante. He didn't know Dante, but Dante's presence alone made him uneasy. Dante's cold eyes rested on Moe like a target pointed at center mass, and Moe began to sweat, even though the room was cold.

"So you cut me out to fuck wit' that triflin' bitch," Chico said.

"It's only business, man. It ain't anything personal with you, Chico. I swear."

Chico paced around Moe like a therapist in a session. "Business, huh?" he replied nonchalantly.

Moe's eyes stayed glued to Chico. He fidgeted with his hands while remaining seated in his chair, trying to calm his nerves.

"I gotta eat too, Moe. You fuckin' wit' that bitch is taking food outta my mouth."

"Chico, I mean, what am I supposed to do? You hot right now. You bringin' too much attention on yourself. I don't need the heat right now, man. I don't! I'm running a good thing here."

"You are, huh?" Chico stopped pacing around Moe and stood close to him, towering over him as he leaned back in his chair. "You remember when your fat, bitch ass was behind in your payments for this shop? You remember a few years ago, when ya bitch ass came crying to me about how the bank was threatening you wit' foreclosure because ya dumb ass wanted to take out a second mortgage on this place to support that ugly bitch you was fucking? Huh, Moe, you remember that? You wanted to live big, nigga! You wanted to show off! And who helped you out?"

Moe remained quiet, his silence and meek demeanor already speaking the truth.

"Yeah, nigga, I'm the nigga that put you on and got you out of debt," Chico said, his voice becoming louder and sterner. "Now you sit ya fat ass in front of me and have the audacity to say you're running a good thing here?"

"Chico, I ain't mean—"

"Shut the fuck up!" Chico shouted, cutting Moe off.

Moe continued to fidget with his hands, rubbing them together and popping his knuckles, an indication of his fear. He couldn't look Dante in his eyes. He knew he was strictly muscle—Chico's shooter. Whenever their eyes locked, he would avert them and look at Chico.

"You betrayed me, Moe."

"Chico, I'll make it up. I'm sorry, man. I ain't mean no disrespect."

"Like hell, you didn't."

"I fucked up. What you want me to do?"

"First, you stay away from that bitch—You only eat off of me—and, second, I need a favor from you."

"What's that?"

"I want you to help me set up that bitch and Cross. I

need for them to go, and ya gonna be the one to help me make it happen."

Moe looked up at Chico and nervously asked, "What you need me to do?" He began to breathe a little easier, knowing he was about to live. His nerves were still on edge, though.

Chico smiled. He continued to talk to Moe, filling him in on when to set up a meeting with Kola. He was about to arrange her death, execution-style. Chico knew it would bring the heat on him and his crew, but bills had to get paid, and he and Apple needed to continue eating.

Before Chico and Dante walked out of Moe's office, Chico turned to Moe and told him, "Don't you ever go behind my back like that again, Moe, or I swear next time it ain't gonna be talk between us, but ya brains on the floor." He shut the door behind him and followed behind Dante out of the tire shop, leaving Moe to ponder about what he'd just said.

The chilly wind made the two men zip up their coats and lower their heads as they walked past the employees outside, hurrying to finish out the day's work. The traffic on Amsterdam Avenue was thinning as the sun slipped behind the horizon.

Dante pulled out a cigarette, lit it up, took a long drag, and walked toward the BMW. He was Chico's chauffeur for the day. Chico needed to relax. Turning to face Chico, he said, "I'm hungry, cuzzo. Let's stop by Applebee's and get somethin' to eat. I'm in the mood for one of their sandwiches and drinks." Dante removed the alarm button from his coat pocket, pointed it at the 5 Series, and deactivated the alarm.

Chico nodded. His mind was on business. It was about to be a busy week for him. He had fifteen ki's to move, and they weren't moving. He was hitting up all the locations he did business with and strong-arming them.

Cross was starting to cut into Chico's pockets heavily. He understood that he had the inferior product, but still, cocaine sold itself. And with Kola flaunting her sex appeal, manipulating his clientele with her slick talk, and Cross having the connect, he felt overmatched.

And it wasn't right that his girl had the disfigured face and was in pain at home, while Cross had the prettier twin sister. And now he had to play bottom feeder to the two people he hated the most.

Chico raged inside. He didn't care about any rules or think about the consequences. The gloves were off. He wanted Kola dead first, and then he would worry about Cross in due time. He wasn't about to give up his hood so easily.

Dante started to walk around to the driver's seat. "Yo, cuzzo, tonight, let's roll out to Sue's Rendezvous and get it poppin'. I'm in the mood to see some strippers and get me some ass."

Chico chuckled.

As Dante reached for the door handle to the car, he turned to see a dark, tinted Chevy Yukon heading his way on the two-way street. With his hand near his gun, he gawked at the car.

Chico noticed the truck and became alert too.

The Yukon stopped alongside Dante. As the front passenger window rolled down, he was ready to extract his weapon and fire, but the smiling face of a beautiful, brown-skinned Dominican woman made him relax somewhat. Still, he kept his hand close to his weapon.

"What's poppin'?" he asked.

"Excuse me, we're lost," the lady with the full, beautiful lips and chinky eyes mentioned with a smile.

The back passenger window to the truck slowly lowered, and the face of another pretty, brown-skinned honey appeared with a matching smile, like her friend. "Hey," she greeted.

Dante didn't return their smiles. He had a straight face while staring back at the girls. "Where y'all tryin' to go?" he asked, trying to look past the cheery girls and into the truck.

"We trying to do something tonight, and we're looking for this street ... um ... Riverside Drive and West One Fifty-Eighth Street. We've been driving all around this bitch for twenty minutes, and we can't find it," the female front passenger said.

Chico told them, "You about ten blocks away. It's on the West Side. Just take Amsterdam Avenue straight up, and when you get to One Fifty-Eighth Street, you make that right."

"Thank you, cutie."

Chico nodded, while Dante kept his eyes on the truck.

The girls continued to laugh and flirt with the men for a short moment. Then the windows went back up, and the Yukon slowly drove away.

As Dante watched the truck, while Chico went to step inside his 5 Series, they didn't notice the young, hooded boy looming from around the corner with his head down. The one who'd reached underneath his hoodie and pulled out a 9 mm, gripping it tightly. He was watching Chico and Dante as they looked at the Yukon. The young boy stretched his hand out, looming closer, his eyes focused on Chico.

Chico turned and locked his attention on the hooded gangster.

Bam! Bam! Bam! Bam!

The windows to the BMW shattered around Chico. Chico jumped back and hit the sidewalk fast.

Dante reached for his weapon to shoot back, but a sudden force pushed him into the side of the car like a gust of wind. His back was on fire, and the only thing he heard was a second round of explosions. He managed to turn. The shot had come from the Yukon. The girl seated in the backseat was poised out the window with a pump-action shotgun in her hand.

Dante's eyes widened. Then he heard the third explosion. *Boom!* The bullet tore into his upper chest and plummeted him across the car. He was dead before he even hit the ground.

Chico scurried for cover. Moving on his hands and knees, he ducked between two cars as the young boy continued firing, his eyes showing no mercy or any hint of fright; he was like a mindless zombie trained to do this.

Chico clutched his pistol. *What the fuck!* he mouthed. He looked to his left and saw his cousin lying dead on the pavement. "Dante!" he screamed out.

Bam! Bam! Bam! Bam! Bam!

As the shots continued to ring out, Chico felt like a sitting duck.

The girl with the pump-action retreated back into the Yukon, and the second hit squad sped away, leaving the lone shooter to finish up. But he didn't get a chance to.

Click! Click! Click! He had emptied out his clip.

When Chico slowly stood up and looked around the car cautiously, the shooter was long gone. He took off running and dropped the gun in a nearby sewer.

The abrupt gunfire had sent people nearby running or hiding. The front of the tire shop was empty; the workers and customers had rushed inside when the shooting started, and the traffic on the street had stopped.

Moe came running out, looking petrified. "Chico, what the fuck happened?" he shouted.

Chico didn't say a word. Seeing his cousin sprawled out on the cold street in thick, pooling blood made him unresponsive. The pistol was still in his hand at his side.

Moe ran over to Chico. "Chico, you need to get the fuck outta here." He pushed the keys to his Range Rover into Chico's hand and pointed to his ride parked across the street. "Take my ride."

Chico turned to look at Moe. He grasped the keys and

didn't say a word. He stuffed the pistol into his waistband and ran over to the truck.

Punk muthafucka! Moe smirked as he watched Chico speed away.

Moe wasn't as stupid as Chico thought. He knew Chico would drop by to pay him a visit after finding out about his dealings with Kola, so he had devised a plan.

When Chico had arrived to meet with him, one of his trusted employees put the word out to Kola and Cross via text message, and then immediately a hit squad was sent out. He had only showed kindness to Chico after the failed hit because he didn't want to look like he was involved with it.

Chapter 16

Kola was looking fabulous in her form-fitting, low-rise leather pants and black V-neck bodysuit that showed off her thick cleavage. She stepped into one of the private back rooms at one of her sex parties, where the muffled bass of Jim Jones' "We Fly High'" could still be heard. The room was off-limits to everyone, except for her security and the hands she trusted to count the money. She closed the door behind her and stared at the piles of money scattered across the large table. It looked like the Rocky Mountains, the way the bills were stacked on top of each other.

She took a sip of Moët. "That's the sexiest shit I've ever seen," she said, referring to the large amount of money within her reach, profit from her parties and drug sales.

Three men stood around the table separating the big bills from the small bills. There was a money machine on a separate table, two small cameras hovering above the room—one aimed at the cash and the second aimed at the door. A stocky armed man holding onto an Uzi stood near the entrance, and a black-and-white security monitor was perched catty-corner on a wooden shelf, allowing the occupants of the room to see who was right outside the thick door.

At her events Kola sold coke, ecstasy, and heroin to willing customers who needed a pick-me-up to be with the girls, so she was making money hand over fist.

The three men glanced at Kola and continued working. They were college kids—nineteen- and twenty-year-old accounting and business majors—undergraduates working on their bachelor's degrees who'd agreed to work for her for some extra cash for books and tuition.

Her new location was at a loft near the Brooklyn Bridge, a waterfront property with a view of the bridge and the river, in an industrial area, surrounded by warehouses, shipping companies, and a lumber yard. The building was close to the Brooklyn/Queens Expressway and the Navy shipyard.. The venue was huge, three floors and many rooms, and was one of her better spots.

The three young men would take subtle glances at Kola, admiring her beauty and figure. And even though she was the youngest person in the room, the college students knew she was way out of their league.

Kola walked over to the corner of the room where two large, empty black duffel bags sat. She said, "I want a hundred and fifty stacks in both bags."

Everyone nodded.

At the sound of a buzz at the door, Kola and everyone else looked up at the security monitor and saw a beautiful, young woman clad in tight blue jeans and a boob-revealing top with long, chic braids standing right outside the door. Kola immediately recognized Candace.

"Y'all finish up in here, a'ight?" she said to her workers. They nodded.

Kola turned and approached the door. She glanced at her one-man security team dressed in black fatigues and nodded, and Rondo returned the head nod.

Rondo, a friend of Cross, was as serious as they came. He was an ex-marine who'd done two tours in Iraq but was fresh home from Attica, where he'd done time for second-degree murder. He'd killed two men armed with guns with his bare hands and claimed it was self-defense. They were trying to rob him, but the DA said it was overkill. One man had his neck snapped like a twig, and the second was stabbed repeatedly in his chest and throat.

Kola opened the thick door and stepped outside to greet Candace, who was from Panama, spoke three languages—Spanish, English, and French—and had a body like Jennifer Lopez.

"Kola, hey," Candace greeted.

Kola knew why Candace wanted to see her. The two walked away from the money room and down the hallway, where they could talk in private.

After glancing around, Kola said to Candace, "Talk to me. What happened?"

"My bitches got one, but Chico, I think he escaped," Candace said in her thick accent.

"What you mean? Y'all missed?"

"We did our job. Tina worked his cousin wit' the shotgun. She put that *puta* down. He don't get back up, but the young boy didn't finish it."

Kola sighed. "Well, at least one is fuckin' down."

"If you want, we finish lookin'," Candace suggested.

"Nah, y'all did good."

Kola passed Candace a thick bulging envelope filled with cash, payment for the hit, and Candace reached out and took it.

"That's the rest of it, twenty-five thousand," Kola said. "Make sure you pay them bitches, Candace. I don't want any problems."

Candace nodded. "We good, Kola. I told you, my girls, we put in work. Niggas see pussy, and they smile. So that *puta* didn't even see us coming."

Kola liked what she heard. She respected Candace. Many niggas and bitches were fooled by the stunning hazel-eyed beauty with the sweet Panamanian accent, but underneath all the glamour and beauty was a hellcat—a woman as deadly as a venomous snake.

Candace had come to the country when she was seven years old and grew up in Edenwald Projects, one of the most notorious housing projects in the Bronx. She learned to fight because she was always bullied for being different and an immigrant. However, by the time she was sixteen, she had a reputation in the neighborhood that made even grown men stay away from her. Candace only fucked with gangsters and killers, and she learned her illicit and deadly ways through them. By the time she was seventeen years old, she was already stripping, trafficking guns for her boyfriend, and had numerous assault and drug charges on her record.

When Kola first met Candace six months ago, she had just gotten out of Rikers after doing a year-long bid for possession and assault. The two met in the strip club, and Candace liked what Kola was saying to her. It didn't take long for Candace to link up with Kola, and at the age of twenty-two, she was a force to be reckoned with.

After her conversation with Candace, Kola walked into the primary room where everything was taking place. The huge area with the high concrete ceiling and towering concrete columns was filled with people. Kola stood above them on a slightly raised platform. She peered down at the crowd and watched to see what was going on.

That bitch will never outdo or outshine me, Kola thought to herself, thinking about Apple.

Kola had the black duffel bag gripped in her hand and walked by the doorman without any problems this time. She strutted toward the elevators wearing a pair of suede pants and a stretch silk shirt underneath her hazelnut Mongolian fur-trimmed sweater coat. She had become a known face to him. He nodded at Kola when she walked by and immediately got on the phone to call upstairs. He said to his employer, "Kola's coming up."

Kola stepped into the elevator and placed the duffel

bag on the floor by her feet. She pushed for the top floor and waited. When she stepped off the elevator, she was encountered by the same three goons like always.

She smiled and greeted them with a teasing, "Hey, boys."

The men perked up but didn't smile. They always knew what she was there for. They had gotten used to seeing her and even liked it when she came by. She was their eye candy.

Kola walked up to them, dropped her bag, and readied herself for the usual search. She looked over at her friend, the only one who took pride in his job and whose hands lingered on her the most. She had gotten used to his deep fondling during his search for weapons.

"Y'all ready to frisk me?"

This time, her friend's hand rested between her legs a little longer, his fingers rubbing against her pussy. Kola released a teasing moan and stared down at Anton. He was a dumb goon, but she thought he was cute.

She was allowed into the room and was ready to meet with Tony. She dropped the duffel bag of cash in the middle of the room and walked over to the floor-to-ceiling windows to take in the picturesque view. Being twenty-one floors up gave her an eyeful of the New Jersey shores, the Hudson River, and the Manhattan skyline. She even saw the George Washington Bridge.

It was a clear, sunny day, and the weather was in the lower forties. Kola wanted spring to hurry up so she could wear her tight skirts and eye-catching clothing. She liked being a tease, and she loved being the center of attention even more.

As Kola stood by the windows gazing at New York City, she thought about business. She was always thinking about ways to expand herself. The parties were profitable, but she couldn't be everywhere at once. Taking over with the connect and networking her business in the streets—going back and forth with her parties and moving so many ki's a week—was taking its toll on her. She thought about who to trust to run her events when she was away on business.

She thought about Candace, but she was too hotheaded and only good for problems, not handling money. Kola missed Bunny Rabbit, her one true bitch who knew how to get money and was a down-ass bitch. It disturbed her that Bunny Rabbit was killed at her eighteenth birthday party in an incident that her sister had provoked.

"I see you like the view."

Kola turned around to see Eduardo approaching her in his long cotton bathrobe, which was open, exposing his chiseled chest. He had on swimming trunks underneath and held a glass of wine in his hand.

"Eduardo, you're back." Kola was surprised to see him.

He smiled. "You miss me?"

"Where's Tony?"

"Back in my country. I needed him to fix something for me."

Kola didn't pry. She understood Eduardo kept his affairs silent.

Eduardo saw the duffel bag sitting in the middle of the room. "It's good to see that business is still good."

"You keep producing that good white, the money ain't going anywhere."

Eduardo nodded. "You look nice."

"Thank you."

"Come, have a drink with me. Relax. I've been gone for weeks."

Kola wasn't sure, but Eduardo walked over to the bar and prepared two glasses. He mixed a scotch on the rocks with a twist and walked over to Kola as she remained standing by the window. He passed her the glass. She took a few simple sips, while Eduardo downed half his drink.

There was a moment of silence between them. Kola glanced out the window; it was hard to take her eyes away from the Manhattan skyline.

"Beautiful, isn't it?" Eduardo said.

"It is."

"The city of dreams."

"Well, my dreams are coming true."

"Cheers to that, beautiful." Eduardo raised his glass in a toast.

Kola raised her too, and their glasses clinked together. "Cheers."

They locked eyes for a moment. Kola felt her heart racing and her panties were on fire. She took a few more sips and tried to control her hormones, while Eduardo stood in front of her with his robe still open. She noticed the bulge protruding from his swimming trunks.

Eduardo finished off his drink and was ready for another one. Noticing Kola's glass was almost empty, he asked, "Would you care for another one?"

She shook her head. "No, I'm good."

"I see that," he said as he walked back to the bar.

Kola wanted to leave, but something inside of her was urging her to stay. She sighed while standing near the floor-to-ceiling windows, feeling the heat of the sun against her.

Eduardo walked over to her and took a few more sips from the short-stemmed glass he held. He stared out the window for a moment and said to Kola, "Come, let me show you something."

"Eduardo, I can't stay long."

"Sure, you can. We haven't seen each other in a while."

Eduardo took her by the hand and led her across the large living room, up the spiral staircase, and into a room down the long corridor. The room was filled with drugs, stacks of ki's—almost three hundred wrapped bricks stacked neatly over each other and lining the walls.

Kola had never seen anything like it. "Oh my God!"

"You like?"

"How do you get it into the country?" she asked.

"It's my little secret."

"Why are you showing me this?"

"Because I can. This is true wealth."

It was a highly secure and large room with one entrance, no windows, and the door was solid steel with a high-tech security system and cameras pointing everywhere.

Eduardo stood in the center of it all with his arms outstretched, still holding his short-stemmed glass in his hand. "This is what fuels America," he said. "This is what many men dream of and will die for—riches and happiness."

"How much is it all worth?"

"At least twenty million."

"Damn!"

Eduardo smiled as he walked up to Kola, who held his stare with a smile. She tried not to look tense, but there was something about him that she really liked. Eduardo was very smart and charming, but she also knew he was a dangerous man. She wondered how many men he had killed over the years by his own hands or by giving the order. She was attracted to him but didn't want to act on it, fearful of the consequences with Cross.

Eduardo took her hand into his and peered into her eyes. "You are a very beautiful woman, Kola."

"Thank you."

"Please, stay for dinner."

"I'm a busy woman, Eduardo."

"And I'm a busy man, as you can see, but I always make time for the things I care for."

They looked at each other. Eduardo didn't want to take no for an answer. He still held her hand in his. "I will change, and you stay. OK?"

Kola sighed, fearing where it was leading. "OK," she reluctantly agreed.

"Good. I'll have my chef prepare a meal straight from the kitchen, and you'll love it."

Kola nodded.

The two exited the room, and Eduardo secured the door with an alarm. She then followed him down the long carpeted corridor and into another room filled with sunlight and decorated with mahogany furniture. Oil paintings on massive canvases lined the room, and a long, rectangular Wynterhall dining room set constructed of hardwood with cherry veneers in a rich, warm, brown finish sat on the shimmering parquet flooring.

Kola was taken aback. The room was worth a million or more in her eyes.

"I go shower and change," Eduardo said to her. "You make yourself comfortable."

Eduardo walked out of a different door and disappeared down the corridor, leaving Kola in the stylish room alone. She felt like she was in a different world. She couldn't believe how far she had come along—the money, the handsome Colombian kingpin trying to romance her, and living the life of a queenpin.

Kola knew Cross would be against her staying. *It's just dinner with a business associate*, she thought, trying to convince herself. She didn't want to be impolite.

Kola didn't have to wait too long. Eduardo walked back into the room dressed in a gray silk shirt, stylish black khakis, and a pair of expensive alligator shoes. He was sharp, yet casual.

"Have a seat. Relax, Kola," he said.

Kola walked toward the dining room table, which was decorated with a long white tablecloth underneath half a dozen taper candles in crystalline glass.

Eduardo slowly lit each candle. Then he approached her, took her hand in his once again, and then guided her toward the table. He pulled out her chair, like a gentleman.

It's only dinner, she kept thinking to herself.

Eduardo sat opposite of her and said, "My chef should be almost done with dinner. You'll enjoy it."

"So you assumed I would be staying?"

"No, I just have him cook big meals all the time."

Kola looked around the room and thought about Cross. She had never cheated on him and wasn't about to start now.

Eduardo lit one of his cigars, took a deep pull, and exhaled. He looked at Kola, his hazel eyes piercing into her soul. "You find me attractive, Kola?" he asked unexpectedly.

"Who wouldn't? You're a very handsome man, Eduardo."

"Powerful too."

Just then a tall, lean man dressed in a dark suit walked into the room carrying a bottle of Cristal Brut in an ice bucket. He set the chilled bottle of champagne in the center of the dining room table then stood next to Eduardo with his arms crossed in front of him, awaiting further instructions, but Eduardo waved him off.

"Champagne?"

Kola nodded.

"It's one of the most expensive in the world, Cristal Brut, also known as 'the Methuselah.' They go for seventeen thousand dollars a bottle."

"Damn!"

Eduardo stood up and reached for the bottle. He removed the foil, leaving the wired hood intact. He grabbed the neck of the bottle, placed his thumb over the cork, and slightly raised the six-liter gold-labeled bottle with it pressed against his hip. He twisted it open quickly, and the bubbles instantly began spilling out.

He walked around to Kola and poured her a glass. "It's the best," he said.

"At seventeen stacks, the shit better taste like platinum in my mouth."

Eduardo laughed as he walked back over to his chair and took a seat. He raised his glass, gazed at Kola with a slight grin, and said, "This is to our success. Money will always be us. And you are—How do your people say it?—a down-ass bitch."

Kola smiled then downed the champagne, feeling seventeen thousand dollars slide down her throat soothingly.

The two then dined on *bandeja paisa*, a typical Colombian fusion dish that Eduardo loved. He wanted Kola to taste it, and she loved it.

Three hours later, Kola found herself standing by the window once again. She had enjoyed the wine and meal. She peered at the city, her mind on her man. She knew she should have left hours ago, but she felt compelled to stay. Eduardo joined her at the window, and they took in the view of the city lights together.

Eduardo took a few sips again. Although he had been drinking all evening, his speech was still coherent, and he didn't look fazed by the wine at all.

He lowered the short-stemmed glass from his lips and suddenly said to Kola, "You know, I grew up poor in Bogotá, my country's capital. My mother was a whore, and my father was a thief. I had many brothers and sister, but I'm one of the few alive. My country is a dangerous country, Kola, but I take pride in where I'm from. I've seen many people killed. Death was an everyday thing for me. At thirteen, I witnessed men cut my father's throat in front of me because he stole from them. When I was fourteen, I killed them both."

Kola glanced at him. She wondered why he was telling her this. He stood extremely close to her, his touch only a fingernail away. Still, she didn't move from him. She just stood there quiet like a mouse in the dark, her heart beating like concert drums. He smelled like fresh roses, and it turned her on, but she wanted to keep it "only business" with him.

Eduardo continued, "I never told anyone this. You're the first. I trust you, Kola. You have this thing about you, and I see why the men love you."

He raised the glass and took another sip. He then said, "I can have anything I want. Everything and everyone is within my reach. With a snap of my fingers, I can give life or death, wealth or destruction. Yet, the one thing I desire the most shies away from me, and she's the most beautiful woman I have ever laid eyes on."

Kola didn't know if he was being sincere or running game on her. She turned to look at him, her eyes showing no hint of emotion.

"I can give you whatever you want, Kola. Just ask for it, and it's yours within the day."

Eduardo suddenly reached out to her and took hold of her wrist, startling her a little. He pulled her closer into his arms like he was Cross himself.

Kola suddenly found herself pressed into the glass of the window, with Eduardo's hand between her thighs. He neared his lips toward hers and invaded her fidelity to Cross. She wanted to resist, but his touch made her melt like butter over a hot stove. She respected his authority and was attracted to his power. She knew that being under his wing, she would be untouchable—a queen to a drug kingpin.

Eduardo cupped her soft breasts and pressed up against her, and they kissed passionately. She felt his bulge pushing into her pelvis. He felt rock-hard and hung.

Eduardo squeezed her ass and continued to keep her glued to the glass. "Damn, you're so soft," he moaned, his hands roaming up and down her body.

Eduardo began unbuttoning her silk shirt, exposing the tight lace bra she had on. He picked Kola up into his arms, and she wrapped her legs around him, and they continued to kiss.

Kola closed her eyes and felt his hands squeezing her ass. She moaned from his touch. Her breathing was heavy with Eduardo pressed against her and his hand now caressing her breast, while his lips kissed her neck.

While Eduardo began fidgeting with his belt buckle, Kola tried to make sense of it all. *How did I get here?* she asked herself.

Eduardo dropped his pants around his ankles and tugged at the buttons around Kola's pants. She was tempted to let him continue, but she suddenly had a change of heart.

"Eduardo, stop," she murmured in his ear, but he continued. She felt his hand sliding down into her jeans, his fingers touching her clit.

Kola knew if she fucked him, she wouldn't be able to look her man in his eyes anymore. "Eduardo, get the fuck off me!"

Eduardo removed his hand from her pants and took a step back. "Is there a problem?"

"I can't."

"You can't, or you won't?"

"Both."

"I see. It's about him, huh?"

Kola remained silent. She knew he had many women and didn't want to be just another one on his roster. She began fixing her clothing. She quickly buttoned her shirt and then fastened her pants. Eduardo had a blank stare while watching her collect herself.

"I can't do this wit' you," she said.

Eduardo pulled up his pants, walked over to the table, picked up his glass, and took a few sips. He then said, "No woman has ever turned me down."

"Well, I'm gonna have to be the first."

"You're a bold woman, Kola, very bold."

"I love him too much."

"Loyalty, I respect that." He nodded.

Kola looked at Eduardo, her heart racing, knowing what he was capable of, but she continued to stare at him bravely. If he wanted to take it from her, she was ready to put up a fight.

"Can I get what I paid for?"

Eduardo chuckled. "Indeed." He motioned for her to exit first. Then he walked behind her, licking his lips, his eyes glued to her ass.

When they were back in the great room with Kola's duffel bag of cash still resting in the center of the room, Eduardo called out for one of his men. One of his goons rushed to his call.

"Bring me what she paid for," he told his suited thug, and the man nodded and hurried off.

Kola reached for her coat, wanting to hurry her exit. Eduardo's deadpan stare was beginning to make her feel uncomfortable.

"I apologize if I offended you in any way, but you are a beautiful woman, Kola, and Cross is a very lucky man."

"I just want it to only be business between us," she replied.

"Business is always good."

The suited thug entered the room again clutching a dark brown duffel bag. He dropped it near Kola's feet and took a step back. She crouched near the bag, quickly unzipped it, inspected the ki's, and closed it back up. Satisfied, she slung the strap over her shoulder and made her exit.

Kola rushed out of the lobby and hurried toward her car. When she had entered the building, it was daylight. Now it was four hours later. Even though nothing had happened, she almost felt like she had cheated on Cross. She tossed the duffel bag into the trunk, and sped out of her parking spot, headed toward the George Washington Bridge.

Across the street, a dark set of eyes observed Kola leaving the towering building. "This bitch is just now leaving," the observer said to himself. He started his car and began to follow Kola toward the bridge and into Harlem.

Chapter 17

Chico yawned. It was 6:45 on a Thursday morning, and he had been driving south all night, headed for Greenville, South Carolina. He had fifteen kilos in the trunk of his car, two semi-automatic pistols hidden in the backseat, and five thousand in cash on him. He did the speed limit, since a search of his BMW could get him a sentence of twenty-five years to life.

He saw the bright green sign: Greenville 165 miles. Reclined in his seat, he took a few pulls from a blunt as he listened to the sounds of Rick Ross. He stared at the long stretch of highway ahead of him and yawned again.

Chico hated to leave New York in a hurry, but he felt he didn't have a choice. The noose was slowly tightening around his neck, and it was getting harder for him to breathe. Harlem and Washington Heights felt like hell on earth for him, and with Dante dead, he was beginning to look weak in the streets.

The night Dante was killed, Chico had rushed home and burst into the door in a panic and a cold sweat. He couldn't believe his cousin was dead. He had tears in his eyes and was seething with rage. It wasn't until he was home that he realized that Moe had set him up. He cursed himself for being so stupid.

The house was dark when Chico had rushed in and called out for Apple. He turned on the lights in the living room and saw Apple standing at the top of the stairway, clad in a long burgundy robe and wearing her mask.

"Chico, you OK?"

Chico stood at the foot of the stairway and looked up at her. "Dante's dead."

"What happened?" she asked nonchalantly.

"We got set up."

Though Apple didn't really care for Dante, she still understood that he was a viable and important asset to their business. Apple could tell Chico had been crying. His eyes were red and puffy, and his face was stained with anguish. He looked distraught. She had never seen him like this.

"You're bleeding."

"It ain't my fuckin' blood," he snapped.

Apple wanted to console her man, but she remained distant, struggling with her own pain.

"Listen, I'm gonna have to take a trip."

"To where?"

Chico moved past her and went into the bedroom. He opened his closet door and began removing his clothes, tossing them onto the bed.

Apple walked into the bedroom behind him. She watched Chico as he began packing his suitcase. "To where, Chico?" she repeated.

"I gotta move these fuckin' ki's, baby. I gotta head down South."

Apple was confused. She hadn't left her home since she'd arrived from the hospital. She had taken comfort in her bedroom and was embarrassed to go anywhere. But with Chico out of town, she would have to continue with her business affairs face to face. "Why, Chico?"

Chico spun around to face her. "'Cause we're broke! The money ain't there, baby. Now, I got fifteen ki's to move, and thanks to ya sister, she fuckin' up our business. So I gotta take this trip down South and get my money right."

Chico didn't mean to be so harsh with her, but he was out of options. He had the product, but no one wanted to deal with him. They were either too scared or just fed up with his weak product.

Apple could only stand there and watch.

Chico stopped moving around for a moment. He noticed the look his woman had on her face. Approaching her with a calmer demeanor, he took a hold of her wrist, held her concerned stare, and said, "Baby, I promise you, I'll be back up here in no time. And when I come back, I'm gonna make it right. I swear to you, baby, it's gonna be like it was before. I'm going to kill your sister and that faggot nigga, Cross."

Apple still didn't want to see him go. She tried not to get emotional. She had done enough crying. She stared at

Chico and had nothing else to say to him. She watched him throw his clothes into a suitcase and then scamper around their home collecting guns and the little cash they had left. He rushed outside to throw everything into his second BMW.

Apple stood in the foyer, her heart aching.

Chico walked up to her and removed the mask. Standing close to her, he said, "I promise I'll be back, Apple, and we gonna get you the best plastic surgeon that money can buy. You'll soon be back to new."

Chico tried to smile, but it wasn't a joyous moment for either of them. The tears started to fall from Apple's eyes. Chico looked into his woman's face. It was hard to leave her alone, but Apple needed to take care of herself for a moment. She was a big girl. Smart.

He neared his face toward hers, and they kissed for a lengthy moment. The scars didn't bother him. She was always going to be his ride-or-die bitch, no matter what she looked like.

He pulled himself away from his woman and moved backwards out of the foyer, his eyes still on Apple. It angered him that he was put in a position to leave his home and his woman, but he had fucked up.

"I'ma be back, baby. I promise."

Chico got into his BMW, started the ignition, and sped down the hilltop driveway.

Before Chico jumped onto I-95 South, he made a quick detour. It was really important. He drove down Amsterdam Avenue toward Moe's tire shop. He couldn't leave Harlem without avenging his cousin's death first.

He parked across the street from Moe's shop and watched everything going on from a short distance. There was no sign of Moe, but Chico was willing to wait. The workers were lingering around in the cold, laughing and joking with each other. It was nine in the evening, and Moe would be closing soon.

Chico lit up a cigarette, reclined in his seat, and listened to Drake. He was watching everything. "C'mon, muthafucka, show ya dumb, fat ass," he said to himself. He took a pull from the cigarette and turned down the volume to the radio to concentrate more on the shop. He didn't want to miss out on Moe leaving.

He perked up when he noticed Moe emerging from the shop twenty minutes later.

"Bingo! I'ma kill this muthafucka." He reached under his seat and removed his pistol. He cocked it back, getting it ready for action, and put it in the passenger seat.

Chico's eyes followed Moe's every movement. Moe walked toward a tricked-out burgundy Acura Legend with spinning chrome rims and dark tint. It was definitely Moe's new ride. He got into the ride alone and pulled off, and Chico followed him.

As Moe drove north, Chico was two cars behind him, looking for the right opportunity to make his move. Moe turned off Amsterdam Avenue onto 155th Street, a four-lane street. When he stopped at a red light on the corner of 155th Street and St. Nicholas Avenue, Chico decided to make his move. There were no other cars around Moe, which gave Chico the opening to strike.

Chico sped up to the driver's side of Moe's ride. His window was already rolled down, and he had the pistol gripped in his hand. Moe was reclined in his seat and smoking a cigarette, nodding to a Jim Jones' track, "We Fly High," and his window was halfway down, allowing the cigarette smoke to air out from his car.

Chico shouted, "Yo, Moe!"

When Moe turned and saw the 9 mm pointed at him, his eyes widened.

Pop! Pop! Pop! Pop! Pop! Pop!

The driver's side glass shattered, and several slugs tore into Moe's frame and into his head like stones ripping through paper. The car started rolling forward with Moe slumped behind the wheel. The Acura jumped the curb of the sidewalk and ran into a light-pole.

Chico stopped his car and jumped out. He wanted to make sure Moe was dead. People were screaming and running, but Chico didn't care who was around. He rushed over to the car with the pistol still in his hand and fired into Moe again.

Pop! Pop! Pop! Pop! Click! Click! Click!

Chico had emptied the clip into Moe. It was certified street justice. He then ran back to his car, jumped behind the wheel, made a screeching U-turn, and sped away, headed for the George Washington Bridge.

Chico pulled into a gas station in Gastonia, North Carolina, right off Interstate 85. South Carolina was only a few miles away now. Hungry and tired, he stepped out of his car, stretching and yawning. He looked around the gas station and sighed heavily, the sun beaming in his face.

He walked into the gas station, dropped a fifty-dollar bill on the counter, and said to the clerk, "Fill me up at pump number seven."

The pimple-faced clerk nodded. He was familiar with Chico's kind—an out-of-towner from the North. His accent already gave him away.

Chico walked back to his car and began to fill his tank with gas. He leaned against the 760 BMW and sighed. "Fuckin' South."

Chico loved the concrete jungle. The South was too slow for him and had nothing but rednecks waving their confederate flags, and country bumpkins longing for the hustle and bustle of New York City. And the trees and grass made his skin itch. He thought it was for the animals and the birds. And all he could hear was the early-morning chirping of the birds.

The last thing Chico remembered about the South was he and Chop barely escaping a half dozen DEA agents who'd kicked down their door during a drug raid in Greenville. It had been years since he'd seen his friend.

They had fled out the back door and ran into the woods before the raid swept through the house. As they hid in the dense woods for hours, the mosquitoes bit Chico, and he was itching from the plants he'd encountered. Eventually he came out of the woods covered in grime and his clothes torn and ruined. That day, he cursed everything about his time with Chop in the South.

Chop was a good friend and a good hustler. The two had met when Chico used to stay the summers in Spartanburg with his grandmother. They became friends when they were fifteen, and as the years went by, they kept in contact with each other.

Chico had gotten into a drug beef in New York, and his rivals shot up his mother's apartment, so his mother sent him packing to live with his grandmother in the South. At the time he was seventeen. His grandmother was strict and tried to rein in her grandson, but Chico was an outlaw and wanted to do whatever he wanted. He ran away from her home and was able to stay with Chop, and the two became inseparable like Batman and Robin, and were into everything, from fights to women and drugs.

Chico had spent barely a year in South Carolina, because it was only a few weeks after his eighteenth birthday when the DEA agents kicked in the doors to one of the stash houses he worked in. He soon learned he had a warrant out for his arrest. That sent him running back to New York, and he never looked back since then. The only thing he respected in the South was Chop.

After fueling his car, Chico picked up a few things to munch on, got back into his BMW, and sped off. His New York plates were a clear indication that he wasn't from around there. He wanted to be in the South as little as possible. His mission was to get with Chop, move the fifteen ki's he had in his trunk through his friend, collect his money, and be back on I-95 North toward New York.

The sun was shining brightly when he drove into Greenville, South Carolina, a few miles away from the highway. He pulled up to a ranch-style home with a sprawling green lawn and a rusty GMC pickup truck parked in the gravel driveway. He stepped out of his BMW and sniffed the South Carolina dew. He looked around the quiet street, the homes spaced a respectable distance from each other, giving neighbors some reasonable privacy, and ample yard space in the front and back. And there was no fencing around any of the homes, just plenty of land, trees, and grass on the long street.

With his pistol tucked in his waistband, Chico stared at the single-floor house, shaded with trees, and the porch wrapped around it to a side door. It was the address Chop had given to him when they'd spoken on the phone briefly.

It had been a few years since Chico had seen Chop. When they had spoken over the phone, Chop was excited to hear from him, but Chico wasn't in the business of keeping up with friends. He was going there for business only, not for a reunion.

He walked up to the door and rang the bell. He remained cautious, remembering the warrants they had on him when he was eighteen. He couldn't afford to get arrested. He had to make this money and get back to Apple. He heard movement from the inside as he stood on the porch.

"Who that?"

"Chop, it's me, Chico. Open up."

The door suddenly opened up, and Chop stood there with a smile. "My nigga, Chico!" he hollered. He pulled Chico into a friendly hug.

Chico didn't smile, though.

"Come inside, my nigga," Chop offered.

Chico stepped into his home. He quickly looked around and immediately noticed the drug paraphernalia on the coffee table, open liquor bottles, and fast food wrappings spread out everywhere. The only furniture in the living room was a tattered couch, and the paint on the walls was chipping. The place reeked of weed smoke and other odors. Chico shook his head.

"What's happening, Chico? Long time."

Chop was all smiles. Tall and lanky with a high-yellow complexion, low haircut, and no facial hair on him at all, he still looked like a young teenager. He was the same as Chico remembered him—a bit cheery and always sloppy. The only thing different about him was that he had cut off his bushy top.

"Yeah, long time," Chico replied dryly.

"I know my shit is a mess right now. Meant to clean

up an' shit, but you know how it is. Nigga get fittin' to do one thang and sumthin' else comes up," Chop said in his thick country accent.

Chop was dressed in a pair of faded blue jeans and a white tank top that showed off his thin frame and several tattoos. He wore a pair of black sandals with tube socks pulled up to his shins. He looked like he hadn't washed in days. Chico instantly knew he wasn't the same Chop he had known years ago. He was clearly using.

"You look good, Chico," Chop said.

"What the fuck happened to you, Chop?"

"What ya talkin' 'bout, Chico? This is me, man."

"Ya usin', nigga," Chico spat.

"I dabble here and there, but I still get my hustle on. I'm still that nigga, Chico. Don't get it twisted, man. I'm here fo' you. I was just fittin' to go to the store. You want breakfast?"

Chico didn't want anything Chop had to offer. He walked farther into the room and continued to look around. He knew he wasn't going to stay. The place was too much of a pigpen. He wasn't comfortable. He knew you couldn't trust a user, even if he was a friend. They would do anything to fuel their addiction and continue with their habit—even betray a friend. He had too much product in his car and too much cash on him. And the look that Chop carried in his eyes said it would not be long until he betrayed him.

"I ain't stayin' long."

"You just got here, man. Why you wanna leave? Ya

my friend, and my home is ya home. I can move that work for you. C'mon, Chico, you can trust me. How many ki's you got in the car?"

"Nah, I ain't come down wit' anything."

"But you told me over the phone that you needed some weight moved."

"Not right now."

"You don't trust me, Chico?" Chop asked, looking offended. "I know it's been a while, but I'm still me, nigga."

"Yeah, it's been a while." Chico's eyes scanned the hallway, searching for anything around him that looked suspicious, his gun concealed and tucked snugly in his waistband.

"I can have some bitches come over. I got drinks and weed. We need to celebrate. My nigga is back in the South."

"Nah, I ain't in the mood to celebrate."

"Chico, ya among family now. Relax, man."

Chico didn't respond. He continued to focus his attention down the hallway. He felt something wasn't right.

"Chico, let me show you around," Chop said.

"Nah, I'm good."

"C'mon, man, it wouldn't be right if I didn't get to show you my place. Ya know, that good ol' Southern hospitality that we known fo'. Let me show you the room you gon' stay in."

"I said I ain't staying," said Chico more sternly.

Chop looked at Chico. The smile dropped, and the cheery attitude dissipated. "Ya hurtin' my feelings, Chico.

I've known you since we were fifteen."

"And I ain't seen you in almost ten years," Chico countered. "Anything could change."

"Well, I ain't change."

Chico was about to speak, but heard a sudden noise that seemed to come from the hallway. He looked at Chop and asked, "We alone?"

"Yeah, Chico, ain't nobody hur' but me and you."

All of a sudden, Chico felt like he had walked into a setup. He knew he fucked up by telling Chop about the large amount of weight he was coming down there with, sounding desperate. And then he was alone. The only good thing on his side was the 9 mm he had on him.

He continued to look at Chop square in the eyes. Chop's eyes already showed what Chico was feeling— mistrust and a setup. "I'ma catch you on the rebound, Chop."

"Yo, nigga, don't go. We suppose to get that money."

"Some other time."

Rapidly, the door to one of the bedrooms in the hallway flung open, and two men came rushing out, screaming, "Yo, fuck this nigga!"

Chico saw the guns.

Chop rushed for Chico to try and grab him, but Chico hit him in his jaw with a hard right, dropping him to the floor. He then reached for his pistol and quickly pulled it out.

The men shot at Chico, and the bullets whizzed by him and ripped into the couch. He jumped back for cover and scurried behind the couch. He had gotten a good look at his two assailants, and he knew they were young.

Chico jumped up and returned the gunfire. The men swiftly moved for cover. One moved against a weather-beaten wall unit, and the other moved into the kitchen. He looked over and noticed Chop hugging the floor tightly, trying not to get shot. Chico couldn't believe the shit he was in.

"What the fuck y'all want?" he shouted.

"Just give it up, nigga!" one shouted back.

"I ain't got shit to give up."

"Fuck that!"

The shooting continued, and Chico felt like a sitting duck. He had half a clip in his 9 mm and needed to maneuver out of the tight situation he was in. It was a moment that he wished Dante was still alive and with him. But, he was alone, and he refused to die in some backwoods house in South Carolina. Chico didn't want to go out like that.

"You set me up, Chop?" Chico shouted.

"You left for New York and forgot about me. I ain't got shit right now. Shit happens!"

Chico wanted to blow his head off, but he needed to save his ammunition for his attackers. Time was ticking. It wouldn't be long before a neighbor called 911 and the cops came rushing to the gun battle.

Think, nigga, think. Chico sighed heavily. He checked his clip and said to himself, "Fuck it!" With his arm outstretched, he sprinted from behind the couch and fired rapidly in their direction.

Chico's gun exploded like a cannon. The first shot hit the wall unit, but the second one was on the money, striking its mark in the chest and pushing him back into the wall. He slid down slowly, dying.

"Muthafucka!" his friend shouted, removing himself from his kitchen cover.

Chico quickly took aim, and before the man could shoot, his body jerked with a slug penetrating his skull. He dropped face forward near his friend.

Chico exhaled with some relief. His adrenaline took over and made him shoot with accuracy. He stood in the center of the room and looked down at Chop, who was still cowering on the floor.

"Get ya bitch ass up!" he exclaimed.

Chop looked up at Chico, panic showing in his eyes. "Chico, I'm sorry, man. I didn't mean fo' it ta go down like that."

Chico wasn't trying to hear out his former friend. He also knew he didn't have too much time to spare. He had to leave the area before it was flooded with cops.

"They made me do it. I didn't want to, man. I didn't want to."

Chico aimed the gun down at Chop. It was paining him to even think about it, but he had done worse. He'd barely made it through the gunfire alive, and now he was put in a predicament where it was him or Chop.

"Chico, c'mon, man, I'm sorry. I can make it up to you. Give me a chance, Chico. Please, give me a second—"

Blam! Blam! Blam! He shot Chop three times and left

him sprawled out across the dusty wood floor in a pool of blood.

Chico stuck the gun in his waistband and ran out the house. He hopped into his car, backed out of the driveway hastily, and sped off.

"Fuck! Fuck! Fuck!" he screamed out as he raced toward the nearest highway. He had just murdered the one source that was probably able to unload the fifteen kilos he had in the trunk.

Chico knew he wasn't staying in Greenville. He leaped onto I-85 and headed north. Time was running out for him.

Chapter 18

Apple had the blackout curtains pulled together, causing the room to be dark. She peered at herself in the mirror. The stress was showing on her.

She had been so blinded by her facial features and yearning for revenge, she had forgotten about her other affairs. There was a third notice from the bank about their mortgage. They were three months behind, and Apple was unaware of it. Their home was about to go into foreclosure very soon, and she feared she was about to become homeless. She had little money to pay any of her bills, and her medical bills were starting to pile up. Chico always kept up with the bills, but everything was falling apart while he was out of town trying to make things right again.

Apple wanted to regain what she had lost focus of before Chico came into her life and the incident with the acid. She needed her loan-sharking business up and running again. Several people owed her unpaid debts, and she was determined to venture out and collect her money.

She thought, *Out of sight, out of mind.* She had been out of sight from Harlem for too long—but now, she was ready to get back on her grind. She didn't have a choice. She needed to become independent again. She needed cash.

She looked at the time. It was late. Midnight. She told herself that tomorrow would be a new day for her. Despite the way she looked, Harlem would once again know and respect her.

Twenty-four hours later, when the sun was down and the moon was up, Apple got dressed in all black—dark jeans, a dark hoodie with an angel-winged crystal design on the back, and a pair of black Nikes. She put on her mask, stepped out of her mansion-style home, and walked over to her McLaren parked outside the two-car garage. It had been a while since she had driven it.

She got in the dusty car and started it; the engine purred like a kitten. The soft leather seats felt nice against her skin, and having her hands around the steering wheel made her lust for the attention it stirred up. She remembered the looks she used to receive while driving it around in Harlem—priceless. She closed the vertical door and revved the engine. The needles on the RPM jumped. The McLaren was ready to go into motion with it still in park.

Apple put the car in drive and sped out of the driveway like a bat out of hell. She turned the first corner hard—a sharp right— and felt the power steering and the strong handling of the car. She continued speeding toward the highway. She didn't care about cops or having an accident.

She arrived in Harlem an hour later. The clock on the dashboard read 9:25 p.m. The night was still young. She navigated the McLaren through the Harlem streets, stirring up the people, their eyes lingering on the flashy ride as she passed by, and her tinted windows making it hard for them to see inside.

She slowly drove down 145th Street in the direction of Riverside Drive. There was little bustling going on in the area where she slowed down and parked. She stopped her car in front of a small hole-in-the-wall lounge between two brick brownstones. The entrance to the place was below in the basement, and there was a long, black awning stretching over the front entrance of the slated brownstone that read, "Restaurant & Lounge."

It was Peon's place. Peon was a well-respected businessman operating in Harlem for years. In his early forties, he had dabbled in drugs during the eighties, done some jail time during the mid-nineties, and after the new millennium, turned his life around, opening up his restaurant and lounge five years ago. But he had a gambling problem and had acquired a mountain of debt in the past year. He'd heard about Apple's loan-sharking business and had a sit-down meeting with her. Apple fronted him a ten-thousand-dollar loan with three points added to it, and Peon promised her that he would be able to pay it back within two months. That was six months ago. He was always trying to duck and dodge her.

Apple pulled the stylish black hoodie over her head and tied it tight around her facial disfigurement, the clear medical mask grasping her face, covering her scars. She tried to hide her wounds as best as possible. She looked at herself in the visor mirror and hated herself. It was obvious she was wearing a mask, and the hoodie over her head only protected the view of her partially.

She got out of the car and tried to keep her mind on business, not her appearance. She looked up and down the block. The area was calm and quiet like a sleeping cat. She stared at Peon's place. Business seemed slow to her, but it was still early. She knew the lounges in Harlem didn't start to get really busy until midnight or later. She didn't want to be around a crowd of people and have everyone staring at her like she was a freak or some science experiment, so she arrived early to handle her business with Peon.

She stepped from around her car and walked toward the lounge like a bitch on a mission. She walked down the short concrete steps, opened the door that led into the small foyer, and passed through into the lounge, where Marvin Gaye's "I Want You" was playing. The inside was quaint and appealing with its laid-back, candlelit atmosphere. The red, brown, and beige combination worked well together to give the place a high-end feel. The bar stretched out from the doorway into the back, and the retro furnishings gave it an eclectic blend.

Apple stood by the doorway and looked around, her eyes scanning every inch of the room. The place was almost empty. An aging gentleman sat on a barstool at the bar with a drink in his hand. He glanced at her when she walked in. He then turned his attention back to the mounted flat-screen TV suspended in the far corner of the bar near the back. Then there was another gentleman seated at one of the tables to her right. He was drinking a beer and looked really rough, wearing a dark hoodie, a do-rag, and baggy jeans.

The male bartender stood behind the bar, polishing glasses and staring at Apple. "Can I help you with something?" he asked her.

Apple moved closer to him, keeping her hoodie over her head, and said, "Yeah, I'm looking for Peon."

The rough-looking man seated at the table quickly averted his attention to Apple when she mentioned the name. He kept his eyes on her like a hawk.

"What you want with Peon?" the bartender asked.

"I need to talk to him. Tell him Apple is looking for him."

The bartender continued to shine the glasses. He dryly replied, "Peon ain't here. I don't know where he's at right now."

Apple wasn't buying it. "He needs to see me ASAP."

The bartender shrugged it off.

"Nigga, you hear me talkin' to you?"

"How old are you anyway?" the man inquired. "And what's wrong with your face? Why you wearing that mask?"

"It's none of your fuckin' business!"

The man sitting at the table quickly stood up. Apple turned to look at him. He was a beastly-looking man, standing over six feet tall and stocky.

"What the fuck you gonna do?" she shouted at him.

"You need to leave," the man said coolly.

"Fuck you!"

The man moved from behind the table and approached Apple, his eyes drilled into her with intensity, but Apple stood her ground. She locked eyes with him and swallowed hard. He towered over her by a foot and outweighed her by over a hundred pounds.

"Little girl, you need to leave right now. This ain't a place for you," he said in a stern tone.

Apple hated to be called a little girl. Still, she was too stubborn to back down from him. "I need to see Peon," she insisted.

"He ain't here," the man said.

"Well, I can wait."

"Not here, you won't," he exclaimed.

"You gonna kick me out?"

"I'm gonna fuckin' toss you out."

Apple slipped her hand in the front pocket of her hoodie and gripped the small, sharp, five-inch blade she had concealed. She was ready to extract it and put it to good use. As the man came forward, she grasped the blade tightly and was ready to defend herself by any means necessary.

Before he took another step toward her, someone shouted, "Yo, Devon, chill out."

They both turned to see Peon standing behind them. He was average height, with a long perm and a high-yellow complexion. They used to call him "Light Bright" back in the eighties. He was wearing a snug T-shirt underneath a purple blazer, with a pair of black leather pants and a pair of black Hush Puppies. And he sported spiky hair and piercings on his nose, eyebrows, tongue, and lips. He was unique with his unorthodox style of dressing. Apple always thought he looked like the singer Prince.

She used to hear stories about how Peon was back in the day. He had street smarts, got money, and had lots of women chasing behind him. But his gambling addiction was his curse.

Peon betted on everything—sports, the racetrack, fights, and he'd lost a fortune playing poker. When he was on the verge of losing his business and was one step away from becoming homeless, he asked for Apple's help when she was at her strongest. He swallowed his pride and took help from a woman, a teenager at that.

Apple glared at the bartender. "I thought he wasn't here, you fuckin' jerk!"

"It must have slipped my mind," the bartender countered nonchalantly.

Peon looked at Apple with contempt. "Why are you here, Apple?" he asked evenly.

"To collect what you owe me."

"And what is that?"

"Peon, don't play stupid wit' me. You know how much you owe me. Ten thousand."

Peon chuckled. He looked at his bodyguard Devon. "You must be mistaken. My debts are paid."

"Muthafucka! Don't fuckin' play me, you' faggot!"

"Like I said, I owe you nothing. Now, I would appreciate if you would kindly leave my place. Your face is disturbing my customers."

Apple lunged for Peon, rapidly pulling the blade from her hoodie pocket and raising it over her head, ready to cut him up. But before she could get close and swing it at Peon, his bodyguard charged at her, forcing her against the long bar, and snatching her by the wrist. He overpowered her quickly and twisted the knife from her hand.

Apple, no match for the 270-pound man, gasped from the hit and soon found herself on the floor on her back, with him smirking over her, his foot against her chest.

"You shoulda left kindly, you little fuckin' bitch!" Devon said through clenched teeth.

Apple cut her eyes at him, squirming underneath his boot. "Get the fuck off me!"

Peon walked over. Smiling, he stared down at Apple. She was trapped like a rat in a trap, and he was the big, bad, hungry cat slowly walking over to devour his prize. He shook his head.

"Dumb bitch! What were you trying to do? Fuck my face up like someone did yours? I heard about the incident." He laughed. "Yo, Devon, take off that bitch mask. I wanna see what she looks like."

Devon was happy to oblige. The bartender came from behind the bar to help pin her down. The old man seated on the barstool continued to sip on his drink, oblivious to what was happening around him. It wasn't his business.

Apple continued to squirm and fight but was once again overpowered. The bartender positioned himself behind her. He was on his knees and held her arms outstretched with his weight on them, so she wasn't able to defend herself.

Devon replaced his foot with his knees against Apple's chest. It felt like a truck was sitting on top of her. He was heavy, and she was barely able to breathe. He leaned closer, reaching to pull off her mask.

Apple turned her face to the side, trying to prevent it from being removed. But it was hopeless.

Devon gripped the mask, smiled, and snatched it off aggressively. He cringed at the sight of her. "Oh shit!".

Peon walked over and stared at her like she was some kind of freak. "Wow! They really fucked you up, Apple. Damn! I ain't think it was that bad. Shit, at least you still got the other side looking right. You fuckin' freak!"

Apple screamed and struggled under her attackers' weight. "Aaaahhh! GET OFF ME! GET OFF ME!"

The mere thought of her looks being exposed in public and then being clowned and laughed at was causing Apple to go mad. Her eyes burned red with rage. She glared at Peon. "I'm gonna kill you, muthafucka!" she yelled.

"Bitch, whatever! Yo, toss this ugly piece of shit out of my lounge. We ain't having no freaks up in here. Bitch might scare away my customers!"

Devon lifted Apple from off the floor like she was weightless and hoisted her over his shoulder. Apple continued to struggle while Devon carried her to the door.

He pushed it open and continued to carry her out, while she yelled, punched, and scratched at him.

Devon tossed her to the sidewalk like she was trash. As Apple landed on her side and skinned her forearm, she cried out.

Devon only laughed. He tossed her mask out afterwards, and it landed near her roughly but didn't break.

Apple slowly lifted herself up from off the ground and tried to hold back her tears. She felt crushed. She had never been so disrespected in her life. If this had happened a few months back, Peon wouldn't have dared pulled the stunt he just did. His faggot balls would've been dangling from her rearview mirror.

Devon continued laughing. He then turned and shut the door behind him, leaving Apple standing in the wind, looking pitiful. She donned her clear mask and then stood alone for a moment thinking about Chico. She wanted him to come home soon. She wanted him to finish killing them all. They all deserved it.

While walking back to her car, Apple stopped suddenly. She caught a chilling feeling that made her skin itch and her stomach turn. She looked around her surroundings frantically, but she didn't see anything alarming to her. She couldn't shake the strange feeling that someone was watching her.

Scared, she quickly hopped into her car, started the ignition, and sped away. She passed through Harlem in a hurry and raced her McLaren onto I-87 North, back to her home an hour away upstate.

Chapter 19

Kola straddled Cross, the satin sheets wrinkling underneath them. She felt his hard-on thrusting into her while his hands cupped her soft breasts. Her body lit up with pleasure from his intense strokes. She felt her man bury himself deep inside of her. She leaned forward and pressed against his chest, her pussy throbbing.

They were naked against each other in the dim glow coming from the vanilla-scented candles spread out strategically in the bedroom, where Cross, a gorgeous specimen of a man, was devouring her sex as if he needed it to live. Moaning and squirming on top of him, riding his dick like she was on a horse moving across clear pasture, Kola spiraled into bliss as he penetrated her.

She wanted to forget about that evening with Eduardo. It was a mistake, even though nothing had happened. She wanted to make up for it by fucking the shit out of her man.

She angled her hips and dug her nails into his flesh. She felt a great heat rush through her body as she tried to force his big dick deeper inside of her.

"Oh shit, baby! Ummm! Ummm! You feel so good!" she cried out.

Cross moaned.

She closed her eyes, gyrated her hips into the dick, and tilted her chin upwards toward the ceiling, her hands against Cross' sweaty chest. She felt her orgasm finally riding its course. "I'ma cum, baby! Oh shit! I'm coming!" she cried out.

Cross gripped her silky-like hips and grunted. Her pussy was so wet and tight, it sent his eyes rolling into the back of his head like he was being possessed by it. He firmly gripped Kola's ass and felt his nut brewing. The pussy was so good that out of the blue, Cross proclaimed, "I fuckin' love you, baby!"

"I love you too," Kola returned, her voice faint from the intensity of the pounding she was enduring.

The couple was unaware that Edge was secretly watching from a short distance through the bedroom door that was slightly ajar. His eyes were fixated on Kola's backside as she rode Cross in a heat of passion. He wanted to know that feeling. Jealousy began stirring up inside of him. He wanted what Cross had.

His eyes narrowed in on the way Kola was positioned on top of her man—the way she straddled him against the mattress—and he slowly touched himself, her fervent moans echoing in his mind.

Edge and Cross had come in late that evening, and Cross gave him permission to crash on their couch. Edge was too tipsy to drive back to his home, so he'd plopped down on the soft couch and closed his eyes. He was supposed to be sleeping on the couch. But he took it upon himself to slowly ease up the stairs and catch an eyeful of his friend fucking.

Kola felt her legs quiver as she came. She pressed her thighs against Cross' sides and felt a surge of relief spread throughout her as between her legs became creamy and her body started to feel spent. She panted, feeling like she was in seventh heaven.

She suddenly turned around with that eerie feeling of someone watching them. She stared at the doorway for a moment, but there wasn't anybody there. She covered up.

"What's wrong, baby?" Cross asked.

"I just got this creepy feeling that we're being watched."

"We good, baby. Edge is probably passed out on the couch."

"He's here?" She was waiting for her man in the bedroom upstairs and was unaware that they had company.

"The nigga was tired. I told him he could crash here for the night."

With the sheets covering her tits, Kola removed herself from off of Cross and quickly closed the bedroom door. She regretted they had left it slightly open, but she'd assumed they were alone in their home.

She looked over at Cross and asked, "Why you have him staying the night? Oh my God, Cross! I could've walked out of here naked and ran into him, thinking we were alone. Don't be doin' that."

"The nigga's 'sleep, baby. He ain't tryin' to watch us. The nigga got his own bitch at home."

Kola sucked her teeth and rejoined her man in the bed. She nestled against him, loving the way he caressed her in his strong arms.

"Besides, that nigga knows better," Cross added.

With the candles still burning and Kola feeling content, she looked into her man's eyes as the dim light shimmered on them like a Caribbean sunset. She positioned herself on top of him and pressed her tits against his chest. She kissed his neck soothingly and felt him squeeze her ass like it was soft fruit in his hands. She smiled.

As Kola lay in Cross' arms, he was drifting off to sleep, but she remained awake and naked in her man's arms. Her mind turned unexpectedly to Eduardo. The room was still. The scented candles continued to glow and dim the room. Her pussy was tingling. She sighed heavily.

Kola tried not to think about Eduardo, but she was worried about the next time she had to re-up. She began to wonder what would happen. Would he try to pull another stunt like before? Would his attempts to try and get into her panties become even stronger? Would he exert his authority upon her, giving her an alternative—some pussy in exchange for the ki's?

Kola didn't want any problems with the two most important men in her life. Business was too good. They were making money hand over fist with Eduardo's potent product, and she didn't want to chance losing such a good connect. She had her sister's man's empire crumbling, and word on the streets was that Chico had been missing in action for over a week now.

What if Eduardo continued to push up on her and she didn't fuck him? Then their business together would dissolve. It was something she tried not to dwell on. She wondered, would she fuck Eduardo just to keep a good thing going? It would probably be her dirty little secret. Eduardo was fine, and she was definitely attracted to him on so many levels. She admitted to herself that it probably would be worth the fuck. It would be some good dick and she would keep a good thing going—solidifying their business connection. But what would be the risk if she were to take things to the next level with him?

Kola looked over at Cross and thought about their future, if there would be any. His gun trial was looming. Edge refused to take the charge for her man, and that infuriated her. Their lawyer had been very successful in postponing the case for as long as he could, but they knew an indictment and trial would be approaching soon. The DA was trying to burn them, and the prosecution was putting together their discovery for the case to incriminate both men on full charges.

Kola didn't want to lose her man. She loved him too much. However, with the way things were going, there was a possibility he might do some jail time. She was willing to hold down the fort, though, if he had to go away for a few years. New York was serious with their gun laws, and one of the strictest states in the nation with regards to the purchase, possession, and carrying of handguns. And even though the gun was clean, with no bodies, and Cross had no criminal record prior to his arrest, they were still trying to prosecute him to the fullest extent of the law. It was going to be a tough battle to fight in court.

Kola couldn't help but to think about her options and her future. She was a smart woman—a sharp businesswoman—but if Cross did get some time, then where would she be? She had some muscle of her own, but Cross' name on the streets was what held her down and got her the reputation she had. Without him around, the wolves would definitely come around hunting for her.

And if she lost Eduardo as her connect, then she would be back where she started and probably fighting for her life. She had made some very dangerous enemies over the years.

Her sex parties were profitable, but they weren't bringing in the type of income she was getting from the drug business. She had grown accustomed to her way of living, and she planned on having it stay that way. She had to play her cards right. She was playing chess, not checkers.

Kola woke up early the next morning. Cross was still out cold lying next to her. She gently removed herself out of the bed, trying not to wake up her boo from his sleep. She donned her long robe and went into the bathroom to pee. She then walked down the stairs and into the shadowy living room, heading toward the kitchen. The clock on the microwave said 8:25. She wanted to make breakfast for herself and her man.

She opened the fridge and removed a carton of eggs and a gallon of milk. She wanted to make some pancakes, scrambled eggs, and sausage.

Kola learned how to burn in the kitchen by watching her little sister cook. Nichols was the best in the kitchen—a certified chef in Kola's eyes.

When Kola wasn't in the streets doing her dirt, she made time to spend with her little sister. Nichols cooked for the whole family and never complained about it. Breakfast, lunch, or dinner, she made it, and everybody loved it. Kola missed Nichols and her cooking a whole lot.

Kola stood by the marble countertop with the milk in her hand, her mind drifting off to the time when her little sister was murdered. So much had changed for her. It had almost been a year since her death. It was painful to think about. She had moved on, but that tragic memory of the way her sister was murdered would always linger inside of her.

She had heard word on the streets that one of her sister's murderers was found shot to death in the Bronx, but she didn't have any real confirmation about her sister's killers. But she did know one thing for sure. She held Apple as the one responsible, and she would never forgive her twin for it.

Kola went over to the stove and turned it on. She

began messing around in the kitchen, looking like a natural housewife, but cooking was something she rarely did. She had been so busy with her parties and the business that fast food and dining out became an everyday thing for them.

She went to put the milk back in the fridge, and when she closed the refrigerator door, she was suddenly startled by Edge's presence in the kitchen.

Kola jumped back and yelped, "Nigga, what the fuck! Why you sneakin' up on a bitch?"

"I heard someone in here and came to take a look," he said.

"What the fuck you want?"

"Just came to take a look and make sure that everything was cool in here."

"I'm making breakfast for my man."

"Can I get some too?" he asked with a smile.

Kola stared at him for a moment. She made sure her robe was tightened and that he was a reasonable distance away from her. "Ain't your bitch waiting for you at your crib?"

"Nah, I'm good. Ain't no bitch in my life right now."

"I wonder why."

"You need help wit' anything, Kola?" Edge started to think about how he caught her riding Cross' dick last night. He smiled to himself. He wondered if her pussy was percolating through her robe.

"No, I'm fine."

"Yeah, I can see that."

Kola cut her eyes over at him, and Edge held her wicked stare with a teasing smile of his own as he stood there shirtless, his jeans sagging off his ass.

Edge wasn't cut like Cross, but had the typical out-of-shape body—a growing stomach, too many tattoos, and no definition to him at all. He continued to look at Kola in an undignified type of way. His eyes followed her every move around the kitchen, and he wanted to push up on her.

Kola already knew what was going through his head. It wasn't anything new that she had to deal with over the years—niggas trying to flirt or fuck her behind her man's back. She grew tired of it, but she didn't expect the same bullshit to come from Edge, who she'd known for a long time. But, in her mind, niggas were going to always be thirsty for new pussy.

Edge was the last person she wanted to see so early in the morning. Still, he was part of their crew and was always around—during the good times and bad.

Kola wanted him to take the fall for the gun. She felt he was being ignorant and selfish about the incident. If he was a true friend, he would be willing to eat the charge for Cross and do the time for his friend. She always felt that Edge had other motives. Things were changing, and she felt he was changing too. She'd had a few words with him before, especially about the gun charge, and she could feel some tension bubbling between the two of them. Kola abruptly stopped what she was doing in the kitchen.

She slammed the pot against the stove. "Nigga, do

you have a fuckin' problem wit' me?" She turned to stare at Edge as he was posted up against the counter, his eyes glued to her.

"Nah. No problem."

"Then stop fuckin' staring like that. It's fuckin' disrespectful."

"It is, right? I ain't mean no disrespect. I was just looking."

"Whatever, nigga."

"I'm sayin', Kola, you know . . . real talk, I ain't mean no harm by looking. You just got a really nice body. My dude Cross is a lucky nigga."

"He is, and I remind him how lucky he is every fuckin' night when his dick is inside of me and he's enjoying my shit." Kola smirked.

"Yeah, I feel that. And I definitely ain't trying to disrespect you. Shit, you like family, ma."

Kola turned from him and began focusing her attention on the stove. She began making an omelet and some bacon.

"I'm sayin', though, was there any disrespect to my dude when you left Eduardo's place three fuckin' hours after you arrived? I mean, it takes that long to get business done?" Edge said matter-of-factly.

"What the fuck you talkin' about?" Kola spun around.

"I think you know what I'm talkin' about. You fuckin' that nigga?"

"You stupid, Edge. It's only business wit' Eduardo. And how fuckin' dare you! You had me followed or somethin'?"

"I just got eyes everywhere, Kola. You feel me? But, I'm sayin', I ain't gonna tell Cross that shit. It could be our little secret."

Edge moved a little closer toward Kola. "I'm sayin', it seems like everybody is gettin' a piece of that ass. Shit, can a nigga get a taste too?"

"You need to fuckin' leave my crib, nigga."

Edge chuckled. "Or what?"

Kola reached for the kitchen knife that was lying on the granite countertop and raised it between her and Cross. When she took a step forward, Edge took a step back. The smile was gone from his face, and he just stared at Kola and the knife.

"You crazy, Kola."

"Try me, nigga. I told you, I ain't fuckin' that nigga. And I damn sure ain't fuckin' you!"

"So it's like that, huh? I'm sayin', you think Cross is gonna believe you? Shit, you already took away his connect. How you think he's gonna feel if words get in his ear that Eduardo might be creepin' wit' his woman too?"

"Edge, I swear to you, I ain't creepin' on Cross. So, if you don't believe it, then I don't give a fuck! But I do know one thing—If you disrespect me in this house again, I'll cut ya fuckin' nuts off," she said through clenched teeth.

Edge's smile returned. "You a crazy bitch, Kola. Cross definitely got his hands full, but we'll talk later."

"How about never?"

"Ain't no disrespect. I'll leave," he said coolly.

Kola kept her eyes on him closely while he began

walking backwards into the next room. She followed him with the knife still in her hand, her eyes narrowed and sharp, her face in a scowl.

Edge collected his things. He put on his shirt and shoes, and then grabbed his jacket from off the back of the couch. He looked over at Kola as he walked toward the door. He grabbed the doorknob then paused for a moment. He turned to look at her and said, "When Cross wakes up, tell my nigga I'll holla at him. In the meantime, we'll talk too."

Kola sighed and lowered the knife to her side. She couldn't believe Edge had the audacity to have her followed, then watched and waited for her to leave. It was only speculation, but speculation in her line of work could get someone killed or incarcerated. It was a careless move on her part, though. Edge was becoming a problem. Kola knew Edge was right about one thing—it wasn't a good look for her even though she was innocent.

Kola walked back into the kitchen. Before she could finish making breakfast, she heard Cross ask, "Where's Edge?"

"He had to go, baby," she replied.

Cross was in a pair of jeans and a tank top. He still had tiredness written all over his face. He didn't bother to hug or kiss Kola at all. He asked, "What you making?"

"I'm making us an omelet. I know you must be hungry, baby."

"Nah, fuck that shit. I gotta run out. I wish you would have woken me up to tell me that nigga was leaving. I woulda left wit' him. It's a fucked-up morning already," he said with a slight attitude.

Kola sucked her teeth and rolled her eyes at him. She was almost done with his breakfast. It really bothered her that he didn't want any of it.

Cross walked out of the kitchen and headed back upstairs. In next to no time, he was dressed and out the door.

Kola stood there looking like she had egg on her face. She took the breakfast she'd made for Cross and tossed everything into the garbage. "Fuck that shit!"

She was a get-money bitch, not a housewife. She was just being nice to her man and wanted to treat him to something special.

Kola quickly got dressed and made her exit right after Cross. She needed to make moves herself.

Chapter 20

Chico took a quick swig from the beer he had in his hand and looked over to his right at Tatiana. She smiled at him, but he didn't smile back.

Tatiana had an oval face with long braids. She was a bit overweight, dark-skinned, and had tits on her like a mountain. She wasn't ugly, but she wasn't a beauty queen. She had connections in Charlotte that he needed to get with; she knew people that mattered. Tatiana had a trustworthy smile, but Chico didn't trust anyone. Especially after the severe fallout he had with Chop, who was someone he once considered a friend.

Originally from Richmond, twenty-four-year-old Tatiana had come to Charlotte with her brothers a few years earlier to help them hustle. Her brothers were once notorious men in Richmond, but a murder charge, warrants, and violent drug rivalries sent her family packing and traveling three hundred miles south. They'd set up roots in the city and soon became known figures in Charlotte, despite not being from the town.

Chico had met Tatiana a week ago at a lounge on Independence Boulevard. Chico was alone. He didn't know anyone in the city, but he had street smarts and knew what to look out for. He had his pistol on him, but he knew he needed to be careful about who he talked to and how he moved. After all, he had fifteen kilos of cocaine in the trunk of his car. Even though he was a notorious figure in Harlem and Washington Heights, New York, nobody knew him in Charlotte. So he was a man without a country for the moment. He wasn't Superman. The stickup kids were heavy in the South, and they wouldn't hesitate to jack him for his supply and shoot him dead, if needed.

He noticed Tatiana seated in a booth. She was surrounded by some men that appeared to be some heavy hitters in the city. She was quiet around them, sipping from her beer and smoking, while her brothers talked shit and laughed loudly. Chico took subtle glances at the crew seated opposite him while he lingered at the bar.

They were perfect. He figured they had the money and the clout to buy the ki's from him. Chico knew from experience that a new face wasn't acceptable so easily or at all even. They would think he was an informer or a cop, or maybe he was trying to set them up. Or worse, they would see him as an easy mark.

He didn't have any muscle to back him. That meant they could effortlessly snatch away everything he had and

not pay him a single dime. He had seen it done before—
men come into the game to hustle, but they end up getting
robbed, gutted like a pig, and left to bleed out and die in
the streets because they didn't have serious muscle around
them.

He refused to become a victim, so he had to map out
a plan. A plan that would assure him his safety and his
money all at once.

He continued to look at Tatiana. He knew she would
be the key to getting connected with the men. She had
that lonely look about her. Her brothers protected her, so
nobody dared fuck with her, but she also had that look as
though she was desperate to find love.

Chico had made his move on her when she left
the booth and walked over to the bar where he sat. She
had nudged in between the two tall bar stools where he
and another patron were seated. She called over for the
bartender and asked for another beer. Chico knew she just
wanted to get away from the men she was sitting with,
because they had a waitress serving them drinks the entire
time. One snap from their fingers, and the petite, short,
olive-skinned lady in the stained black apron and curly,
bushy ponytail would quickly come over with her round
serving platter in her hand, ready to take down any orders.

Tatiana was dressed in a pair of blue jeans, a black
T-shirt, and some white Nikes. Chico quickly noticed the
diamond bracelet with the matching diamond earrings.
She was fresh, nothing old, but everything looked new on
her, no matter how plain it appeared. Chico had an eye for

fashion, and even though her jeans looked like they came from Macy's, he already saw that they were pricey by the way they highlighted her wide, thick hips.

Chico had caught Tatiana's eye, but she didn't say anything at first. She already knew he was a new face in town. Mostly regulars came to The Jackpot Lounge on the strip.

"Nice bracelet. Tiffany's, right?" Chico asked.

Tatiana turned to him. "How you know?"

"I bought my *ex*-girlfriend almost the same one a few years ago. You got taste," he said. He emphasized *ex* to Tatiana, not wanting to give off the impression that he was already taken.

She smiled. "Thanks."

"So what's ya name?"

"Tatiana."

"Nice name."

She continued to smile. "What's your name?"

"Chico."

The two greeted each other with a handshake, and Tatiana was thrilled to meet him. She figured he was from up North, with his accent and his style of dress.

Chico knew not to rush things with the woman. He had to play it out smoothly and take his time with her, make it believable. They spoke briefly and exchanged numbers.

Tatiana walked back over to sit with her brothers, but as she sat with them, her eyes would periodically look over at Chico. She really wanted to get to know him. He was new. He was different.

Having accomplished the first part of his plan, Chico downed his drink and left. He just needed to execute the rest of it really carefully. He got into his car and drove to the motel he was staying in, a Super 8 Motel that wasn't located too far from the lounge.

Two hours later, Tatiana gave him a call. She made it known that she wanted to see him that same night, if it was possible. After Chico told her what hotel he was staying in and the room number, she said to him that she would be there in twenty minutes.

Chico had been extra cautious while staying at the motel. He had rented two rooms for the week. In one room, he kept all of his private possessions and cash. It was also where he slept. The second room, which was on the same floor, was just a trap room he only used if he had company coming over or if he had business to take care of. He knew not to shit where he ate. The rooms were down the hall from each other.

Before Tatiana arrived, Chico placed a phone call back home. He needed to talk to Apple. He had called from the first room he rented. Her phone rang several times before she picked up.

"Apple."

There was silence over the phone. Chico knew Apple had picked up, but she wasn't saying anything.

"Apple, talk to me."

He thought he heard some crying over the phone and started to worry. The pit of his stomach was in knots. It felt like the Nikki situation all over again, with him not being there to protect Apple. His pride was hurt.

Apple finally spoke. "Where are you, Chico?"

"Charlotte, North Carolina, right now."

"They tryin' to take our house away from us, Chico," Apple cried out.

"I'ma take care of everything, baby. You know that."

"When? I'm alone up here. You need to come home."

"I will, baby. I just need to move this work down here, and then I'm back on the highway as soon as possible."

"I'ma be homeless, Chico. They tryin' to take everything away from me. Our house has gone into foreclosure, and muthafuckas is threatening to bring the marshals to evict me from my fuckin' home, Chico. They fuckin' with us. I'm about to have nothin' up here. Even you."

"Baby, I'ma take care of this shit. I promise."

"Whatever!" Apple hung up.

Chico was almost in tears. He had the urge to just get back on the highway and drive straight back to New York, but he needed to get his money right. His cash was dwindling. He needed to either strike a deal with some serious consumers or cook the crack in his room, bag it up, and sell it on the streets himself. Every day he drove around dirty, it was a risk to his freedom, and possibly his life, if the stickup kids caught wind of what he was driving around with.

Tatiana came knocking on Chico's motel room door after midnight. Chico was lying in bed. The television was off, and the room was silent. He was thinking about Apple and their situation, when the knocking had suddenly disturbed him. He got out of bed and looked to see who it was. He had forgotten about Tatiana.

He looked around the trap room and made sure it fit the part he wanted her to see—an out-of-town hustler, which he was. He had a few clothes and jewelry laid out on the bed and dresser, along with an ounce of weed. He wanted the place to look lived-in.

Chico answered the door, and Tatiana was standing there smiling at him.

"Did I wake you?" she asked.

"Nah, I was just chilling. Come in."

Tatiana stepped into the room.

Chico closed the door behind her and stared at her plump figure. She was far from his type of woman. She was a thick girl from head to toe. He even got the impression that maybe she was whorish.

"So what's up?" she asked with a grin.

"You tell me."

Tatiana looked around his room and noticed the ounce of weed on the dresser. "I see you smoke."

Chico removed the two blunts from his back pocket and flashed a smile.

Tatiana smiled. "My kind of guy already."

He sat on the edge of the bed and began breaking open the blunt down the middle. When Tatiana sat down next to him and placed her hand on his leg, he already saw where things were going.

Soon, the two were getting high and laughing. Then a half-hour later, Chico had his dick down her throat as she sucked him off. She was seated on the edge of the bed, while he stood over her with his hand knotted around her braids. He fucked her that night too.

Chico had two things going for him with Tatiana. One, he was from New York, and two, he had that hustler's mentality. She was feeling his swag and ate it up. She connected with him quickly. In fact, so quickly, she allowed him to move in her three-bedroom condo off of Bellhaven Boulevard near the I-485. Chico knew that her lavish living—the burgundy Benz she drove, her style, and her condo—was all funded through drug money. She moved through Charlotte like she owned it. Her brothers had the city on lock with fear and were making so much money, people were calling her family "The Untouchables."

Chico crashed at her place for a week. He kept the duffel bag with the ki's of dope locked inside the trunk of his car. The alarm was always on, and the BMW was always parked in front of her door where he could look out the window and see what was going on. Chico wanted to unload everything in a hurry, but he understood it would be time consuming. He didn't want to rush anything and fuck it up. He didn't want Tatiana to be too much in his business.

The first stage with her was through sex. They fucked almost every night, and Chico made sure she became infatuated with him. He would dick her down like he was a porn star. Chico had to admit to himself that the pussy was good and Tatiana was a freak. She did anything he wanted her to do—fuck her up the ass, deep-throat, tea-bagging. If he mentioned it, she did it.

Two weeks went by, and Chico became familiar with her routine. He had gotten to know a little more about her family, where she came from, and what they were about. She was close with her brothers. She even told Chico about their illicit business ventures. The money. It was definitely sloppy on her part. While they would be nestled together in bed, Tatiana would do a lot of talking.

She had three brothers, Jonathan, Ryan, and Tito. Ryan was the oldest and the brains of the three. Jonathan was the right hand and the moneymaker, while Tito was the youngest and the shooter/killer. Tatiana was their baby sister. They had grown up without parents. Their mother was serving a life sentence in jail for killing two cops, and their father was dead, killed in a police raid.

Through her brothers, Tatiana owned a beauty salon and a local diner right off Wilkinson Boulevard, only a few short miles from Charlotte Douglas International Airport. She was caked up, flossing, and trying to become a businesswoman.

Chico was more interested in hearing her talk about her brothers than anything she had to say about herself. He wanted Tatiana to introduce him. He needed to somehow move into their circle and gain their trust somewhat. Whatever Chico needed to know, Tatiana provided him the information. Like about the drought the South was having.

A month ago, the feds and DEA agents did a huge raid on an upcoming shipment coming in to Miami. They seized over 9,500 pounds, or nearly five tons of cocaine with an estimated street value of up to 186 million dollars. It was a crucial blow to every hustler in the South. The effects of the raid in Miami gradually spread north to states like Georgia, Tennessee, South Carolina, and North Carolina. The local hustlers were hungry for some action. The product they had was drying up in the streets, and it was the right kind of news Chico needed to hear. It was like he had a full well of water in the hottest desert. He saw an opening in North Carolina, and he needed Tatiana to butter her brothers up for an introduction.

Tatiana lay next to Chico in her queen-size bed. They had just finished fucking for the umpteenth time, and she was spent. Her thick flesh was glistening with sweat as she tried to catch her breath. Chico was a good fuck. She looked over at Chico and loved every inch of him. They had been together for two weeks, and Tatiana didn't want anything to change between them.

Chico got up, planted his feet on the carpet, and sat on the side of the bed hunched over. He looked despondent for a moment. His cell phone began to ring. It was Apple. He didn't want to answer it in front of Tatiana.

"You gonna answer that, baby?" Tatiana asked.

"Nah, it ain't important right now."

"Why? 'Cause I'm the only thing important to you right now?"

Chico didn't reply.

Tatiana moved closer to him and stroked his back, being playful toward him.

Chico wanted to call Apple back. He needed to know what was going on with her in New York. He stared at her number in his cell phone, while Tatiana slowly began kissing the small of his back. He was unresponsive to her kisses and her gentle touch against his skin. He had making money and Apple on his mind at the moment.

Chico turned to look at Tatiana. He was ready to push his plan into action. He slightly shifted his weight over to his right arm, putting his weight down on his right hand so he could catch a better look at her. She propped herself up on her knees with her sagging double-D breasts dropping like heavy sandbags. One of her wrinkled thick thighs was almost the size of Chico's torso, with her stomach rolls protruding.

"What's goin' on wit' this drought I keep hearing about?" he asked.

"You know, baby. I already told you. Miami got hit hard a few weeks back, and that shit is fuckin' up business right now. I mean, we still caking and shit, but they tryin' to find some weight to hold down the streets. It's gettin' ugly out there. Our connect got caught up in that shit, so it's like critical for the moment."

"Oh, word?"

"Why you asking?"

"I want you to introduce me to your brothers."

"Why? I mean, they know about you 'cause I told 'em, but they don't know you like that. My brothers are dangerous, Chico. I don't want them fuckin' wit' you. I love you too much."

"I just wanna talk to them."

"About business?"

"I got a proposition that I want them to listen to. I might be able to help them out wit' this drought. I got a connect—"

Tatiana intervened before he could finish. "In New York?"

"I'm about my money, too, love. You feel me?"

"What you tryin' to offer them?"

"How many ki's does your brothers move on the average?"

"I don't know. Seven, maybe eight, a month."

Chico knew they were lightweight. At his peak, he was moving that in a day. Still, he knew it was the South and he had to work with them. Tatiana's brothers looked like the only reliable crew that would be able to purchase from him in large quantities and probably have the cash on hand. He wasn't trying to do anything on credit.

"I can get them fifteen ki's."

Tatiana looked at him confused. "What are you talking about?"

"Tatiana, what do you think I'm about? Where I'm from?"

She held his stare. She knew by his look and demeanor that he was serious.

"How you think I get my money?"

"So you really want to meet them?"

"I'm not talking to you just to hear myself talk, baby. I'm fo' real wit' this."

"You better be, because my brothers are serious. If you bullshit them, they'll fuck you up. I love you, Chico, but when it comes to business and my reputation, if you embarrass me wit' them, I'll fuck you up!"

Tatiana was stern in her tone, and her eyes quickly changed from loving and caring to a hard, vigorous stare at Chico. Chico wasn't intimidated by it, though. The eye contact between them showed the type of world they came from. He was just as ruthless as her brothers. The only difference was, he was outnumbered.

"Tatiana, I ain't the nigga to fuck wit', but I like that about you. That's why I'm wit' you, baby, 'cause ya a go-getter."

"And don't you forget that. But I'll set it up for you to talk to my brothers."

Chico nodded. "You won't regret it."

"Oh, I know I won't," she said. "So now that we done wit' that business, ya need to come over hur and finish ya business," Tatiana said, propping herself against the headboard and spreading her thick thighs, her pink pussy throbbing.

Chico strained a smile. He slowly climbed on top of Tatiana as she wrapped her thunderous legs around him, pressing against him as he thrust into her. He felt like he was being wrapped in a long blanket.

"Ugh!" he grunted.

"Ooh, fuck me, baby," she cooed.

As Chico fucked Tatiana, his mind drifted to Apple. He needed to call her back, but he had to take care of his business with Tatiana first. He needed to keep her happy for the moment. She was a freak, and her pussy was always throbbing. He threw her thick legs back, gripped her ankles, arched his chiseled frame, and fucked her while he stood on the balls of his feet, his big dick burrowing inside of her like a worm.

Tatiana panted. "Oh God!" She wiggled underneath him, her toes curling.

Chico stared at her intensely and fucked her vigorously, like a jackhammer smashing into concrete. Her pussy felt like it was being ripped open, causing her to come quickly.

He came right after, pulling out and exploding on her stomach.

Tatiana loved the way he spread his semen on her. "Shit, nigga!" she said, smiling.

After he got off of her, Tatiana rolled over on her side. She was finally depleted.

Chico lay next to her for a moment. A short while later, when Tatiana began to snore lightly, Chico got out of bed, put on his jeans, and snatched up his cell phone. He went downstairs and called Apple. The phone rang a few times before he heard someone answer.

"Apple," he uttered.

"Baby, where you at?" Apple cried out.

"I'm still in North Carolina. How you holding up?"

"Come home, baby. They gonna take our house, and I can't do it anymore. I thought I could, but I can't."

"I'ma be back soon, Apple. Just do what you gotta do."

"And what's that? I have nothing left up here. These muthafuckas disrespected me, Chico. They put their hands on me. Can you fuckin' believe that? And they treated me like I was trash to them. I can't collect 'cause I ain't got the muscle anymore, Chico. I ain't got you up here wit' me."

Chico sighed. "Who the fuck was it? When I get back, I'll take care of them. Just give me their names, baby."

"How, muthafucka? You down there, and I'm up here!"

"Apple, did you forget who ya' talkin' to and who I am? You remember what the fuck I'm about? I'm still a threat to niggas up there, no matter where the fuck I am, you hear me? You just give me their names, and they gonna be dead by tomorrow night."

"Don't worry about it."

"Fuck you mean, don't worry about it? They put their muthafuckin' hands on my bitch, and they think that shit's gonna slide like that? Apple, this is my fuckin' reputation. I need to worry about it."

"If I'm that important to you, then you need to bring ya ass back up here and come take care of ya business and me."

"And I will!"

There was brief silence over the phone. Chico was fuming. His mind was telling him to just get on the interstate to New York and murder everyone. But with the drought going on, Chico saw an opening he could take full advantage of.

"Baby, just let me come down there wit' you," Apple suggested.

"Nah, now's not a good time."

"Why not? I can't be up here anymore."

"It just ain't a good time, Apple. Trust me. I'm not gonna be down here fo' too long. I'm workin' on somethin' now. Just trust me, baby."

"Fuck you, Chico!" Apple ended the call.

Chapter 21

The streets of New York were starting to become a very cold place for Apple. Spring weather would be breaking soon, but there wasn't anything warm stirring inside of her heart. Her mind was spinning. It felt like the walls were coming down around her. Apple's heart was becoming disfigured like the damaged side of her face. She was a bitter bitch. The streets were cold to her. Her loan-sharking business was no longer profitable or respected. She had over twenty-five thousand dollars owed to her.

But what bothered Apple the most was her sister Kola, who was ahead of the game. Kola was winning. The streets still had respect for her, while Apple was slowly withering away in the city's gutter.

Apple sat in the dark and still bedroom. The shades were drawn tightly, so there was no sun in the room. She carried a deadpan look. It was mid-afternoon, and the door was shut. The room was untidy. There was no more money. There was no Chico. No respect. The only thing she had left to feed on was her bitterness and animosity.

She had tried to collect money from the people who owed her, but it was the same thing like Peon. They stared at Apple like she was a child, and then a monster.

One individual spat on her the minute she showed her face in his barbershop.

The man that owned the barbershop on Morningside Avenue was kin to Ayesha, and they were close. There was speculation on the streets that Apple was behind the murder, but Apple was at the peak of her power when the speculation was traveling from ear to ear. Sony had cried for a long time over his cousin's death. He used to like Apple, but when Ayesha was killed and he heard through the grapevine about who was probably behind it, his dislike for Apple started to boil over like an overflowing pot.

One day, he had to set aside his anger and pride to borrow five thousand dollars from her. The IRS had run an audit on him, and agents went through all of his books thoroughly and found out that he hadn't paid taxes in three years and was hiding money, including winnings from Atlantic City. In total, he owed Uncle Sam eight thousand dollars. He didn't have that much money on him. So he reached out to Apple. She had given him the loan with the stipulation that he had to pay her more than five hundred dollars per week in interest on his initial five-thousand-dollar loan and other subsequent loans. Sony knew it was highway robbery, but he was in a bind with the IRS and reluctantly agreed to the terms.

When Apple had walked into his Harlem barbershop to collect, Sony had exploded on her. He had rushed up to her face and spit on her, while his customers and employees all looked on. No one said anything or got in the way. Everyone just minded their business and felt that Apple had gotten what she deserved. However, a few were still scared of her, knowing that Chico was still around.

There was heckling and laughter at Apple. She had worn the mask, and everyone stared at her like she was some freak show. They were seeing with their own eyes that the rumors about her were true.

"You put ya fuckin' hand on me again, Sony, and I'll cut it off," Apple said through clenched teeth.

"You fuckin' monstrous bitch, get the fuck out my shop! I don't owe you shit in here!" he yelled. Sony's voice was breaking, and he was becoming emotional. Seeing Apple again reminded him of his cousin's violent death. He wanted to kill Apple himself. Shoot her in the back of her head like she had someone do to his cousin, but he didn't have the heart. The only thing Sony had for Apple that day when she came to collect was resentment and cruel words.

Apple stormed out of the shop, vowing she would be back, and quickly jumped into her McLaren, unaware she was being watched closely by three sets of eyes from a short distance. She had made enemies in Harlem, and she was drawing unwanted attention to herself, driving around in a half-a-million-dollar car.

Apple started the ignition and was ready to pull out the parking spot, but she was suddenly blocked in by a dark blue Chevy. She turned her head swiftly to look and felt it was a hit.

She was ready to reach for her pistol and protect herself. Until she noticed that the man exiting from the driver's side wasn't a threat. She quickly recognized him. He was a cop. Detective Rice. She relaxed and sighed with relief.

The detective walked over and tapped on her window, indicating he wanted her to roll down the window so they could talk. Apple did so.

Detective Rice stared at her face. He didn't mean to stare so hard, but it was a shock to him to see how much her features had changed. Apple's face was framed by dark shoulder-length hair, and her clear mask was highly visible. Detective Rice was mute for a short moment. He remembered how beautiful she was once, and looking at Apple now, he felt sorry for her.

Detective Rice peered at Apple with a deadpan expression. "You remember me?" he asked.

Apple nodded.

"Why don't you shut the car off so we can talk?"

"I'm not going anywhere. You have me blocked in, Detective."

Detective Rice turned and glanced at his car. He then focused his attention back on Apple. "Nice car. It definitely stands out around here. How much does something this flashy go for?"

"Look, Detective, what do you want with me? I'm a busy girl."

"Well, first, I'm sorry for what happened to you. I know it's a tragedy. And then with your sister, we're still—"

"Look, Detective, er . . ."

"Rice," he reminded her.

"Detective Rice, am I under arrest?"

"No, not right now."

"So what's this about? Because I got somewhere to be."

"It's about you, Apple. I know you're angry. A lot has happened to you within the year, but these murders going on around here point back to you."

"Can you prove it?"

Detective Rice was quiet. Apple had her answer.

"How long do you think you'll last out here? You're still a little girl, Apple. People are out here to kill you. Is this the way you want to carry out the memory of your little sister, through sheer bloodshed and revenge? You're just eighteen."

Apple quickly snatched the mask from her face to give the detective a closer look at her wounds. "Do I look like a little girl to you right now?" she shouted. "Huh, nigga? And you think I give a fuck? Look at what the fuck they did to me! To my fuckin' face! You see it, detective? This is my fuckin' reality!" She angled herself closer to him so he could get a better look at the burns entrenched into her skin.

He didn't cringe though. He had seen worse. Apple held his stare. Detective Rice knew it wouldn't be long before the morgue was scraping her body off the pavement, or charges would be pending against her.

"What happened to you?" he asked.

Apple smirked and replied, "Harlem."

"Here's my card."

Apple took his card and tossed it out the window. "Fuck ya card!"

"It doesn't have to be like this. You need help."

Apple put her mask back on, adjusted the straps, then turned to the detective and asked, "Can I fuckin' go now? I ain't got time to play this cat-and-mouse wit' you." She revved the engine, indicating her impatience.

Detective Rice slowly stepped away from the pricey vehicle, his eyes still on Apple. He shook his head knowing that he wasn't going to get anywhere with the girl. She was too badly damaged, inside and out.

Meanwhile, a burgundy Tahoe parked across the street from the barbershop with keen eyes fixated on Apple and her high-end car. The three men in the truck were about to make their move on her when the detective suddenly pulled up. They were forced to hesitate on their plan to carjack Apple. They wanted her McLaren with a hard-on.

"This muthafuckin cop! Ooooh, this fuckin' cop is in the way right now," Hayden exclaimed. "I want that shit, yo. That bitch needs to come out that fuckin' car."

"Yo, we on it, Hayden. We definitely on it," Mann said.

Hayden was a twenty-four-year-old ruffian who stood six feet even with a bald head and narrowing eyes that were always scheming on something or someone. He'd never known his parents, and the only thing he knew how to do well was steal and fight. Hayden had his eye on Apple's McLaren for the longest. He had a wild crew under his wing that did stickups and stole cars, sometimes with the driver still behind the wheel. It didn't matter to his crew if it was broad daylight or in the shadows of the night. If they wanted something, they took it brazenly.

Hayden had the .45 gripped in his hand and was waiting for the detective to leave. His attention was only on the McLaren. He knew the retail on the car would make his payday. He also knew about Apple and her sudden reputation in Harlem. He had already said to himself, if he had to shoot the bitch to get the car, he was ready to do so.

After Detective Rice pulled off in the Chevy, Hayden had made his exit from the truck and rushed over to do the deed, but Apple had sped out the parking spot before he could even get close to the car.

"Fuck!" he shouted. He ran back to his car and tried to cut a sharp U-turn in the street, but before he could complete it, an oncoming car approaching in the opposite direction abruptly cut off the Tahoe, halting Hayden's chance to follow behind the McLaren.

Hayden had cursed, but he knew it wouldn't be long before he would see Apple again. He was going to take that car away from her by any means necessary.

Apple heard the hard knocking at her front door. It boomed throughout the house like loud thunder, but she chose to ignore it. She already knew who was waiting for her outside. It was early morning. The nightmare had finally arrived. After countless letters and warnings about their mortgage and the lagging behind in payments, the bank finally decided to make their move and carry out an eviction. They were taking her home away from her. They had come to embarrass her. She no longer had any sanctuary in her home. It was being ripped away from her, just like everything else.

Apple had peered out her bedroom window and saw the sheriff and marshals standing outside with a team of men ready to barge into the house.

"This is the sheriff! Open up!" the voice roared with conviction. "We will come in!"

She didn't want to believe it. The tears of anguish stained her face, and many worries were playing constantly in her head. Everything she owned was there, and even though she hadn't been in the house long, it was her home. It was away from Harlem, and it gave her comfort.

The marshals continued to shout and bang at the front door.

Apple continued to ignore them. She wanted to take a pistol and shoot them dead, or put the pistol in her own mouth and squeeze, since it felt like she had nothing to live for. They were violating her. It looked like there was a drug raid at her home, with all the uniforms and commotion happening.

Apple sat in her bedroom butt naked, staring at the walls in the dark. She wanted to be consumed by it—the darkness. It was the story of her life. The mask was off and lying on the dresser. She wanted the marshals to see the scars on her face and the core of her skin.

The bedroom looked like it had been hit by a whirlwind. Her clothes were scattered everywhere. The plasma TV was smashed to the ground. The closet doors were kicked in and hanging from their hinges. The walls had holes the size of basketballs in them. The bedroom showed it had clearly been vandalized. It was a straight "fuck you" from Apple to the bank and the people forcing her out.

The knocking intensified, but Apple wasn't getting up to let men trying to evict her into her home. If they wanted in, it would have to be by force. She wasn't going to give them the satisfaction.

The front door was forced open with a thump, and the men came rushing into her home. They searched the house looking for her. It didn't take them long to find Apple in the bedroom. The bedroom door was forced open, and four men clad in flight vests and windbreakers that read U.S. Marshal and Sheriff came rushing in. They were quickly shocked by what they saw. Apple was seated Indian-style on her bed. She didn't even acknowledge that they were in the room. She carried her deadpan demeanor and continued to sit there.

"Ma'am, you gotta get dressed and leave this residence immediately."

It was evident that the men were disturbed by what they saw. They didn't expect Apple to be so young, and the burns on her face, the mess to the bedroom, and her nakedness had them taken aback.

The alpha male of the four men approached Apple as she sat. "Ma'am, you got to get dressed and leave here now. I'm not going to tell you again," he said harshly, his blue eyes shooting into her, showing his aggravation.

As Apple sat and continued ignoring them, the man turned to look at his fellow officers. They hated to carry out brute force, but Apple wasn't giving them a choice. They had the writ of restitution, an official court document that directed them to immediately remove the occupants of the specific premises, inventory the property located therein, and turn the possession of the property over to the plaintiff, which was the bank. Everything was being videotaped for their well-being. If things got ugly, then the marshals would have video documentation that they did everything by the book.

The marshal sighed heavily. He glanced at his fellow officers again, his eyes indicating that they had to use force with her, which he seemed to be against. The silver-haired marshal approached Apple in a stern manner. She remained seated. He reached out to grab the young teen. He wrapped his thick, chubby fingers around her thin right arm, tightening his hold onto her.

Apple suddenly reacted. "Get the fuck off me!"

She tried to pull herself away from the marshal's stern hold, but he was too strong. When he dragged Apple out of the bed, a loud thud was heard.

Apple continued to fight them off, but she was immediately overpowered by the three husky men, while the fourth videotaped the incident. She tussled and shouted but was instantly subdued and covered up.

"You can't stay here!" the silver-haired man said to her roughly.

Apple looked up at him with a steely glare while still on the floor. She remained quiet.

"Now, take what you need to take. You have thirty minutes to pack it up and leave the premises," he said. "If not, then you will be arrested and charged for trespassing. Do you understand me?"

Apple was still quiet.

"Do you understand me?"

She was in a no-win situation. Apple didn't want to go to jail. She reluctantly nodded.

"OK. Please put some clothes on, and you have thirty minutes."

Apple was lifted off the ground and handed a shirt and some jeans to put on. She got dressed while the men waited outside her bedroom. She looked around but didn't know what to take. Teary-eyed, she grabbed a large trash bag and started throwing some clothing into it.

Fifteen minutes later, she had packed a few things, mostly clothing and some shoes. Apple just wanted to forget about everything. The marshals came in and escorted her out of her home like she was on her way to death row.

Apple tossed what she could into her McLaren. Trunk space was almost nonexistent in the stylish sports car, so Apple wasn't able to take much. The marshals stood guard outside of the house like they were soldiers standing watch outside of a castle.

"Where the fuck am I supposed to go now?"

"It's not our concern, but you can't come back here," the marshal said.

Her tears were dried, but she was crushed. She had it all once, but now everything was gone. She went from the gully projects to enjoying the picturesque view that the West Side had to offer, to living in an extravagant home upstate, and now she was homeless.

Notices of eviction were posted on her home along with a padlock on the front door. It was embarrassing for Apple. She didn't know where to go or who to turn to.

Chico had suggested that she go live with her mother for the time being, but Apple was against it. She refused to go crawling back to her mother after the way she had treated her. Apple didn't want to give Denise the satisfaction, and she knew her mother would rub the entire incident in her face.

Apple got behind the wheel of her car. It was the only thing she had left that reminded her of the wealth she once had. She glared over at the marshals and sheriff standing outside of her home and shouted, "Fuck y'all! Y'all some fuckin' bastards!"

The men kept their composure. They had a job to do and didn't allow their emotions to intervene with the task.

Apple sped out of the driveway like she was in the Indy 500 and hit the corners doing 40 mph. As she drove farther away from her home, her tears began to resurface. She was hurting. She was scared. She didn't have anywhere to go. She only had a few hundred dollars on her, and that wouldn't last but a week for her.

She drove around aimlessly for a moment and tried to pass the day away by just driving. But gas wasn't cheap, and it would be costly to fill up her gas tank. She parked on a tree-lined block in a secluded section in the neighborhood, the sun slowly setting behind the horizon.

Apple wanted to disappear like the sun. She nestled in the driver's seat, trying to find some comfort in the McLaren. But the car was for show, not for living in.

It got cramped after a few hours, and her joints started to hurt from the constant fidgeting. She ended up falling asleep in the parked car in tears, suicide not far from her mind.

Chapter 22

The meeting with the Johnson brothers was in an hour. Tatiana had done her part and had gotten her brothers to meet with Chico, and it didn't surprise him that they'd agreed. North Carolina was going through a drought, and there was desperation among the hustlers to get their hands on something right away.

Chico wanted to become their pipeline. He could monopolize the South if he made the right moves. He probably could start fresh in Charlotte; there wasn't any Chico or Kola down there. He was a new face. He wasn't warring with anybody. Yet, Chico's pride prevented him from staying away from home for too long. He was ready to travel back to Harlem after the deal and finish off what he had started. He vowed revenge, and he was a man who kept his word. His gun was ready to do the talking for him.

Chico wanted to let the Johnson brothers know that he was the real thing and definitely serious about doing business with them. One way to solidify his name among the brothers was to have something tangible at their reach. Showing would make them believe him.

He removed a kilo from the duffel bag that was locked in his trunk, placed it inside of a smaller bag, and got into Tatiana's truck. Everything Chico was doing was a risk, so he was trying to stay two steps ahead of any troubling situations.

Tatiana turned her cocaine-colored Yukon into the parking lot of a strip club on West Woodlawn Road. Chico was in the passenger seat, the small bag resting on the floor between his legs. It was a Thursday evening, and the parking lot was crowded. The Champagne Room was a huge one-story building that looked like a large warehouse and had its name lit up in bold neon lettering over the front entrance.

Tatiana parked her truck directly outside the front entrance, where there was valet parking. One of the parking attendants recognized her vehicle right away and came rushing over to assist her. Chico stepped out of the truck clutching the bag, and Tatiana walked around the vehicle to hand her keys over to a short Mexican man wearing a bright red vest, a black shirt, and black pants. He nodded and greeted Tatiana with a smile then jumped behind the wheel to park the vehicle.

Chico followed behind Tatiana toward the front entrance. The three-man security detail out front all stood over six feet tall, weighed over two hundred pounds, and every one of the men was clad in tight black T-shirts that highlighted their strapping physiques. Tatiana gave them a head nod and briskly moved past them with Chico right behind her, knowing she was exempt from the searches or the cover charge. It was her brothers' club, and she was a well-known figure throughout the establishment.

They walked through the short foyer where there was a man in black clutching a handheld security detector wand and a small booth with a young girl seated behind it that took the cover charge for the door. Smiling, the man waved them through with ease. Tatiana and Chico walked into the adult entertainment establishment and were greeted with the blaring music of Piles and Jeezy's "Lose My Mind."

The thunderous bass ripped through the vibrant, dimmed club, causing the walls to rattle. Naked women moved around dancing with the ballers, who were popping bottles and tipping the girls spread in every corner of the room. The place had attitude with an upscale décor. It had a full bar and a large, luxurious upstairs VIP area overlooking the main floor, and titillating tableside dancing. The customers were able to enjoy different selections of champagne and fine imported cigars with the lovely girls, along with catching major sporting events on wide-screen televisions.

The stage had dual gold poles centered on each end with blue illuminated lights trimmed around it. Two voluptuously endowed strippers were on stage twirling around the poles and making their booties clap. There were a total of thirty young, beautiful, and scantily clad women of all flavors circling the club and providing private dances with bottle services being offered.

Chico followed behind Tatiana. The place was thick with male patrons. The Champagne Room was a very popular spot in Charlotte. It was only one of the few businesses that the brothers owned. They also had a mechanic shop on Old Pineville Road, a moving service, a dry cleaner, and a grocery store. They were about their business, legal and illicit. Chico understood that the brothers were a force to be reckoned with. They came from Richmond and took over a different city, which took skills, heart, and pure muscle.

Meeting with the Johnson brothers didn't scare Chico. He was far from intimidated by them. He was only cautious. He understood he was in their world now, and not his own. With Tatiana being his only connection and the only woman who could vouch for him in the city, it was like moving through a land mine. He had to be careful with every step, because one wrong move, and it was his ass. He wouldn't leave Charlotte alive.

Tatiana moved through the crowd with authority. They stared at Chico like he had the plague, but because he was with Tatiana, they gave him a pass and didn't bother or question him.

Tatiana headed toward the back of the club, to a narrow hallway. On the left were the stairs that went up into the VIP area, and on the right were two doorways with black doors. A stout man guarded the entrance. He wore the same close-fitting black shirt the other bouncers wore, "The Champagne Room," written across the front of the shirt.

Tatiana walked up to him and asked, "Are my brothers in there already?"

He nodded.

Tatiana went through, and Chico walked behind her. He locked eyes with the man for a moment, and the glare in his eyes showed the mistrust he had for Chico. Chico didn't care for the man's feelings against him. He paraded a smirk as he passed him and was four steps behind Tatiana.

When they walked into a room, her brothers were seated around a large round table playing cards. They were amongst friends and associates, smoking, drinking with a few beautiful, scantily clad, exotic-looking women moving about in the room. This room was off-limits to everyone in the club, even those who had the money to splurge in the VIP area. It was the brothers' private domain, where gambling and business transactions went on, and where the girls performed sexual favors for the brothers and their guests, since it was forbidden throughout the club.

Two mounted plasma flat-screens hung on the walls, and they had a private bar with their personal female bartender clad in a skimpy bikini. A safe was hidden underneath the bar, and security cameras were plastered all over.

Once Tatiana walked into the room with her friend, all eyes were on him. Chico was a fish out of water. They had seen him around with Tatiana in passing, but there was never a formal introduction. The brothers knew he was there for business, though.

Tatiana locked eyes with her brother Jonathan, who

was the oldest.

Jonathan nodded then suddenly stood and shouted, "Everybody, get the fuck out this room now!" He didn't have to say it twice or give an explanation why.

Everyone swiftly started to pile out the room, knowing what was about to go on wasn't any of their concern.

When the last person that didn't matter stepped outside, Tito shut the door, locked it, and looked over at Chico harshly. His dark black eyes ripped into Chico with some doubt. He then turned to look at his sister and exclaimed, "Yo, Tatiana, who is this fuckin' fool anyway?"

Tito already showed that he was the hothead, the one with the temper. He turned to glare at Chico, his face twisted into a scowl. Tito stood five eight and had a lean build, along with brown eyes. He had long braids and smooth, dark skin. He could be mistaken for a pretty boy, but he was deadly like a venomous snake.

Jonathan leaned back in his chair and looked up at Chico, his eyes heavy with some concern. "So you the muthafuckin' nigga fuckin' my little sister," he said.

Chico casually replied, "I'm the nigga that's gonna get ya outta this drought."

"Says who?" Tito shot back.

Chico turned to look at him, but didn't say a word.

"He's cool, y'all," Tatiana intervened.

"Why? 'Cause you fuckin' the nigga, Tatiana?"

Tatiana cut her eyes at her brother. "Whateva, Ryan."

Ryan took a drag from the imported cigar he was smoking, his eyes darting back and forth from his sister to

Chico. Ryan was the heaviest of the brothers. He weighed over two hundred and forty pounds, had a protruding stomach, chunky arms, and thick legs.

He blew out smoke from his mouth and looked over at Jonathan. If Jonathan said Chico dies, then he dies. If he said let him sit and talk, then he would sit and he would talk. Jonathan was the shot-caller. The figure that many men in the city didn't want to cross. He was smart and he was vicious.

Jonathan had smooth, dark skin like his little brother Tito. He had a neatly trimmed moustache that matched his perfectly manicured hair—peppered with small tufts of gray. The patches at both temples gave him a distinguished look. He was in his mid-forties. He had soft eyes at times and was the one you could reason with, if he liked you. But he was just as deadly as Tito. He had been acquitted of three murder charges over the years and ran his empire with an iron fist.

The room was quiet for a moment. Everyone waited for Jonathan to give the word. He cut his eyes into Chico, locking into his stare. He knew how to read a man. He studied body language and looked for signs of weakness or mistrust in everyone, even his own family. The way Chico held his stare said a lot about him.

"Sit down," Jonathan ordered.

Clutching his bag, Chico walked up to the table and took a seat opposite from Jonathan. Tatiana sat next to Chico. She glanced at her brother. Her nerves were jumping. She knew anything could go wrong in a heartbeat. She had witnessed her brothers do the unthinkable at times, even against her ex-boyfriends.

Jonathan lit up a cigarette and then turned his attention back to Chico. "My sister tells me that you're official. Where are you from, Chico?" he asked coolly.

"Up top, New York," he said.

"Fuck y'all New York niggas," Tito barked. "Muthafuckas think they can come down here and take over shit!"

Jonathan cut his eyes at his little brother and said, "Relax, Tito." Jonathan said to Chico, "You wanted to meet us, and because of my sister, you got your chance. So talk, nigga."

Chico had to humble himself. He was just a nigga trying to move some ki's and trying not to get killed. He wasn't much for speaking. He knew showing was better. He reached into his bag and dropped a brick of dirty white in front of Jonathan, who stared at the ki.

"That's what I'm about and what I can do for you," Chico said.

Tatiana smiled.

"What the fuck I'm gonna do with one brick?" Jonathan asked.

"I can get you much more where that came from."

"You know what? Why don't we just pop ya fuckin' ass and take it from you?" Tito spat.

Chico turned and looked at Tito. He was getting tired of his mouth, but he had to keep his cool. He calmly replied, "That's a fool's way of thinking. Profit off the short term, never the long. And when that ki is done, then what?"

"I'll tell you then what, muthafucka!" Tito barked, stepping closer to Chico and raising his shirt to reveal the butt of a gun.

Chico didn't budge.

"Tito, I told you to chill the fuck out!" Jonathan shouted.

Tito looked at his older brother, and the seriousness that Jonathan showed in his eyes warned him to take a step back and be quiet. Tito didn't like it, but he knew his brother didn't give out too many warnings. He was lucky to get the first one. His face remained in a frown as he stood against the door.

Jonathan focused his interest back on Chico, admiring what Chico had said to Tito about fools and their shortcomings. He believed the same thing. Chico's body language showed Jonathan that danger was nothing new to him and he was from the streets. Jonathan had been paying attention to the little things about Chico.

"Before we were rudely interrupted," he said, continuing. "We don't know you. My sister may vouch for you, say you're legit, but that only gets you this meeting with us. How can we trust you?"

"Yeah, ya right. You don't know me and I don't know you. But I'm from Harlem. You got peoples out there?"

"I got peoples everywhere," Jonathan replied.

"Well, make a phone call to your peoples out that way and ask about Chico. My reputation is fierce out there."

"It ain't fierce down here," Jonathan countered. "You police?"

"I should be asking you that. Ya the one with all the questions."

Jonathan chuckled then looked at his sister. "Your friend here is funny."

"That's why I love him," she replied.

"Look, I came here thinking maybe I could do business with some serious people that are about their money. I got product to move—lots of it. I ain't for games."

"I'm not for games either."

"So let's talk."

Jonathan was quiet for a moment. He looked into each of his brothers' eyes. They were quiet with hard stares. He then turned to face Chico. He had something on his mind.

He leaned forward, clasped his hands together, looked intensely at Chico. "So what you working with?"

"I got a straight Haitian connect in New York, right off the boat. I've been dealing with them for a few years now. They're legit. Sixteen a ki. A minimum purchase of ten to get the pipeline open."

"Sixteen with a minimum of ten? Nigga, you trying to extort us?" Ryan chimed. "You think 'cause our connect got caught up in that Miami sting that we supposed to be some fools in desperation?"

"I'm just about my business," Chico replied.

Jonathan was quiet for a moment. He was thinking.

Chico remained cool while patiently waiting for his reply.

Jonathan took a pull from his cigarette, blew out smoke, and kept his eyes on Chico. He then glanced at Tatiana but remained quiet. The room was itching to hear his response.

Chico knew he was their only connect for the moment. It was a sweet deal for them. The drought was critical. Rival hustlers would be looking to re-up soon, and the streets would be thirsty for some action. His cocaine wasn't as pure, and it was stepped on too many times, but when the streets are hungry, anything was better than nothing.

Chico pushed the ki of coke over to Jonathan and said, "Go ahead. Test it out if you want."

"I don't use," he returned dryly.

Chico shrugged.

Tito was itching to take a hit, but he wasn't about to do it around his brothers. Jonathan was against his family using, saying it made them look weak and bad. He believed a man became sloppy and careless with business and his life when he went to getting high.

But Chico already knew that, because Tatiana had already told him so much of her brother's business.

Jonathan turned to look at Ryan, who glanced at Chico. Then he whispered something in his brother's ear.

Jonathan nodded, looked at Chico once more, and said, "We can try you out, for the moment."

Chico nodded. He was expressionless, but Tatiana was the one smiling.

"I can have up to ten or more for you in a few days."

"No. First, I make that phone call to New York to ask about you, because I do have peoples out there," Jonathan said. "Then if you're not who you say you are, guess what?" Jonathan looked over at Tito.

Tito smirked and lifted his shirt, revealing the butt of a 9 mm he carried.

Chico remained nonchalant and simply replied, "You do that." He removed himself from the chair.

The room was still tense even though a transaction had taken place. Jonathan, who continued to smoke, dismissed Chico, but asked his sister to remain behind for a moment.

Chico walked out the room.

When the door shut behind him, Jonathan looked at his sister. "If this nigga ain't legit, baby sis, you gonna kill this nigga for us."

Tatiana was silent for a moment before saying, "You don't have to worry about him, Jonathan. He's official."

"Yeah, we'll find out," Ryan added.

Tatiana walked out of the room and saw Chico waiting in the hallway. She just looked at him for a minute.

"Everything cool?" he asked.

She nodded, but before they exited out the hallway, Tatiana said to him, "You just better deliver like you said you would and have someone to vouch for you up north."

"Everything is already taken care of."

Tatiana had a little nervousness spreading throughout her when she started to realize that she really didn't know him too well, but for only two weeks. She had gotten so sprung by the wild sex they were having, it actually clouded her judgment. She began to wonder if she had made the right choice by introducing Chico to her brothers. Some doubt started to settle in. Tatiana knew if he turned out to be false, then she would pull the trigger on him her damn self.

Several days went by, and Chico was finally able to make the delivery. They agreed on twelve kilos at sixteen apiece. Chico would walk away from the deal with a hundred and ninety-two thousand in cash in a black duffel bag. Even though he had the ki's on him, he made them wait a few days because he didn't want it to look like the deal was done in desperation. He had to make it look like he had taken a trip up North and met with the Haitians.

Jonathan had made the call up North to a few well-known associates of his in New York. He asked about Chico, gave his peoples a description, and the word came back that he was for real. His status was legit. Not a snitch, but a high-end mover. Jonathan trusted his peoples' word and felt a little more at ease doing business with Chico.

Tatiana was relieved that everything worked out smoothly. Her brothers didn't show their satisfaction. It was business, not a friendship.

Tatiana wanted to celebrate with Chico in the confines of their bedroom, but Chico wanted to rush back to New York and check on Apple. He had accomplished what he came to the South to do—get rid of his product, get his money, and head back to New York. He had opened up a pipeline in Charlotte, and figured it would only be one of many places to come. He had his eye on the South now. And he would be back. Regardless of how he felt about it, it was a newfound hustle for him.

Chapter 23

Kola had fucked plenty of niggas and had done things that would go down in history books. But once Cross came into her life, her wild ways stopped, and she became more business-minded and faithful to her man.

At first, she only got with Cross to piss off Apple. She was well aware of the strong crush that Apple had for Cross, and when the sisters were at war with each other, she used Cross to her advantage. But Kola didn't expect to fall in love with him. It came unexpectedly, and when it came, she didn't know what to do with it. Cross was her king. He was a man that had all the qualities she looked for—street-oriented, a hustler with respect, and a good lover. It would soon be a year that they'd been together, and she was looking forward to their anniversary. Cross had made her into something she thought she would never become—a faithful bitch.

Kola got the phone call from Edge late one night.

"You know where ya man is right now? Laid up wit' the next bitch in Brooklyn," he told her. "And you wanna be down wit' that nigga."

"You is a fuckin' snake, Edge!" Kola barked. "I thought he was your boy."

"I'm the snake? Shit, I thought you were his number one bitch. He playin' you, Kola, and this nigga just had a baby by his Brooklyn bitch."

"You fuckin' lyin', Edge! Get the fuck off my phone!"

"Go check it out yourself. I got the bitch address."

Kola didn't want to believe him. She figured Edge would say anything to get into her panties. But hearing about Cross' infidelity was hard to swallow. She still took the address from Edge.

"I'm sayin', ma, I thought you should know. He's my boy and all, but he shouldn't be doin' you dirty like that."

"Fuck you, Edge! You think you scored some points wit' me by tellin' me this shit? Nigga, I don't give a fuck what you say to me about Cross. I ain't never fuckin' you, and that's a fact, muthafucka!"

"It's whateva, Kola. I just thought you should know."

The phone went silent, and Kola was left sitting there with many worries and doubts in her head. The tears began to fall, as uncertainty and concern about her relationship with Cross settled in.

Men came at her all the time, but she turned them away, believing she had developed something special with Cross. Then she thought about Eduardo and how guilty she felt just kissing him that night. It could have gone further, but thinking about her man made her stop and come to her senses. What hurt her the most was hearing about the baby. It felt like she had acid in her stomach, hearing that Cross got some next bitch pregnant.

Kola wanted to find out for herself. She wasn't going to lie around and get herself worked up over speculation. She needed the facts. Remembering the address that Edge had given to her, she decided to take a trip out to Brooklyn really soon. And if Edge was telling her the truth, there would be hell to pay.

Kola and Candace were parked across the street from the Fort Greene projects in Brooklyn, New York in a black Chevy Trailblazer with tinted windows. The sun was casting down, and the weather was warm in the notorious Brooklyn hood. Candace was itching for some action. She was down with Kola a hundred percent. She was ready to call her team of bitches and regulate on a few Brooklyn hoes, but Kola just wanted to be low-key and take everything in for the moment. She wanted the truth.

Kola stared at the address in her hand. It was on the fourth floor, apartment 4B, and the girl's name was Cynthia. Edge had given her a clear description of Cynthia—five five with caramel skin, soft, chinky eyes, and long, sinuous black hair—telling her, she couldn't miss her because "shortie is beautiful."

Kola didn't like coming out to Brooklyn unless it was for business with her parties. Brooklyn was a savage place in her mind. The bitches were prehistoric, and the men didn't know how to get money like Harlem niggas.

In Kola's eyes, Harlem was where everything started and ended, and she was offended that Cross would even fuck with a Brooklyn bitch, let alone have a baby by one.

"You ready to do this?" Candace asked.

Kola wasn't sure if she was ready to see the truth or if she could handle it. She looked at the time. A quarter past seven. She then looked at Candace and said, "Fuck it! Let's see this bitch!"

Both girls stepped out of the truck and hastily walked toward the building on St. Edwards Street. The area was quiet. They walked into the projects like they owned the place. Candace had her .380 tucked in her jeans like a nigga. She was as hood as they came.

They entered the lobby and proceeded toward the elevators. Both girls were silent. Kola didn't have a plan; she was going off a whim. She knew Edge had a motive and figured it was probably much more than to just get into her panties. He was still upset that she had grabbed a hold of the connect and had made his feelings known about Kola associating with Eduardo.

As the elevator ascended toward the second floor, Kola's nerves were shaking. She wanted to talk to the bitch and see the baby for herself. She brought Candace along for backup just in case the situation escalated into something much more serious. But she just truly needed to see for herself.

After the elevator came to a stop on the fourth floor, Kola stepped off first, with Candace right behind her.

"What apartment is this bitch in?" Candace asked.

"4B."

The girls looked for 4B, which was two doors down from the elevator. When they approached the door, they heard rap music blaring from inside.

Kola glanced at Candace. "I just wanna talk first."

Candace smirked and nodded.

Kola turned to the door and knocked. The girls were ready for anything. Their hair was styled into long ponytails, and they were dressed in sneakers and jeans, but no jewelry. In a fight, earrings and chains would be the first thing to grab for, easy to snatch off.

Kola knocked harder after no one answered the first time. The rap music lowered, and they heard a woman's voice shout out, "Who is it?"

"I wanna speak to Cynthia," Kola shouted in response.

"Who's asking for her?"

"Just someone that wants to talk to her about something important," Kola said.

"Like what?"

Candace was getting impatient, but Kola gestured for her to be quiet and chill out.

Kola then said, "It's about Cross."

The door suddenly opened up, and a young, beautiful-looking woman emerged, whose looks alone could give Kola a run for her money. Kola was shocked herself. Cross definitely had good taste in picking his women.

The two ladies looked at each other silently. Cynthia stood the same height as Kola and had the same curvy figure. She was wearing a skimpy T-shirt that exposed her cut abs and pierced belly button and a pair of tight-fitting jeans that highlighted her hips and round ass. Her hair flowed down to her back, and her facial features were flawless.

"What about him?" Cynthia asked.

"You know him?"

"How do you know him?" Cynthia countered.

"Bitch, I'm asking you the question," Kola returned.

"*Bitch*?"

"How you know Cross?" Kola's eyes looked past Cynthia and gazed into her apartment momentarily. From where she stood, she knew the apartment was well furnished, and the diamond bracelet around the girl's wrist and the necklace she had on looked expensive.

"Bitch, you fuckin' her man?" Candace stepped closer to Cynthia, in a threatening way.

"Her man?" Cynthia raised an eyebrow. "Bitch, that's my nigga. Cross is my son's father."

Kola's heart sank into her stomach, and she wanted to throw up.

Cynthia stood with a posture that let it be known she wasn't about to be bullied in front of her own home. She was pretty but carried that hood mentality. She was a Brooklyn bitch to the fullest.

"Y'all bitches need to step away from my fuckin' door. My son is 'sleep, and I ain't tryin' to explain myself to y'all. I've been fuckin' wit' Cross for two years, so who the fuck is you, bitch, to come up in my crib wit' that bullshit? Step the fuck off!"

Candace couldn't tolerate the insult to her friend any longer. She lunged forward, striking the girl upside her head with her closed fist and a hard blow. Cynthia stumbled back into the apartment, throwing her arms up in defense, but Candace was all over her like flies on shit.

They tussled in the short foyer, with some hair-pulling and their clothes getting torn. Candace had the advantage for a moment, but Cynthia was far from being just a pretty face. She pushed Candace off her and let off a right hook that connected with Candace's jaw. The blow knocked Candace back, and then Cynthia charged forward, hitting her again repeatedly with a series of blows.

Kola jumped into the fight, snatching Cynthia by her long, flowing hair and yanking her back like she was pulling on a rope. Cynthia jerked from the pull and screamed out. Kola tore into Cynthia like a lion. They were in the living room falling over each other and knocking into the furniture, beating on each other like a Vegas fight. Cynthia was holding her ground, but Kola was the more skilled and brutal fighter. She had Cynthia on one knee with the girl's hair knotted around her fist tightly.

"Get the fuck off my fuckin' hair!" Cynthia shouted, trying to free her long hair from Kola's clutch. Cynthia was relentless and refused to be beaten.

Kola tightened her grip.

Candace was furious. She had a bleeding lip and a bruised eye. She pulled the .380 from her waistband and charged at Cynthia with the intent to kill. Before Cynthia could look up and defend herself, Candace gun-butted her savagely, and Cynthia went down.

"Stupid bitch!" Candace screamed. She continued to pistol-whip Cynthia until her hands were covered in blood.

Kola had to pull Candace off Cynthia, who was sprawled out on the floor and not moving, her face caked with blood.

"Fuck that bitch, Kola!" Candace said, breathing hard like a marathon runner.

Kola looked down at Cross' side bitch, unconscious and lying on her side, blood trickling from the open wound that Candace had caused. At that moment, Kola wasn't the savvy businesswoman with the intense sex parties that high-profile men attended or the queen bitch that moved drugs in the streets. At that very moment, she was a young girl in love. A teenager with a crushed heart. Her true colors were exposed in Cynthia's apartment. Her ponytail had been pulled loose from the fighting, and she had scratches on her face.

The sudden sound of a baby crying made Kola spin her head in the direction of one of the bedrooms in the hallway. She slowly proceeded toward the sound.

Candace stared at Kola and asked, "Kola, where you going?"

"I gotta see him," she answered gruffly, her back turned to Candace.

She continued down the hallway and walked to where the baby was heard crying. She walked into one of the two bedrooms in the apartment. The walls to the room were painted a light blue, and it was decorated with a stylish white crib near the window. Many toys and teddy bears were scattered about, and an old-school wooden rocking chair was near the child's crib. The room looked like something out of a Macy's catalog. *It took money to style the baby's room the way it is*, Kola thought.

Kola walked over to the crib and peered down at the baby crying. He wore blue pajamas ornamented with small teddy bear heads. He had a full head of dark, black hair and was the color of peanut butter. He was a cute baby, and Kola couldn't help but to notice the resemblance to Cross.

She reached down and carefully picked up the crying infant. It brought back painful memories of the abortion she'd had without telling Cross. Then she lied to him, telling him that she was pregnant with his baby, so he wouldn't take a plea and end up in prison. Kola assumed that lying about a pregnancy was a sure way of keeping him around. But her heart felt like it was being twisted in a pair of vise-grips as she actually held the child that her man had fathered.

Kola soothed the baby in her arms, trying to calm its piercing screams. She gently rocked the infant in her arms, and it was actually working. The child's screaming grew fainter, and his eyes began to slowly close again.

"Kola, c'mon. What the fuck you doing?" Candace exclaimed, rushing into the bedroom.

Kola turned with the baby in her arms, and Candace was taken aback.

"Yo, what the fuck, Kola!"

"Ssssshhh!" Kola whispered. She put her index finger against her lips.

The baby was soon asleep, and Kola gently put him back into the crib. She stared at the boy for a moment.

Candace rushed over and grabbed Kola by her arm, spinning her around. "C'mon!"

Both girls dashed out the room and ran out the apartment, leaving Cynthia unconscious on the living room floor.

Hearing the commotion, a few neighbors began to step out their apartments, but the girls were already retreating down the concrete stairway and running out the building.

They jumped into the truck, and Candace sped away while Kola was in a daze, slumped in her seat. She stared out the window of the car as it moved hastily on Myrtle Avenue. When Candace came to a stop at a red light, Kola couldn't hold the hurt in any longer. She burst into tears with the realization that everything Edge had told her was the truth. She was so naïve to think she was the only woman in Cross' life.

"Yo, don't even worry about that, Kola, 'cause you still gonna get yours," Candace said, trying to comfort her friend.

Still, Kola's tears continued to trickle. She felt exposed. She hadn't cried like that since her little sister's murder. It was a feeling she tried to control, but it came out on its own.

Candace steered the Trailblazer across the Brooklyn Bridge as she raced back to Harlem.

Kola felt betrayed. She didn't know what to do with herself. *Love don't live here anymore*, she thought.

Kola didn't go home. She got a room at a five-star hotel in the city. Her phone had been ringing nonstop; it was Cross calling. She knew he had gotten the word about the incident, but she didn't feel like talking. She felt like a fool.

As she spent time alone in the elegant hotel room, a sinful smile crept across her face. She had the upper hand. She had the connect—Eduardo. He was only dealing with her and not her man. She thought about the night she turned down his sexual advances. *Was it a mistake?* she asked herself.

Things were changing in her crew—the loyalty was crumbling. The empire she dreamed about having with her man was becoming a lie for her. Edge was a snake and a hater, and Cross was even worse, she felt. He was a cheater and a backstabber. She gave him her love and trust, while he was wifing the next bitch. Kola now regretted having the abortion and not giving Cross the child he wanted.

Kola's phone rang. She looked at the caller ID and saw a New Jersey number. She had an idea who it was. Eduardo. It was time for her to re-up, but she had missed the day to meet with him. Kola figured Eduardo must be concerned about her.

Kola's heart was too troubled at the moment for business to be on her mind. She sat on the bed and stared at the number that had called previously. She had choices to make. She could easily fuck Eduardo and solidify her position with him in the drug world. But she didn't want to become just another one of his mistresses. She wanted to be a queen.

And while she loved Cross with all her heart, he was becoming a different man, almost careless and indecisive about things. He had a snake in his camp that he failed to pick up on his radar, and then with the pending gun charges, she didn't know if he would see the light of day anytime soon.

She got up and got dressed. She had made her choice.

Chapter 24

Apple woke up startled and frightened from her uncomfortable sleep in her car. Sweaty, she looked out the window frantically. She couldn't shake that odd feeling that someone was watching her up close—stalking her—but she didn't see anyone lurking around. She had been having the same feeling for several days now. She had made plenty of enemies in the past year, so it was a long list to choose from.

One name was constantly popping into her head—Guy Tony. He was still out there and hadn't been seen or heard from in months. He was still a dangerous man, and he had a crucial grudge against Apple that made her feel the need to look over her shoulder wherever she went.

Apple was parked on a shaded tree-lined block a few miles south from the Tappan Zee Bridge in White Plains, New York. The sun was just rising, and the morning air was fresh, but Apple felt the total opposite. She felt sick. Her stomach was upset and churning. Her eyes were red and sunken in from the lack of sleep that she was getting.

Her body felt frail, and she was constantly tired from not eating enough. She could barely move from out the car.

Apple straightened herself out and sluggishly stepped out her McLaren to stretch her legs. She looked around at the few cars on the block where she had parked. It had been two days since she was evicted from her home, and with nowhere to go and having less than fifty dollars to her name, each passing day was critical and hard.

She was washing up in public places, using the facilities at rest stop bathrooms, fast food restaurants, chain stores, and other public places to clean her face, wash her clothes in the sink, and brush her teeth. She would try to do these things early in the morning or late at night when there was less of a crowd to stare at her like she'd stepped off the freak bus, and to avoid some of the kids making fun of her or becoming frightened by the simple sight of her.

"Mommy, what happened to her face?" a four-year-old had asked his mother, pointing at Apple as she exited a public restroom early one morning.

Apple turned her head in embarrassment and rushed out the store, once again trying to hold back her tears.

Sometimes, Apple would sit in her car for hours clutching her pistol, wanting to commit suicide. But she always hesitated in doing the fatal action, thinking about her sister. Kola couldn't win. She wouldn't dare give her twin sister the satisfaction of killing herself, knowing she would spit on her grave and laugh. Besides, she had a score to settle. No matter how tempting it seemed and how rough it was getting for her, Apple's pride wouldn't allow her to take it that far. Still, every day it was one thing or the other.

She was constantly calling Chico and begging him to get her out of the situation she was in. Chico would assure her that things would get better and told her that he would be in New York within the week. Apple felt she wouldn't last that long. He had promised to send her some money via Western Union, and when the money came, it gave her little comfort. But she was able to afford to stay in a motel for the week.

Apple checked into a seedy, dilapidated motel in the outskirts of Hackensack, New Jersey, a popular hangout spot for punks, penny-pinchers, and pimps. It was such a step down from where Apple was staying before. The dirty room reminded her of the home in Harlem she once shared with her sisters and mother.

A sullen cashier behind bulletproof glass in the vestibule turned over the key to Apple in exchange for cash, no questions asked. Apple walked into the 10'x10' room that was dimly lit by a single bulb in the ceiling fixture, and smelling heavily of sweat. A small mattress rested on a chipped particle board bed frame. The blanket was stained, the bedspread torn, and the filthy brown carpet on the floor was littered with cigarette burns. There was an old television set with a broken antenna and a non-working remote, and the windows were so dirty, they blocked out the midday sun.

Apple sighed heavily while staring at the two towels

on a small dresser. Her temporary home for a week was an ugly, destitute place, and with her McLaren parked right outside underneath the room's window, she felt an uneasiness inside of her that traveled to the bottom of her feet.

She walked farther into the room and twisted her face. "Hurry up, Chico," she said under her breath.

Apple was a little nervous about going out into the streets, but she was from the hood, and with her scarred face, it made her blend right in with the undesirables that frequented the seedy motel, although her car was a magnet for attention.

She still couldn't shake the feeling of somebody watching her. Therefore, she stayed in the room and only came out when she needed food. She could only afford to buy a few things to hold her over, though, like potato chips, cookies, cakes, juices, and cups of noodles.

Two days went by slowly for Apple. Time for her felt like it had stood still. The TV and a newspaper became her only source of entertainment, and her mind was heavily on Chico. The nights were lonely like a castaway's stranded at sea, and her days were long and drawn out with nothing much to do. Apple barely got any sleep, and when she did, it was only in intervals.

As day number three in the motel slowly approached, Apple woke up from her sleep in a chilling sweat. She was having the same recurring nightmare—there was an entity chasing her and slowly tearing her apart. It was wicked, and it was fast. Apple could feel her flesh being torn from her, and her burns coming alive on her face—taunting her, digging into her skin and spreading. She was becoming uglier and uglier, and she couldn't stop it. Whenever she felt overwhelmed by the entity engulfing her, she would jump up from her sleep screaming, only to see it was just a nightmare. But she would be shaking and looking around the room with paranoia.

"It's a dream. It's only a dream," Apple told herself, trying to find some reassurance and calm her breathing. She needed someone to hold onto, but Chico wasn't there.

It was one in the morning, and the room felt too still. It was dark. The television was off. She could hear a few pimps chatting outside her window. They lingered around in and outside of the motel while their hoes worked the track until sunup.

Apple then had a sudden urge to go to the window and look out. She had a bad feeling about something. She drew back the blinds and peered outside. That's when she noticed an empty parking space where her car was once parked was. Her eyes grew big with the realization that her car was gone. It was stolen.

"No, they didn't!" she screamed out.

She hurried to put some clothes on, rushed out of the lobby, and ran to where she had last parked the McLaren. She was hysterical. Her head was spinning in every direction, hoping to get a glimpse of the car somewhere, but the only thing around her were barren streets and working girls.

One of the young pimps sauntered up to Apple. He was clad in sagging blue jeans and an Atlanta Falcons throwback jersey, his braids showing underneath the baseball cap he wore backward. He looked only a few years older than Apple.

Smoking a cigarette, he looked at Apple for a moment. "Yo, shortie, that was ya car, right?" he asked.

"Yes!"

"That shit got towed like an hour ago, shortie. I think it was the repo man or somethin'. Shit, it was either that, or them stickup boys were gonna snatch that shit from you eventually."

Apple stood there looking despondent.

The young pimp stood there focused on watching his girls walk the track. He was used to seeing her disfigured face, so the burns meant nothing to him. In fact, he even had a sick thought about trying to put her to work on the track. The pimp knew of a few tricks who would pay for her, having some kind of sick, twisted fantasy about sexing a freak with a tight, succulent body. She was damaged goods, but he looked at her with a gleam in his eyes.

With no car to get around, things were hopeless. Apple jumped on the phone to quickly call Chico. She was so upset, her voice was shaky, and she began to tremble with the phone in her hand.

The pimp was playing her closely. He saw some potential in the girl. Apple didn't pay him any mind, though.

The phone rang in her ear as she waited for Chico to pick up.

"Hello?" he finally answered.

"They took my fuckin' car, Chico!" she yelled into the phone, sounding hysterical.

"What?"

"They took my fuckin' car! I'm fucked, Chico! What am I supposed to do now, huh?"

"Apple, listen, it's just a car. We'll get you a new one."

"It was your gift to me, and now I don't have shit!"

"You still at that motel in Jersey? I'll be there in two days."

"You know what, Chico? Fuck you! You ain't shit! I don't give a fuck about ya fuckin' promises. Keep ya fuckin' promises. You supposed to be a man! You ain't a fuckin' man! You a bitch-ass nigga for lettin' all this shit happen!"

"Ya blaming me?"

"I just don't give a fuck anymore! Fuck you and go to hell!" Apple screamed out.

Apple smashed her phone on the pavement and stormed back into the room.

The young pimp watched her with a smirk, taking a pull from his cigarette and nodding. He said to himself, "Yeah, I could work wit' that. She ain't that bad. Body fuckin' tight though."

Apple stormed into her room and slammed the door so hard behind her that it echoed throughout the hallway. She fell backwards, leaning against the door, and abruptly broke down in tears. She slowly slid down to the floor with her back pressed against the door. She couldn't move. She didn't want to move. She pulled her knees into her chest, hunched herself over, and wrapped her arms around her shins with her face lowered between her knees as she continued to let the tears fall. It was hell on earth.

She heard an unexpected noise in the room and looked up. She wasn't alone. Someone was inside with her. Her eyes scanned the place in the dark, but it was hard to see. She slowly stood up, and as she got to her feet, a large shadow lunged at her from out of nowhere. It was fast.

Apple tried to fight it off, and there was a quick tussle, but she quickly succumbed when a handkerchief soaked in chloroform was put over her mouth. The vapors depressed her central nervous system, and she quickly passed out into the arms of her attacker.

Chico arrived at the motel in Hackensack two days later, his heart filled with worry. He had been calling Apple's phone repeatedly, and was only getting voice mail.

When he drove up to the sleazy motel on the barren New Jersey block, it was mid-afternoon, and the place looked like a ghost town. He rushed out of his car and hurried into the lobby, where he saw a young girl sitting at the front desk reading a magazine. The lobby was empty.

The girl was standoffish when Chico approached her and started asking questions. He wanted the keys to Apple's room, but she told him she wasn't allowed to do it. Chico slipped a hundred-dollar bill under the glass for her to take, and she didn't hesitate snatching up the money and pocketing it. She then took a set of room keys from off the hook behind her and handed them to him.

Chico hurried up to the second floor, opened the door, and went inside. The room was empty. He noticed all her things were in the room, but she wasn't around. He figured she probably went for a walk to cool off. He decided to wait around. He continued to call her cell phone frantically, but there wasn't any answer. Her phone was going straight to voice mail.

Chico waited around the motel for Apple for several days, questioning people, looking around, hoping she would show up. He knew something had to have happened to her. Keeping his emotions contained, he got into his BMW and raced toward Harlem.

Chico crossed the George Washington Bridge and was in Harlem late in the evening. Lincoln Projects was quiet. Spring was in the air, the leaves were blossoming, and the warm air was soothing. He was parked across the street from the projects. It had been over a month since he was in Harlem.

Looking at Apple's old building, he reached under his seat, removed a pistol, and stuffed it into his pants. He still had enemies in the hood despite his short absence.

Chico stepped out of the car and proceeded toward the building. He was cautious, though, keeping his hand close to his gun and alert with every step he took.

He walked into the lobby and decided to take the stairs instead of the elevator. He knew Denise's apartment and knocked on the door roughly. He could hear H-town's "Knockin' Da Boots" playing from behind the door. He knocked again, steadily looking over his shoulders.

The locks began to turn, and the door opened with Denise in her robe, exposing a glimpse of her nakedness underneath.

She tied her robe. Glaring at him, she barked, "What the fuck you doin' at my door, Chico?"

"I'm looking for your daughter, Apple. You seen her around?"

"What the fuck you comin' here for asking about that bitch? I ain't stressin' that bitch!"

"She ain't been around."

"If the bitch doesn't wanna be found, then that's because she don't wanna be found. Why the fuck you comin' to my door wit' this bullshit and disturbing me from tryin' to get my fuck on?" Denise slammed the door in Chico's face.

Chico was ready to put holes in her door for being so disrespectful, but he didn't want to draw too much attention on himself. He casually walked away, exited the building, and jumped back into his car. But he didn't start the ignition right away. Chico sat in the car with his pistol clutched in his hand and steadily looked around. He had no idea where Apple was, nor did he know if she was safe or in any danger.

Chico took out a pack of cigarettes from his jacket,

removed one, and lit it. He took a much-needed drag and exhaled. Apple had him concerned, but he couldn't stress about her anymore. He had done what he could for her. He still loved her, and wherever she was, he was just hoping she'd come back safe.

He looked around Harlem. He had to get back to business and focus on his return. This time, Harlem would feel his wrath. He was angry, and the only thing on his mind was payback and making money.

Chapter 25

Apple slowly opened her eyes and found herself in a strange place. She had no recollection of her surroundings. She was still drowsy and disoriented from being unconscious for such a long time. She felt weak. She couldn't remember what had happened. The last thing she remembered was crying and yelling at Chico. Then things around her went completely black.

When she tried to move, she realized she was tied four bedposts, her arms and legs outstretched, and she was completely naked. She couldn't scream because her mouth was covered with duct-tape. She struggled to free herself, but the thick rope was knotted securely around her wrists and ankles.

Apple was able to turn her head and look around. The barren room was nasty and run down, with peeling paint and black mold. There was one badly fitted small window in the room with the curtains drawn closed, and it reeked of every odor. There was a clogged sink that had partly fallen off the wall and hung at an odd angle.

Apple squirmed violently against the stained bed, trying to free herself, but it was hopeless. She mumbled under the duct-tape, but it was all incoherent. She wasn't going anywhere. She turned her head to the right and quickly saw a shadowy figure seated in an old chair. Her eyes widened. His face was unclear in the dark. She focused her undivided attention on the stranger, feeling her heart beat a thousand times in one second.

Apple became frightened. She thought it was Guy Tony.

"It's about fuckin' time you woke up," the figure spoke.

Apple didn't know the voice. It wasn't registering in her mind.

"You know how long I waited for this moment? A long fuckin' time," he added.

Apple kept her eyes trained on him. She didn't blink. She couldn't turn away. He proceeded to step forward, and slowly but surely, he revealed his image from the darkened corner where he was seated. Apple was shocked.

"You fuckin' remember me?" he said. "Huh? You dumb bitch!"

Apple did. It was Ayesha's oldest brother, Shaun. Apple continued to squirm. She knew Shaun wasn't there to do her right. The menacing look he carried in his eyes sent chills all through her naked body.

Shaun moved closer. He was scowling. "I lost a fuckin' sister and my brother Memo because of you!"

He was in a pair of beige cargo shorts and a tight-fitting tank top that showed off his strapping physique and tattoos. He had on dusty black sneakers and sported a bald head.

Apple remembered when Shaun was a scrawny peewee kid running around Harlem since they were ten years old. He was older than her by two years, but she remembered him always being a nerd. He went away two years ago. Ayesha always said he went off to a private school. He had changed a lot.

Shaun had been watching Apple closely for months and had been planning his revenge. Ayesha was his heart, and when Apple took his sister away from her because of a petty beef between them, it changed him.

Their grandmother had a small insurance policy taken out on each grandchild, and when Ayesha was gunned down, the family had gotten ten thousand dollars. Her brothers Memo and Shaun paid off their bills and a few debts with the money, and what was left over, they invested in weed.

Shaun became a small-time hustler, until he stumbled upon a new hustle in Mexico. He owned a whorehouse with underage girls in Los Mochis, Mexico, a dusty small town a few miles south of the border, where the summers were extremely hot, reaching over a hundred degrees during the day and overnight lows of eighty degrees.

Shaun had some status in the city with his illicit business of selling sex. The Mexican police would frequent his place for sex or to get their weekly payoff. He had a good thing going.

"Yeah, you stupid bitch, I ain't that young, nerdy nigga anymore. You better start getting used to me, because you're gonna see a whole lot of me from now on. I got plans for you, Apple—something special."

Shaun took a seat next to her on the bed and placed his hand on her thigh. He smiled. He then moved it up a little bit, toying with her, making her fidget under his touch.

"Still nice," he uttered. "I wanna know, though, who fucked up your pretty little face? Shit, they did me a favor. Started something I plan on finishing."

Shaun picked up a small leather pouch from off the floor and unzipped it. He removed a syringe and a packet of dope. The glint in his eyes showed how much he was enjoying the moment.

Apple wanted to speak. She had so many questions. She pleaded with her eyes. She continued to fidget, wanting to break herself free.

Shaun began mixing and cooking the dope right in front of Apple's eyes. She could only watch on helplessly as Shaun planned her vicious fate. He used a silver spoon to dissolve the heroin in. He then took a piece of cotton and dropped it into the heroin to filter out any particles. Shaun took the tip of the syringe and pushed it into the center of the cotton. Then he slowly pulled back the plunger, until all of the heroin was sucked in.

Next, Shaun chose where to shoot it into Apple's body. Apple began to tear up as her eyes followed the syringe.

Shaun neared the tip of the needle closely to where

her arm folded because it would be easy to get it into one of her veins properly. He held the syringe flat against her skin and slowly inserted it, and the dope went pouring into her bloodstream like a running river.

Apple felt a sudden burning sensation, and her head fell back against the mattress. She was no longer watching Shaun closely.

Shaun pulled the plunger from her arm and only a slow trickle of blood was released. He smiled.

As if on cue, the door to the room opened, and a tall Mexican clad in a police uniform stepped inside.

"There you go, my friend. She's all yours," Shaun stated.

"*Mi amigo, ella es fea!*" the officer said, meaning she was ugly.

"She's what you asked for. She's American and black, Pedro. Besides, the damage is only one side to her face. *Ella es todavía muy bien ir.*"

Pedro shook his head and sighed. He stared at the drugged Apple and smiled. He walked closer to the mattress and observed her body.

"She's your freak, Pedro. Enjoy her," Shaun said with a conniving smile.

The officer licked his lips, admiring the young body of the teenage girl. He passed Shaun a few pesos for payment and began unbuckling his pants. He was excited.

"I'll leave y'all two alone," Shaun said, making his exit.

Pedro was bottomless. His pants were on the floor, and his dick was hard and clutched in his hand. He climbed between Apple's listless legs and thrust himself into her.

The heroin had Apple feeling euphoric. She didn't fight off the man on top of her. In fact, she wasn't even aware that she was being raped.

"Ugh! Ugh! Ugh!" the Mexican officer grunted, violating Apple in the missionary position.

His sexual episode was quick. He was in, and five minutes later, he was pulling out. He quickly got dressed and hurried out of the room.

Shaun peered in on Apple and smiled. "Yeah, you and me, we gonna have lots of fun." Then he closed the door to his prize.

Epilogue

Harlem had two major figures vying for control of the streets—Chico and Kola. Apple had been forgotten. It'd been a month since her sudden disappearance, and many people thought she'd run off because she was too embarrassed to face anybody.

Chico was gaining his control again over his city streets. He had a strong pipeline to the South, via the Johnson brothers, and a new chick by his side. Apple was becoming nothing but a memory for him.

Kola was the queen of New York. She didn't care who she had to cross, even if it meant killing those closest to her. She didn't want to end up like her sister, missing and her reputation ruined. So when she gave the order to have Edge killed, it didn't disturb her. She considered it a cost of doing business.

TO be continued

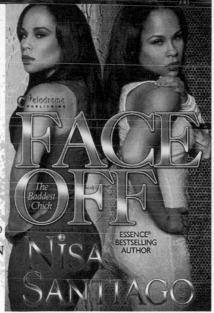

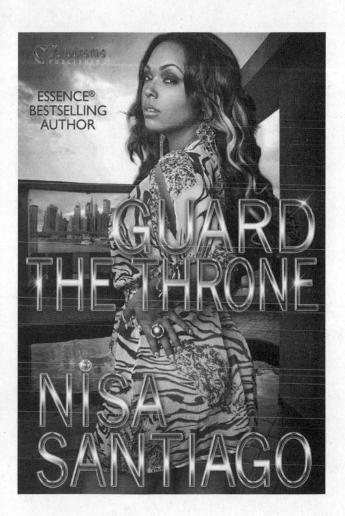

ESSENCE®
BESTSELLING
AUTHOR

GUARD THE THRONE

NISA SANTIAGO

Melodrama PUBLISHING
WIFEY
I Am Wifey
FROM THE ORIGINAL PUBLISHER OF WIFEY
ESSENCE® BESTSELLING AUTHOR
ERICA HILTON

RISE OF AN AMERICAN GANGSTRESS

Kim K.

NATIONAL BESTSELLING AUTHOR OF *SHEISTY CHICKS*